THROUGH THE S̶C̶O̶P̶E̶, McCARTER SAW THE SNIPER'S HEAD EXPLODE

But a second later, an explosion of a different type erupted.

As if from out of nowhere, men bearing assault rifles, sawed-off shotguns and handguns shot up fifty feet farther down the line of brush and wrecked vehicles. And, unlike McCarter, they had no reason to hesitate.

"Down!" McCarter yelled. It was an unnecessary order. The men of Phoenix Force, the Special Forces soldiers and their guide had all dropped into the grass behind vehicles of their own accord.

McCarter felt his elbows sink into the damp earth behind what had once been an army jeep. He'd had no time to make an actual count. But quickly assessing the enemy, he estimated their number at roughly two dozen.

Two dozen that he could see. There could be more—many more, in fact—who had simply been slower to show themselves.

In any case, Phoenix Force and their companions were outnumbered.

DON PENDLETON'S

STONY

AMERICA'S ULTRA-COVERT INTELLIGENCE AGENCY

MAN®

ATOMIC FRACTURE

A GOLD EAGLE BOOK FROM
WORLDWIDE®

TORONTO • NEW YORK • LONDON
AMSTERDAM • PARIS • SYDNEY • HAMBURG
STOCKHOLM • ATHENS • TOKYO • MILAN
MADRID • WARSAW • BUDAPEST • AUCKLAND

Recycling programs
for this product may
not exist in your area.

First edition April 2014

ISBN-13: 978-0-373-80444-3

ATOMIC FRACTURE

Special thanks and acknowledgment to
Jerry VanCook for his contribution to this work.

Printed in U.S.A.

ATOMIC FRACTURE

PROLOGUE

A twisted smile fell over Emad Nosiar's face and adrenaline shot through his body as he glanced at his watch.

Quickly he moved across the carpet of the eleventh-story hotel room to the window. Far below, at the corners of Ujaama and Sadaquee streets, he could see the cars and trucks flowing freely through the busy intersection. The sidewalks on both sides of the streets were crowded with pedestrians. Mixed in with men wearing Western-style business suits were others in traditional Muslim robes. The former were, for the most part, clean-shaved. The latter had long, untrimmed beards.

The women were of a similar mix. Some were outfitted like Western whores, wearing clothes that left their ankles and calves—not to mention their bared faces and hair—exposed for all to see and lust after. But other females had remained true to the faith in their dark burkas and veils. Behind the faithful women trailed what seemed like a dozen children each, moving along the sidewalks at a slower pace as they tried to keep together.

In the reflection off the glass, Nosiar saw his smile widen even further. The busy traffic of Ramesh, Radestan, was about to come to a screeching—and exploding—halt. And it would be of his doing.

Raising the walkie-talkie in his left hand to his lips, he pressed the binoculars to his eyes with his right.

Through the lenses he could make out two ancient Ford pickups, one loaded with bales of hay, the other piled high with lawn-care equipment, parked on opposite sides of Ujaama Street. Behind the wheel of the lawn-care truck sat a man wearing a khaki shirt with military epaulets on the shoulders. In the other pickup was a long-bearded man with dark brown hair falling down his neck. Both men had removed their headgear so as not to attract attention. Though he could not see them, Nosiar knew that an eight-point Radestani army officer's cap rested on the seat next to the man in the military shirt. A more traditional Arab headdress—known as the kaffiyeh—would be next to the driver of the other pickup.

The thought added a chuckle to Nosiar's grinning face. One of the men would don his headwear as soon as the action started. The other would remain bareheaded as they moved their vehicles into position. Which one did which depended on who came along the streets in the next few minutes.

Nosiar turned the binoculars slightly, letting them stop on a black Buick Enclave parked in an alley a half block farther down Ujaama Street. Though he could not see it from his position on the eleventh floor of the hotel, he knew another Enclave was also in the alley almost directly beneath him.

His men were ready. He pressed the transmit button on the walkie-talkie. "Ali One to Three, Four, Five and Six," he said in Arabic.

The acknowledgments from each driver came back in the same language. But Nosiar also needed to contact his second in command; his man on the ground who would step in and take up the slack if anything went wrong. And to contact the man he would address simply as "Two," he needed to switch frequencies.

A simple turn of the dial on the walkie-talkie accomplished that.

"One to Two," Nosiar said into the small portable radio. The line crackled with static. Then a somewhat hoarse voice, slightly higher in pitch than Two's usual deep baritone, answered. "Yes, One. I am in place. All is ready. At *both* sites."

Nosiar smiled to himself. The tension in Two's voice came from the stress of the operation they were about to conduct. The man would not have been human had he not been at least a little nervous. "Good," said Nosiar. "Remember, you will have to move swiftly between the first and second sites as soon as we have finished at the first."

"I understand," said the man using the simple call number Two.

Nosiar was about to speak again when he caught sight of a trio of army trucks a quarter of a mile farther down Ujaama. Quickly he switched back to the frequency that connected him to the operatives below.

The three vehicles were moving toward the intersection. And they all had canvas sides covering whatever it was they were transporting. Nosiar prayed silently that their cargo was more troops—*men*, government soldiers—and, therefore, his enemies. He pressed the button once more. "Three targets approaching from the south," he said. "Strike time, approximately ninety seconds."

"Ali Three to One," came a voice as soon as Nosiar let up on the button. "Military or People's Secular Opposition Forces?"

"Government vehicles," said Nosiar. He watched through the binoculars as the man in the hay pickup quickly donned his kaffiyeh and secured it in place with a double-wound cord known as an *agal*. The man in the uniform slumped down in the driver's seat, hiding the military epaulets on his shoulders and leaving his head bare.

The Radestani army trucks caught a green light at the intersection before reaching the corner where the vehicles were set up. They made good time, passing beneath Nosiar's binoculars with twenty seconds to spare on his ninety-second estimate. But his men were ready. As soon as the third truck passed the alleys, both of the black Enclaves pulled out behind them onto the street. Then, a second or so before they reached Sadaquee Street, the pickups suddenly darted out from the curbs to block their forward progression.

The technique was known as a "flying block." And it worked almost exactly the same way every time Nosiar employed it.

The army trucks screeched to a halt.

And gunfire erupted immediately.

Dark-haired, dark-skinned men—obviously of Arab descent but wearing jeans, T-shirts and other forms of Western dress—suddenly appeared from the Enclaves behind the trucks and rose from hiding in the beds of the pickups. AK-47s, some of Russian origin, others Kalashnikov copies made in China, began to sputter out 7.62 mm bullets to penetrate the canvas sides of the military trucks. Nosiar caught himself breathing faster and deeper as his men moved forward, still firing, to surround the trucks and shred the canvas.

Emad Nosiar was pleased to see that his prayer to

God had been at least partially answered. Two of the three trucks did indeed contain Radestani soldiers. While the rifle fire from his men continued, he watched through the threads of canvas as the surprised troops jerked back and forth in death throes, having no time to bring their own weapons into play.

The third truck in the small army convoy appeared to contain rations. As the men who had appeared from the Enclaves poured round after round through the canvas, Nosiar saw cans of food explode and fly through the air. Ragged metal cans and broken glass bottles became impromptu shrapnel in the assault.

The odors of canned meat, vegetables and other food—rations that would never reach the government soldiers for whom they'd been intended—rose with the wind, all the way to the eleventh floor of the Hotel Sala-hudden to penetrate the cracks around the window and enter Emad Nosiar's olfactory glands.

Along with those smells came the stench of death in the form of blood, expelled feces and urine. Not to mention the screams of terror as completely innocent and unaligned men, women and children along the side-walks fell to wildly aimed rounds.

As Nosiar continued to watch through his binoculars, a large shard of glass flew through the air. It sliced into the hoodlike covering of a woman's black burka at the throat. Then, unseen behind the garment, it severed her jugular and slammed her to her back on the sidewalk. Nosiar turned his binoculars downward and watched as blood raised the material in front of her neck, pushing it upward with each beat of her petrified heart. When the fire-hose stream had reached its height above her neck, it splashed back down, then ran to the sides, creating huge black pools on both sides of her head.

Her burka stayed in place and she died faceless.

Breathing even harder as he watched, Nosiar wondered for a moment if it was the will of God that he take such delight in such things. Especially with a woman who was undoubtedly a fellow Muslim. But the thoughts were disturbing so he attributed them to Satan. Yes, such thoughts *had* to come from Satan. The great enemy of God shoved them into his mind to slow his progress in the never-ending jihad.

There was always going to be collateral damage. That was simply life in the jihad. He could not afford to worry about it. The dead in God would go immediately to paradise as martyrs. Let the demonic Westerners—especially the Great Satan America—worry about collateral damage. They were the ones who would burn in the fires of hell for all eternity.

When the woman had bled out and lay still on the concrete, Nosiar turned his binoculars back to the trucks. All but one of the soldiers in the first two trucks was now dead. Some had fallen forward onto the floor of the vehicle; some hung awkwardly out over the sides, while others had fallen to the ground. The shreds of canvas tarp that had hidden them earlier now flapped in the breeze.

The one man who remained alive had been shot in both legs. He lay sideways on the street, the OD green battle dress pants of his uniform soaked black with blood. He was trying valiantly but vainly to pull himself to the curb with both hands as sweat ran down his forehead into his convulsively blinking eyes.

Nosiar continued to watch. One of his men, wearing faded blue jeans, a plain white T-shirt and carry-ing one of the AK-47s, broke off from the front of the truck and walked purposefully toward the lone survi-vor. Through his round glass lenses, Nosiar could see a sadistic grin on the face of that man. He glanced into the glass window once more at his own face. It was smiling very much like the man below who was about to commit murder.

The man in the white T-shirt stopped next to the bro-ken soldier. Aiming his rifle downward, he shot him first in the right elbow.

The government soldier fell forward for a second. Then he raised his head slightly and tried to scratch his way forward using his left arm.

The muzzle of the AK-47 pressed into the injured man's other elbow. Then it jumped slightly again with recoil.

Blood, tissue and bone fragments shot out from the now quadriplegic soldier. With no way left to crawl, he twisted at the waist and fell back against the concrete, looking up at his torturer.

Nosiar's blue-jeaned man jammed the barrel of his rifle into the soldier's forehead. For a moment Nosiar thought the AK-47 would end the man's life right there. But the man in the T-shirt appeared to change his mind and pulled the rifle back toward him. Instead of aim-ing at the head, the 7.62 mm weapon was now pointed at the soldier's lower abdomen. A 3-round burst ex-ploded out of the weapon and the man on the ground grimaced in pain.

The trio of gut shots would ensure the man died before help could arrive. But it also ensured a slower, more torturous and lingering demise than a head shot would have provided.

Nosiar's chuckle became an audible laugh. He had trained his men well. The screams of the dying soldier would send a message to the civilians on the sidewalks who had survived the attack.

The gunfire was over now. The Radestani military men had been vanquished. So Nosiar raised the walkie-talkie to his mouth and said, "Ali One to Three through Five. Did we sustain any casualties?" he asked.

"Negative," came the responses from the men below.

"Good," Nosiar said. "Gather up all weapons and extra magazines. If the trucks are still drivable, assign drivers and bring them with you. And make sure you shout enough ridiculous PSOF slogans so the civilians hiding along the street will believe you are from the People's Secular Opposition Forces." He could still feel the excitement in his chest and had to force himself to breathe shallowly. "Then proceed to the second site. Team Two may need backup."

Without waiting for any answers, Nosiar let his binoculars fall to the end of their strap and picked up his own AK-47 from where he had rested it against the wall by the window. Without further ado, he left the hotel room and walked down the hall to the elevator. On the way, he passed a young couple who had undoubtedly heard the gunfire outside the building. Both stared at his rifle, then closed their eyes in terror and pressed their backs against the wall to let him pass.

Nosiar walked onto the elevator and took it to the twelfth floor, then walked down another hall to the other side of the building where he had rented another room. Inserting the key card, he entered and walked directly to the window, pulling back the curtains.

Below, he saw two more streets. Another busy intersection. And more parked vehicles that he recognized. As he waited, he saw the two pickups and Buick Enclaves turn the corner, their drivers looking for places to set up again.

Excitement still filled Nosiar's chest as the vehicles pulled into parking spaces. The intersection would again be closed, and other vehicles would pull in behind to prevent a retreat. Again, the words "flying block" crossed his mind. The term had been coined by someone in the press when it had first begun to be used in the Syrian civil war. The technique, and the term for it, had caught on all over the Islamic world.

Nosiar stared down through the window once more. There was one small difference between this assault and the one he had just orchestrated on the other side of the hotel. This time, he had received prior information that the People's Secular Opposition Forces—or PSOF as the loosely allied, poorly organized rebels fighting the Radestani government were called—were definitely bringing a truckload of supplies down the street.

That intel proved correct.

Less than two minutes after Nosiar's men had set up he saw the semitrailer come lumbering forward a block away. Pressing the key on his walkie-talkie again, he said, "Ali One to all units. There will be great amounts of supplies in this truck. But unless there are men hidden in the trailer, we expect only a driver and perhaps a guard in the cab."

"Ali Four to One," came back to Nosiar. "We left dozens of dead soldiers on the other side of the building when we masqueraded as PSOF rebels. Now that we are to play the part of soldiers ourselves, we will not create as much hatred or emotional response if only two men are killed."

"That is correct," said Nosiar. "So you know what to do." He paused a second. "Do I need to spell it out for you?"

"Negative," was the response from the man on the ground. "You have trained us to know."

As the semitrailer neared, the pickups and other vehicles pulled into place just as they had done before. But this time the men—the same men who had emerged earlier in the clothing of the rebel PSOF—appeared wearing the military uniforms of the Radestani army. One of the men on the ground—Ali Three it appeared to be through the binoculars—fired a burst of 7.62 mm fire through the side window into the driver and another into the man riding shotgun.

Another of Nosiar's men shot the lock off the door at the rear of the trailer, then fired his own burst of autofire into the storage area. Perhaps there had been only one man in the back of the trailer. Perhaps none at all. Nosiar couldn't tell from his vantage point. All he knew was that there had not been enough killing to suit him. There had not been enough carnage to keep the balance of power between the government and rebels going. Nosiar stared down at the sidewalks. The men, women and children had not even had time to take cover. So he spoke into the radio one final time. "Do it," was all he had to say.

Immediately the imposters in government army uniforms turned toward the people on the sidewalks. The AK-47s from both Russia and China spit out their deadly automatic fire, cutting down innocent civilians before they could hide.

But not before they could scream.

The massacre went on for less than sixty seconds. But to the few people on the street who survived it by diving under cars or darting down the steps to basement establishments, it would seem like hours for the rest of their lives.

When it was over, Emad Nosiar simply said, "Bring the truck," into the walkie-talkie. Then he switched frequencies again and said, "One to Two."

"Two," said the voice on the other end.

"It appears that everything went well," Nosiar said.

"Perfect," said Two. "The rebels will blame the government and the government will blame the rebels. Both sides are weakening more every day."

"Then God should be praised," said Nosiar.

"Indeed," said the man going by Two.

"I am signing off the air," Nosiar said. "We will speak when we meet again in a few minutes."

"We will indeed."

Nosiar smiled as he switched the walkie-talkie off, lifted his rifle and started out of the hotel room. Adrenaline still shot through his veins and he thought of Two still on the ground at the flying block site below.

Harun Bartovi was Two's actual name. And he had truly been a gift from God. The man had worked his way up the ladder to become Nosiar's most competent and trusted assistant. Bartovi could be counted on not only to carry out orders but also to give them, and he had the ability to think on his feet, changing plans in the middle of an operation when the unexpected happened. No one could coordinate the flying blocks the

way Bartovi did, and these last two were perfect ex-
amples of his efficiency. He had remained below as a
backup, ready to take up the slack if any part of his
plan fell apart. But it had not. His careful and strategic
planning had meant he had not had to fire even one
shot himself.

Nosiar walked down the hall to the elevator. More
than a few civilians lay dead below, and he would more
than likely have to step over their corpses when he left
the hotel. That was unfortunate because most of them
would be fellow Muslims. But as he had done before,
he pushed such uncomfortable thoughts from his mind.

Casualties were inevitable. Some had to die so that
others could live. And the end of the jihad would certainly justify the means. He would fight on and continue to prepare for whatever happened. Nosiar wanted
the current semi-Islamic government to be overthrown.
It was weak and needed to be replaced by a total Islamic
theocracy. But he could not afford to let the godless rebels win, either. If they ever became organized enough
to take over, they would set up a satanic democracy. For
some time now, Nosiar and his fellow al Qaeda brothers had planned to do their best to keep the war going.
The two sides would eventually destroy each other, and
when they did, al Qaeda would take over and set up the
Islamic government that God wanted.

Nosiar pushed the down button and waited on the
elevator. The problem he faced was that that plan was
taking too long. So he had come up with an alternate
course of action. One that would speed up the process
of al Qaeda's takeover.

Or destroy Radestan altogether and provide the

means for al Qaeda to start the country anew from the very foundation.

The elevator doors opened and Nosiar stepped inside.

Either way, God's will would be done.

CHAPTER ONE

The violence had started in Syria but soon bled to Lebanon and then nearby Radestan. What had begun as political demonstrations against a repressive, semi-secular, semi-Muslim government soon turned into riots. Then the rioters quickly morphed into loosely organized private armies led by men who were charismatic leaders but seemed incapable of agreeing on anything among themselves. Joining forces, they knew, was imperative if they were to overthrow the government. But until egos could be satisfied, and some sort of chain of command put in place, they remained little more than well-intentioned brigands.

So all-out war had become the norm. Brutal and savage, as all wars are. Soon neighbors were killing neighbors, and occasionally even brothers shot brothers. Radestan became a fuzzy, confused and chaotic country. For the most part, it was soldiers versus rebels. But determining exactly who was who became impossible, for there were still citizens who sided with the government and military personnel who sympathized with, and even fought for, the disorganized PSOF rebel forces.

The cause was as old as mankind itself: should the people of a nation be governed neutrally, and be free to practice the religion of their choice, or should theocracy rule the land, creating all laws and demanding that each individual adhere to that belief system?

And to confuse things even more, there were rumors of more and more al Qaeda troops crossing the border into Radestan every day. They were reported to be pouring fuel on the fire of both government and rebel forces, lying in wait for the time when both sides had weakened each other enough to give the terrorists the chance to take over themselves.

All of these thoughts flashed through David McCarter's brain as he free-fell through the sky just outside of Ramesh, Radestan. Below, the former British SAS commando turned Phoenix Force leader could see the capital city several miles away from where he and the other members of Stony Man Farm's crack counterterrorist team, Phoenix Force, would land.

The city looked peaceful enough from two thousand feet in the air. What he knew to be a mixture of ancient mud-and-clay structures with more modern houses, soaring office buildings and other structures appeared now only as tiny indiscernible spots. But McCarter knew that even if violence was not in progress beyond his limited vision, it only meant the government and rebels had taken a brief respite to rest and regroup before plunging back into gunfire, explosions and other attacks and counterattacks.

McCarter turned his eyes upward as he continued to fall. The aircraft that had brought Phoenix Force to Radestan was now only a tiny speck in the distance as Jack Grimaldi, Stony Man Farm's ace pilot, steered the plane out of the country's airspace. McCarter shifted his eyes to four other, closer, spots in the sky. Rather than moving away from him like the plane, these spots followed a descent similar to his toward the ground.

The sight brought a hard grin to McCarter's face. He believed firmly in the adage that a true leader led from the front—which meant he had jumped from Grimaldi's plane first. And that fact, in turn, meant he could see the other four members of Phoenix Force still above him.

Rafael "Pescado" Encizo was a Cuban refugee who had earned the Spanish name for "fish" due to his expertise under the water.

Calvin James, a former Navy SEAL, could kill enemies faster with a knife than most men could with a machine gun.

The barrel-chested Canadian, Gary Manning, could bench press close to five hundred pounds—on a *bad* day—and his expertise with explosives had saved Phoenix Force and thousands of innocents countless times since the inception of Stony Man Farm.

Thomas Jackson Hawkins—better known simply as "Hawk" or "T.J."—was the youngest and newest member of the attack team. A man with a family military history he could trace back to the Revolutionary War, Hawkins spent what little time they ever had between missions engaged in any danger sport he could find.

McCarter felt his chest fill with pride as he watched the spots in the air gradually become larger. He was proud of his men. And he loved them like the brothers that they were.

The Phoenix Force leader glanced at his altitude gauge and saw that he had a few more seconds before he pulled the ripcord and allowed the parachute canopy to shoot out and fill with air. He had chosen a HALO—

High Altitude Low Opening—jump to keep his team's entry into the war-ravaged nation as low-key as possible. There would be shooting before this assignment was over, he knew. Lots of it. But the thought of his team drifting slowly down beneath open chutes—silhouetted against the sky as clearly as shooting range targets—held little appeal to him. There was nothing, McCarter knew, more vulnerable than a paratrooper as he neared the ground.

Another glance down and the Phoenix Force leader could make out more details of the city buildings in the distance. They were approximately ten miles from Ramesh, Radestan's capital city. He twisted his neck to look straight down and saw what was obviously a small house and a larger barn.

It appeared that Phoenix Force would be landing exactly where they'd planned to do so.

A weathered, wooden-fenced corral stood adjacent to the barn's own aged wood, and a dozen or so undernourished cattle stood inside that fence. As McCarter dropped closer, several of the bovine heads, their mouths moving up and down, back and forth, as they chewed their cud, looked up to watch him as intently as he watched them.

The Briton didn't have to check his altitude gauge again to know it was time to pull the cord.

The sudden jerk as air filled the canopy lifted McCarter back up in the air. Then he leveled off and began to fall again—this time much slower. He took a quick inventory of the other members of Phoenix Force to make sure they had experienced no equipment failures, and mentally ticked them off in his head as he continued to glide to the ground.

His men were fine.

McCarter flipped a switch on his belt and activated the two-way radio. The team had all tuned in to a secure frequency while still on the plane, and now he made use of it. "Phoenix One," McCarter said into the headset microphone positioned in front of his mouth. "Sound off, mates."

One by one, the men known on the airwaves as Phoenix Two, Three, Four and Five, checked in.

McCarter looked down again at the cattle inside the corral and immediately steered his canopy toward a flat area outside the fence and away from the barn. "I'm nearing the ground," he said into the mike. "And I'm angling away from the animals. I suggest you blokes do the same." No sooner were the words out of his mouth than David McCarter's boots hit the hard dirt and sparse grass. Landing hard after the lower-than-usual opening of his parachute, the Briton automatically threw himself forward into a shoulder roll to spread the impact across his body. Then he popped back to his feet in time to watch the others return to Earth a few seconds later.

All except T. J. Hawkins, who had been the last to jump out of the plane, While his chute had opened fine, he seemed to have had some sort of trouble with his steering toggles. Instead of landing outside the corral with the rest of the team, Phoenix Force's airborne ops expert touched down inside the rustic wooden fence, barely missing one of the cows.

McCarter couldn't help but chuckle. Neither could the other three Stony Man Farm operatives who were gathering up their chutes next to him. The three men under McCarter's command knew why their leader had suggested they sail clear of the corral.

It was ankle-deep in cow manure.

Hawkins had seen what was on the ground where he would land, too. And he'd chosen a bone-jarring "stand-up" landing over a roll-through in the cow dung. Even then, his boots sank as if he'd landed in some muddy, foul-smelling swamp.

With a look of disgust on his face, Hawkins pulled in his chute, doing his best to avoid the manure that had clung to the light material. Once he had control of the mess, he climbed over the rickety fence.

"Be sure to walk downwind of me, would you, Hawk?" Gary Manning said.

"Yeah, you probably should keep about a hundred yards behind us on the way into town," said Calvin James. Rafael Encizo nodded and smiled.

Hawkins was irritated. "Unless things have changed since our briefing," he said, "we're due to change clothes anyway before we head into town." He reached down and pinched the material of his combat black-suit, pulled the stretchy material out, then let it snap back into place. "These things just *might* draw a little unwanted attention. They practically scream, 'We're Westerners—shoot us.'"

James sucked in a deep breath of air, which caused his nostrils to flare in, then out again. "I'm thinking about shooting you right now myself," he quipped. "I'm not sure just changing clothes'll be enough to disinfect you."

"Of course every cloud has a silver lining," said Encizo with a straight face. "If we come across any Radestani bomb-sniffing dogs, you're sure to end their careers."

Hawkins shook his head and stared first at James and

then Encizo. When he spoke, his voice was heavy with sarcasm. "What are you two doing risking your lives with the rest of us when you could be making bundles at the comedy clubs? I mean, I can see you on Letterman, Leno and—"

Before he could finish, the creak of an old wooden door opening came from the small frame house twenty yards away. As if he had heard the conversation and realized it was time for him to make an appearance, a short man wearing khaki work pants and a woodland-camo battle-dress-uniform shirt appeared and walked toward them. The checkered *kaffiyeh* on his head was held in place by a red *agal* that rested just above his eyebrows. The two distinct "looks" appeared to contradict each other.

"Dude looks like *Lawrence of Arabia* guest starring on *Duck Dynasty*," James whispered.

None of the men responded, but couldn't suppress smiles. The comment even seemed to get Hawkins over his bad mood.

A light breeze was blowing through the area, and it caused the khaki-and-kaffiyeh-clad man's long, stringy gray beard to dance as he approached. Stopping five feet from where Hawkins stood, he looked down at the Phoenix Force man's dung-covered boots and grinned. "If that is the worst thing that happens to you during your time in Radestan," he said, "you will be very lucky." Then, turning to McCarter as if he somehow sensed that the Briton was in charge, he carefully pronounced each syllable of the first line of the code phrases that had been set up by Stony Man Farm.

"Someone's in the kitchen with Dinah," the man said in heavily Arab-accented English.

"Someone's in the kitchen I know," McCarter answered immediately. "Someone's in the kitchen with Dinah."

"Strummin' on the old banjo." The words sounded strange with a Radestani accent.

Hawkins turned to McCarter and said in a low voice, "Did Hal come up with all that?"

The Phoenix Force leader knew he was referring to Harold Brognola, Stony Man Farm's Director of Sensitive Operations. He nodded.

Hawkins shook his head. "He'll have these Arabs square-dancing and making moonshine before it's all over," he said, again under his breath.

With their identities established, the old Arab stuck his hand out in greeting. "I am Abdul Ali," he said. "As you can see, I was told you would come."

McCarter nodded as he shook the man's hand. "I understand you were once in the Radestani army?" he said.

Abdul Ali's shoulders straightened slightly. "I was," he said. "I rose to the rank of major."

"So what happened?" McCarter asked. "You don't look old enough to have retired."

"I did not retire," said Ali. "I simply resigned. Our government has become corrupt, and the armed forces have followed in that corruption."

McCarter nodded. The Farm's cybernetics genius, Aaron "the Bear" Kurtzman, had checked Ali out six ways to Sunday and believed the man was truly on the side of the rebels. So until something pointed him away from that view, McCarter would stick with it. "So you've been helping train the rebels?"

"We are trying to train them, and organize them into

one central force to overthrow the present government," said Ali. "There are also Special Forces Americans—Green Berets, I believe you call them—in Ramesh who are working with them, as well. But, of course, we are not publicizing that fact."

"And Russia and China aren't shouting it to the roof-tops, either," said McCarter, "but they're supporting the current regime with money, equipment and advisors."

"That is correct," said Ali. "It is the same here as it is in Syria, Lebanon, Egypt and elsewhere. There may no longer be any Soviet Union, but Russia is up to its same old tricks, as I believe you Americans say." He paused and blew air out between his closed lips, making them flutter. "It is like the Cold War all over again. As if Russia and the U.S. are playing chess on a giant chessboard and Radestan is just one of the pieces."

The two men had begun shaking hands during the brief discourse and now they dropped their arms to their sides. "How's the training been going?" McCarter asked.

Ali rolled his eyes. "Forming the rebels into a cohesive unit has not been easy," he said. "Most of the time I feel like a junior high school principal or an umpire at one of your American Little League baseball games. They do not take to military discipline very well and one bunch—I call them bunches because they are too disorganized to call them anything else—cannot agree with another bunch on anything past the fact that they all want to overthrow the government."

David McCarter nodded. "Well, we'll just have to work with what we've got," he said.

"We'll be leading the PSOF rebels into battle once

we meet up with them. So I hope at least some of the training has rubbed off."

Ali stared at the Phoenix Force leader with his dark brown eyes. "I was told to meet with you—not to take orders from you." He cleared his throat. "I am used to being in charge myself."

"Some wires must have been crossed along the chain of command, then," said McCarter. "But I'm sure we can get things cleared up." He reached over his shoulder into the backpack he'd worn during the jump. "Hang on," he said, pulling out a sat phone and tapping the speed-dial number for Stony Man Farm.

A moment later he said, "Sorry to bother you, but we've got a small problem defining the chain of command between us and our Radestani contact. Would you mind speaking to Mr. Ali for a moment?" He handed the phone to Ali.

The former Radestani major looked slightly confused as he accepted the phone and pressed it to his ear. "Hello?" he said.

The expression on the Radestani's face told McCarter that Abdul Ali was being told in no uncertain terms who was in charge and the penalties he would risk if he continued to question the chain of command. McCarter knew that Brognola could even summon the President's personal involvement if need be. Clearly, from the look on Ali's face, no such intervention would be necessary.

CHAPTER TWO

It had taken years of hard labor—not just regular hours but often evenings and weekends—for Mani Mussawi to work his way up the ladder at the nuclear storage facility just north of Colorado Springs, Colorado. Even though he had been hired years before the al Qaeda strikes against the World Trade Center and Pentagon, there had been some reservations on the part of his supervisors to employ him. After all, there had already been other Islamic extremist terrorist operations against the U.S. abroad, and while political correctness forbade them from openly acknowledging it, Mussawi's name and the dark brown color of his skin had made them uneasy.

So the former Saudi Arabian subject, now a naturalized U.S. citizen, had been forced to start at the bottom in spite of his impressive MBA from Yale.

Mussawi had begun his career working for the United States' government in the mail room, sorting the envelopes and packages that came and went each day, then pushing a clumsy cloth-and-aluminum cart around the facility to deliver each piece of correspondence to its rightful recipient. The routine had become monotonous very quickly. But Mani Mussawi had soon realized that he could not have been placed in a better position in which to begin his career.

It afforded him the opportunity to meet each and every one of the workers at the facility and to get to know them on a first-name basis. He had made a point of learning the first names of the lower-echelon employees, and made sure to always address the higher-ups as "Mr." or "Ms." or, in the case of the many former military men and women who worked there, by their former titles. Mussawi always had a broad smile on his face as he delivered the mail. The warm facial expression, combined with his frequent inquiries about the workers' children, parents and other family members had soon endeared him to the staff.

Oh, Mussawi thought as he lifted the can of disinfectant that he kept by his computer screen, there would always be a few of the hundred or so men and women whom he now worked with who would always view him with suspicion.

And there had been a short period right after the Boston Marathon bombing when people had once more taken a step back from him. But eventually they had begun to regard him as one of their own again. And those in the position to continue to promote him year after year had learned to trust him once more. Or at least act as though they did.

Mussawi sprayed his keyboard liberally and began to wipe it down with a clean cloth.

By showing their trust for him, his fellow employees could then sit back in their chairs and think, *See, we are not racists. Not at all. We even have a man of Arabic origin working in a position of trust.*Which, considering the real reason Mussawi was working where he was, made his mission a hundred times easier.

Mussawi used the cloth to push the button that would

start his computer, wondering briefly if anyone might have touched it since he'd left the day before.

As the computer worked its way through boot-up and other programs for which it was preset to utilize, Mussawi caught a glimpse of navy blue out of the corner of his eye. He looked up, smiling the congenial smile that had become second nature to him since he'd begun to work his way into the hearts of the other storage facility employees at the desks crowded into the large underground office. The smile widened further as he recognized Catherine's blond hair and blue eyes. The woman wore a navy-blue suit, and looked far more professional than she had only a few hours earlier.

Without the suit. In his bed. But she was every bit as sexy, Mani realized, as she set a disposable cup of steaming coffee on his desk.

"I thought you might need a little pick-me-up," Catherine said right before she took a sip from her own cup. Then, in a much quieter voice, she added, "After all, you expended a lot of energy last night."

Mussawi stared at the bright red lipstick that had just been transferred from Catherine's mouth to the white foam cup. In his mind, he pictured her as she'd been last night, squirming under his touch and gyrating to the rhythm of their love-making. "I have a lot of that same energy left," he whispered back, glancing quickly around to make sure none of the other people at their desks were paying them any attention. "But a little caffeine never hurt."

The two nuclear storage facility managerial position employees' eyes met for a moment and Mussawi felt a combination of lust and guilt flow through his veins. Fraternization such as theirs was forbidden between the men and women who worked together in this facility. Which, of course, made an affair such as theirs all the more enticing. They had been flirting for weeks, and the former Saudi knew that the rumors about them had run rampant. But they had not consummated their attraction until last night.

And as they'd lain together afterward, with the moonlight through his bedroom window causing the Anglo woman's light skin to glow against Mussawi's darker flesh, she had said, "We'll have to be extra careful now, my love. We need to distance ourselves from each other at work."

Mussawi had shaken his head. "That is the *worst* thing we could do. People have talked about us for weeks now. If we suddenly start ignoring each other, they will know it has finally happened."

Catherine winked at her new lover, jerking his mind out of the reverie. "Tonight?" she asked softy.

Mussawi nodded. "By all means." But even as he said the words an uneasiness swept over him. American women were promiscuous. Had he picked up any germs or even some sexually transmitted disease from Catherine? He had insisted on using condoms. Still....

Mussawi sprayed more disinfectant on his hands and rubbed them together. It was too late to worry about that now, he thought as Catherine turned and disappeared behind one of the dozens of dividers that separated the office cubicles from each other.

Mussawi's computer was now ready and he tapped in the complicated set of codes to access the facility's inventory lists. He began a second set of carefully encoded entries that would eventually lead him to the whereabouts of several hundred small, easily portable nuclear bombs. "Backpack nukes," he whispered under his breath, thinking of how very American the nickname was. He was about to access the list when Jason Hilderbrand suddenly appeared at the side of his desk. "Morning, Mani," the man said. Hilderbrand wore a button-down collared shirt beneath a V-necked sweater-vest, and shining brightly at his throat was a silver Christian cross. "How's it going, my man?"

Mussawi shook his head slightly. "It will be a boring day, I'm afraid," he said.

"Inventory, you know." Without thinking, his hand rose to his neck and he grasped the cross dangling from a silver chain around his own throat. It had been given to him by Hilderbrand soon after he'd expressed an interest in Christianity.

Hilderbrand smiled and Mani could tell that his eyes had dropped to the cross. "And how about the other thing?" he said. "The revival is still going on at my church. Great evangelist they've brought in. Patsy and I'd be honored to take you with us tonight."

Mussawi thought briefly of the hot, stuffy, tent meeting to which Hilderbrand was referring, then of the soft white flesh now hidden beneath Catherine's navy-blue work suit.

"I am sorry, Jason," he said. "But I have a previous engagement."

Now Hilderbrand reached up and touched his own cross. "But you've thought about it some more, right?"

Mussawi didn't want to pour it on too strong. So he said, "Yes, Jason. I do think about it. A lot. But it is very difficult to reject things you have been taught since birth."

Hilderbrand nodded. "I understand," he said. "But

keep thinking about it, okay? Sooner or later, the Holy Spirit will bring you the Truth."

"I am doing my best," said Mussawi, his mind still on Catherine.

"I know you are." Hilderbrand smiled. He patted Mussawi on the shoulder, then walked away.

Mussawi returned to his computer screen and keyboard and pulled up the page listing the backpack nukes. The page had been flagged, and when he hit the icon to open his top-security interoffice email, he found an order to transfer an even dozen of the small nuclear devices to another secret storage site in the Florida Keys.

The smile that covered his face now was not for anyone else's benefit. It was for him, and him alone. He had kept up with the ongoing hostilities in both Central and South America and had suspected for several days now that he'd get an order such as this.

Just because they were called backpack nukes didn't mean they had to be carried to a detonation site like a college student on his way to English composition. They could be dropped from an airplane or encompassed in the nose of a rocket just like any other bomb. For that matter, they could be rigged with a timer and simply left somewhere.

Mussawi closed the email and began the next long, tedious series of codes and passwords that would get the ball rolling for the transfer. He knew the United States had no intention of using the small nukes as a first strike against any of the countries south of Mexico. But they had to be prepared for the unlikely event that Iran, or North Korea, or one of the other "axis of evil" nations with nuclear capabilities but short-range delivery systems could cut a deal to launch at the U.S. from a closer site.

After all, it was hardly a secret that the rebels in South and Central America were being backed by America's enemies. And considering the unstable leaders who ran such countries, the decision to attack the U.S. could come based on nothing more than a sudden whim.

Mussawi stopped typing as another form appeared in his peripheral vision. He looked up to see John Karns standing patiently next to his desk. "How about lunch today, Mani?" John was a retired Marine drill sergeant who had let himself go somewhat since leaving the service. His white shirt hung over his belt both in front and on both sides.

Mussawi beamed again. "Sounds good, Sarge. But it's your turn to pay and my turn to pick."

Karns shook his head and chuckled. "That's a hard one to guess," he said. "You never want to go anywhere but McDonald's."

"I like Burger King, too," said Mussawi. "But Mc-Donald's… It always just seems more…*American.*"

Karns leaned over the desk and rested both hands next to the keyboard. "Can I tell you something, Mani?" he said, whispering almost as softly as Catherine had done.

"Of course," Mussawi said, letting his eyebrows furrow slightly to show concern.

"It's a little embarrassing," Karns said, then cleared his throat. "But I didn't like you much at first. I suppose I was something of a bigot. Especially after 9/11, I looked at all Arabs with suspicion. Even hated them."

He coughed a little nervously, then went on. "But we've been pals for what now? Ten years or so?"

"Something like that," Mussawi said. He feigned interest. He'd heard the same no-longer-a-racist speech from several other men and women who worked at the facility, and knew practically word for word, what was coming.

"Well," said Karns, "you've changed my attitude."

And now I know we're all brothers under the skin, Mussawi mentally predicted would be the man's next words.

"You've made me realize we're all the same no matter what we look like," said Karns.

"We're all individuals regardless of our ethnic backgrounds. Some people are good, some bad. But we're all brothers and sisters."

More elaborate than usual, Mussawi thought, but essentially the same self-serving speech. "That is a great compliment, Sarge," he said. "Thank you."

"You're welcome," Karns said before walking away.

Mussawi returned to his computer screen and keyboard. As quickly as he could, he moved through the next complex set of checks and balances to access the twelve backpack nukes that were to be shipped to Florida.

Twelve. An even dozen. Mussawi's hand moved to the cross suspended around his neck. Twelve was also the same number as the apostles of the Jesus that Hilderbrand kept trying to sell him on.

Mussawi made several more entries to the file. And one deletion. And when he was through, only ten of the original dozen nuclear weapons had been cleared for shipment from the Colorado Springs facility.

The other two had simply disappeared, as if they'd never existed.

Mussawi sat back and clasped his hands behind his head, stretching his back as his most genuine smile of the day curled his lips upward. It was impossible to completely erase the trail he had left in his wake. His deception *would* be discovered. But today was Friday, and it would be Monday—at the soonest—before the backpack nukes would be missed. And by then he would be long gone from this facility in the side of the mountain.

With the two missing nukes. On his way home to Radestan.

As if ordered by God himself, Ralph Perkins—Mussawi's direct supervisor—walked past as Mussawi closed his files and made his screen go black. "Ralph," he said, his voice sounding slightly weak. "I am not feeling so good."

Perkins stopped in his tracks, then took a slight step back from Mussawi's desk. "What are your symptoms?" he asked.

"Nausea. Sore throat. And it feels like a headache's coming on."

"There's a lot of flu going around," Perkins said. He glanced at an air duct in the ceiling. "Get out of here before it circulates through the vents and makes everybody else sick, too."

Mussawi nodded, stood and started toward the door. He wanted very badly to smile again. But it would not fit the illusion of pain and illness he had just created. So he looked down at his feet, shuffling slightly as he walked.

In his heart, however, he celebrated.

Now it was time for the final leg of his mission. The fulfillment of the destiny God had for him. He had been placed here as a mole more than fifteen years ago. To do exactly what, he had not then known. His job had been to lie low and wait for orders when the correct opportunity arose.

And finally that opportunity *had* arisen. The insane political correctness and tolerance of all belief systems that had infected America like the HIV virus had made it possible. Political correctness had been the most crucial element in the sham he had just pulled off.

Americans were so afraid they might offend someone that they opened themselves up to all manner of attack.

Mussawi reached the elevator in the hallway and pressed the up button. As he waited, he thought of a passage he had read in a philosophy class years before when he'd still been an undergraduate student at Yale. It had been by Friedrich Nietzsche, an atheist who God would banish forever into the tortures of Hades. But like all nonbelievers, Nietzsche had mixed truth with blasphemy to confuse the righteous. And one of those truths came back to Mussawi now.

Mussawi could not quote the philosopher verbatim but essentially Nietzsche had said that when a nation reaches a certain level of power it begins to feel sorry for, and sympathizes with, its enemies.

Which was exactly what the United States of America was doing right now.

As the elevator doors opened and Mussawi began what would be his final exit from the nuclear storage facility, the irony of it all struck him and, now alone, he laughed out loud. For years the Americans had worried that nuclear weapons might be smuggled into their beloved country. What was about to happen, however, was just the opposite.

Mussawi was about to smuggle two nukes *out* of the United States. They would go to Radestan. One would be set off in the desert as a demonstration of power. The other would then be used as a bargaining chip. A *big* bargaining chip. His Islamic freedom-fighting brothers would threaten to detonate the other backpack nuke in downtown Ramesh if the current president did not immediately step down and turn the country over to al Qaeda.

The mole rode upward in the elevator, watching the numbers above the door light up, then go dark again as he passed each floor. The situation would never get to the point where Ramesh had to be destroyed; Emad Nosiar had assured him of that. The current government was weak, and the president *would* give in. There would be no need for the second bomb. No innocents would die.

Mussawi whistled the "Star Spangled Banner" softly as he walked toward his car. Nazis, Communists, Islamic terrorists—none of them could ever really bring down the United States. Not completely, anyway. But his adopted country was about to implode when it was discovered that the nukes going to Radestan had come from America.

Because Nietzsche had been right. The U.S. felt so guilty that they were successful that they tried to make up for it with political correctness.And political correctness would be the downfall of the United States.

Blue Ridge Mountains, Virginia

AARON "THE BEAR" Kurtzman grasped the arms of his wheelchair and swiveled it slightly as he picked up the telephone next to the computer. Stony Man Farm's number-one cyber expert pressed the receiver to his ear. "Yeah, Hal?" he said into the mouthpiece.

"I'm on my way in," Brognola advised in his familiar, deep, level voice. In the background Kurtzman could hear the rotor hum of what he knew must be a helicopter.

"I'll be here," Kurtzman said, then hung up the phone.

Fifteen minutes later Hal Brognola came through the door to the Farm's Computer Room and walked up the wheelchair ramp that led to Kurtzman's long bank of computers. Clamped between Brognola's teeth was the stub of a well-chewed cigar—one of his trademarks.

The atmosphere at the top-secret counterterrorist facility known as Stony Man Farm was serious but familiar. Each individual who worked out of the Farm was a top expert in his or her field, and everyone else was aware of that fact. So while there was still a sort of paramilitary order to be followed, the warriors—both on the home front and in the field—were on a first-name basis with one another thanks to mutual respect.

So when Kurtzman said, "Hello, Mr. Director," over his shoulder without looking toward Brognola or stopping his fingers, which were flying across the keyboard, it came out sounding more like a nickname than a title.

"Ah," said Brognola as he stopped next to the wheelchair at the top of the ramp. "We're being formal today, are we?"

"Why not?" said Kurtzman. "It might class this joint

up a little now and then." Strands of his wild, prematurely white hair had fallen over his forehead and he swept them back with one hand.

"Okay, then, *Mr. Bear*," the director said, referring to Kurtzman's nickname earned for his massive physique. "What have you got for me?"

"A lot. And not much."

"Maybe I should address you as Mr. Dickens, then," Brognola said. "That sounded an awful lot like, 'It was the best of times, it was the worst of times.'"

Kurtzman whirled the wheelchair almost 180 degrees to face the man. "There's internet chatter like crazy among the crazies," he said matter-of-factly. "Almost an eight hundred percent increase in what we're used to." He inhaled a deep breath. "So we've got to assume *something* bigger than usual is in the works."

"But you don't know what it is?" Brognola chomped down a little harder on the cigar stub.

Kurtzman nodded and more strands of hair bounced on top of his head. "Precisely," he said. "Which I guess would fall under your Dickens' quote as being in the 'worst of times' category. However I did pick up the word *nuke* encoded in one email. But for the most part, they—whoever *they* are—have gone to a whole new software program."

Brognola's eyebrows lowered. "We can thank that little weasel Edward Snowden for that," he said. "I'd like to get my hands around his throat. He's the reason our enemies have changed software and everything else they can." He clamped down harder on his cigar, then changed the subject slightly. "Nuke, of course, is our abbreviation for nuclear. Do you mean—"

"Yes," Kurtzman interrupted the big Fed. "Most

everyone in the world, regardless of language, calls nuclear weapons 'nuclear weapons.' And they use the same shorthand version of the word—nuke—just like we do. The atom was first split by men who spoke English and so the word has become integrated, without change, into just about every culture on Earth."

"Was the word used in any sort of context you could make out?" the director asked.

Kurtzman shook his head. "Negative. But keep in mind it's also a word that gets kicked around all the time in cyberspace slang. It *could* mean our worst fears—some terrorist group has gotten its hands on a nuclear bomb and is planning to use it somewhere in the world. But that's not necessarily the case. There's a lot of bragging, and posturing, and bring-on-the-jihad-high-school-pep-rally-type crap thrown around between the terrorists these days, too."

"Now I see what you mean by having a lot and having nothing," Brognola said. "But we've got to always assume it *could* mean something disastrous."

Kurtzman nodded. "Of course we do," he said. "The bottom line is that I just don't know exactly what's going on at this point."

The SOG director stared the computer genius straight in the eye. "You aren't telling me you can't decipher this new software cyber babble, are you?" he asked, a puzzled look on his face.

Kurtzman almost smiled. He did his best to remain modest about his abilities with what he often referred to as his "magic machines." And most of the time he was successful in that modesty. But he also knew there was no one in the world quite as skilled in both the science and art of cyberspace as he was. That wasn't his ego speaking, either. It was just the way it was. Or as Yogi Berra had once said, "It ain't brag if it's true."

"No, Hal," the man in the wheelchair said, "I'm not telling you I *can't* decipher it. I'm just telling you that because of all of the intelligence information Snowden leaked about how we follow terrorists, they've gone to whole new programs and it'll take a little while for me to figure them out." He paused and took another deep breath. "The terrorist groups—all of them—are getting much better at covering their tracks than they used to be. There are so many of them, and they've linked up with dozens of Third World countries in the Middle East and Africa. Which means they've gained access to more sophisticated electronics than they used to have.

"They're also getting more and more help from former Soviet computer experts who hire themselves out as sort of cyber mercenaries." The Farm's cyber genius shook his head slowly as he scratched the side of his face. "It's a lot like the difference between what we were when Stony Man first started and where we are today. In the beginning, we were lucky to have computers that could even access the internet, send email, whatever. And now…" He turned slightly and swept a hand across the front of the dozen or so computers to which he had access. "We've progressed," he said. "But so has the enemy."

A thin smile curled the corners of Brognola's mouth and the cigar stump rose at a steeper angle between his teeth. "In the old days we were lucky to have two-way radios with face transmitters and headphones," he agreed. "So yeah, we've come a long way." The cigar stub had almost disappeared inside his mouth now and he took it out and dropped it into a trash can just to the side of Kurtzman's desk.Then, reaching inside his jacket, he pulled out a leather cigar carrier, slid the top off and produced a fresh stogie—which wouldn't be smoked any more than the last one had been. Sticking the cigar in his mouth, he returned the case to his pocket and said, "But the world was a safer place in those days, overall. I never thought I'd miss the old Soviet Union. But at least they were more practical when it came to things like nuclear warfare." He chomped down on the cigar. To Kurtzman, it looked as if he was only a few tobacco leaves away from biting the cigar in two. "Moscow knew that a nuclear strike would mean nuclear retaliation, and be disastrous for both countries and the whole world. These terrorist organizations either don't realize that or don't care. They think they're on a mission from God."

"They're about as much on a mission from God as the Blues Brothers were on *Saturday Night Live*," Kurtzman said.

Brognola chuckled. Then his eyebrows lowered and his voice turned serious. "Okay," he said. "I'd better get going. I've got to track down Able Team. They're test-firing some new weapons with Kissinger off-site, and I think we'd better get that done right away. Because when you decipher this chatter flying back and forth across computer land I suspect they'll be on an immediate flight out of here to…wherever." Kurtzman turned back to his keyboard. "Will do, *Mr.* Director," he said as his hands once again flew across the letters, numbers and symbols with lightning speed.

"Thank you, *Mr.* Bear," Brognola said as he started walking away. He had gone only a few steps when a computer in the bank in front of Kurtzman suddenly rang out with a siren not as loud, but not unlike an emergency tornado warning in the suburb of some Southwestern U.S. city. Kurtzman wheeled to it, then tapped a few keys and stared at the screen.

Brognola stopped and turned back.

A moment later Kurtzman's head swiveled and he stared at the big Fed. "You know that 'wherever' you said Able Team would be flying off to, Hal?" he said.

Brognola nodded.

"I know where it is," said Kurtzman.

CHAPTER THREE

Carl "Ironman" Lyons raised his hands to cover his ears as soon as the first shot was fired. In his peripheral vision, he could see that John "Cowboy" Kissinger—Stony Man's chief armorer—had done the same. Kissinger wanted to test some new weapons not just on the Stony Man firing range but under more realistic battlefield conditions, so had arranged for a visit to a "kill house" used by SWAT teams both local and federal. Covering their ears had been an instinctive reaction to the thunderous noise. Even coming from inside the enclosed walls of the kill house the outside effects of the explosions were painful. Not unlike synchronized swimmers, each man outside the house ensured their earplugs and coverings were secure before the next round was fired.

More shots exploded inside the walls and the Able Team leader pictured Rosario Blancanales—better known to his fellow Able Team members as "Politician" or simply "Pol"—making his way through the rooms of the practice range. The kill house had three levels and each room, hallway and staircase was equipped with "pop up" targets that featured good guys, bad guys, hostages and innocent bystanders—all of whom had to be shot or passed by with less than a second's consideration by the brain.

More shots rang out. Now that his ears were covered, Lyons dropped his hands to his sides and moved quickly to where Kissinger stood, leaning against one of the pickups in which they had arrived. The Stony Man armorer held a laptop computer in front of him, and on the screen the Able Team leader could see the interior of the house. Blancanales was making his way cautiously up the steps to the second floor. In his hands was a Yankee Hill Machine Company's Model 15.

A head and shoulders—then two arms holding an AK-47—suddenly appeared at the top of the steps and Blancanales fired one shot directly through the forehead. A ragged hole appeared in the paper face of a terrorist wearing a turban. Then the target disappeared as quickly as it had appeared.

Lyons continued to watch as Blancanales made his way through the rooms on the second and then third floor, carefully picking out the good guys from the bad and putting holes through the paper images of the enemy targets. The Able Team leader noted, however, that each time his fellow warrior pulled the trigger, he winced slightly.

The Yankee Hill Model 15's short ten-inch barrel combined with powerful 6.8-caliber rounds, was loud even outside the facility. It had to be deafening for the man inside.

Almost as if he'd read Lyons's thoughts, Blancanales suddenly stopped and turned around. On the screen, Lyons saw him flip the short-barreled carbine's selector to the safe position. Then, the YHM held barrel down, the Able Team member retraced his steps and exited the building without completing the course.

As soon as Blancanales emerged, he shook his head

in what looked like an attempt to clear the ringing in his ears, then walked swiftly toward the pickup where Lyons and Kissinger stood. Handing the YHM-15 to Kissinger, he said, "It shoots great. But if I'd finished the course I'd have been as deaf as my ninety-year-old grandfather." He shook his head again. "Give me the standard M-16 A2 anytime."

Kissinger smiled, and Lyons sensed that the armorer had anticipated just such a reaction. Turning, he set the YMH in the bed of the pickup. When his hands came back in sight, he held a similar-looking rifle. But this weapon bore a long tubular device on the end of the barrel and there was a small scope mounted in the top of the receiver.

"Try this one, Pol," Kissinger said, extending the rifle in front of him. "I think you'll find it a little gentler on the eardrums."

Blancanales took the weapon and looked down at it. "Sound suppression," he noted.

"Right," Kissinger agreed. "And while you won't be able to appreciate it fully here in the daylight, it cuts down considerably on the muzzle flash from the short barrel."

Blancanales nodded. "I'll go back and give it *one* shot," he said. "But if it isn't quiet enough…" His voice trailed off for a moment. "I'm not sacrificing my hearing for it."

"I think you'll be happy with it," said Kissinger. "Yankee Hill's making some with permanent suppressors. But I've altered several so you can take them off if you *want* to create noise and confusion."

Blancanales lifted the rifle slightly in his hands.

"Not much heavier than the unsuppressed model," he said. "The suppressor titanium?"

Kissinger nodded. He cradled the laptop in his left arm long enough to hold his other fist to his mouth and cough. "Adds about eight inches to the barrel length. You put that on the end of the standard M-16 and you've got 22 to 24 inches beyond the receiver. That's bumped the weapon up to sniper length—*without* sniper rifle accuracy."

Hermann "Gadgets" Schwarz, Able Team's electronics expert, joined the group and studied the look on Blancanales's face.

Blancanales wasn't convinced. "It doesn't look like a problem on this 10-inch barrel," he said. "It'll still be relatively easy to maneuver inside tight spaces. But a 10-inch tube means a sacrifice in sight radius."

"That's what the optics are for," Kissinger said, pointing to the scope.

Schwartz smiled and said, "You suppose the boys over at the BATFE would approve?"

"Alcohol, tobacco, firearms and explosives? Of course not," Lyons growled. "But luckily we don't answer to those Bureau yo-yos."

Blancanales stared down at the new rifle as he retraced his steps toward the entrance to the kill house. Lyons watched Kissinger tap several keys on the laptop's keyboard and knew the armorer was changing the pop-up targets to give his fellow teammate a new challenge. A moment later he saw Blancanales appear on the screen at the starting point.

Kissinger pressed a button on the chronometer on his wrist and shouted, "Go!"

Blancanales carefully navigated his way through a

mock laundry room without incident. But as soon as he stepped through the door to a hallway, a full-size target popped into view as if from out of nowhere. Blancanales swung the sound-suppressed weapon that way but didn't fire.

A little girl stood holding a lollipop to her lips less than ten feet to Blancanales's left. A second later, the paper target disappeared.

Blancanales moved on, his back against the wall as he navigated the corner past where the girl had stood. The screen in Kissinger's hand changed again and Lyons could see a large bedroom just ahead of his fellow Able Team warrior. Blancanales had just stepped into the room when another target—this time a criminal-looking guy wearing a striped T-shirt, appeared. He held a large revolver in his right hand. His other arm was wrapped around the neck of a woman whose face looked terrified.

This time Blancanales tapped the trigger and three rounds of 6.8-caliber hollowpoint ammo spit from the weapon. The sound of each round was barely audible over the microphone Blancanales wore in front of his mouth. But three holes appeared in the hoodlum's face, two inches above the frightened hostage's head.

When Blancanales said, "Much, *much* better, Cowboy," his voice seemed loud by comparison.

The words had barely left his mouth when two new targets raised their heads above the other side of the bed. The first showed only the face and neck. Blancanales passed it by. But the second target rose higher, exhibiting shoulders wearing a desert-tan camouflage BDU blouse. Blancanales turned the YHM that way but hesitated again.

A split second later the target rose slightly higher and the butt of a folding rifle stock could barely be seen. It was still impossible to ID the target as friend or foe, and the Able Team operative held his fire as another second passed.

Then the target behind the bed rose higher and began bringing the weapon up toward the Able Team warrior. Finally, he was clearly the enemy, and Blancanales put a 3-round burst into his head. The camouflaged target dropped down behind the bed.

Suddenly the first target began to rise. It wore the same style BDU desert-tan blouse. But when it rose, Lyons could see that its hands were empty.

Blancanales let it live.

The Able Team warrior moved on through the kill house, shooting the bad guys and rescuing the good. Each new room, each hall and stairway, presented new and increasingly confusing targets. But by the time Blancanales had finished clearing the third floor of the house he had a perfect score.

And while he had not set a new personal record with the unfamiliar weapon in his hands, he had come close.

Lyons was about to speak when the Farm-secured cell phone in the belt holster behind his Colt Python .357 Magnum began to vibrate. Drawing the phone much like he would the revolver, he looked at the screen. He pressed the answer button and held the device to his ear. "Yeah, Hal?" he said.

"If you're finished playing Cowboys and Indians, I need you back at the Farm," the Stony Man director said. "I've sent Jack to pick you up."

"What have we got?" Lyons asked.

"Two backpack nukes have disappeared from a nuclear storage facility in Colorado," Brognola said.

"Okay," said Lyons. "We're on our way." He holstered the cell phone as Blancanales appeared from the kill house and walked forward, holding his new YHM and grinning ear to ear.

The man known as Ironman looked up at Kissinger. "Yankee Hill Machine has made an incredible weapon, here, Cowboy," Lyons said. "And you've made it even better. We'll take three." *Outside Ramesh, Radestan* THE MEN OF Phoenix Force and Abdul Ali kept away from the blacktop highway, using the trees and brush lining the roadway to hide them as they made their way toward Ramesh. But along with the natural concealment, they passed a seemingly endless stream of wrecked and burned-out military vehicles representing both sides of the conflict in Radestan. Old and broken-down jeeps—looking as if they'd been left over from World War II and repeatedly repaired—lined the ditch every hundred feet or so. Most still bore the spray-painted eagle-and-scimitar seal of Radestan.

But other vehicles looked more civilian in nature. Well-worn pickups and bullet-ridden sedans—many so old that the paint had worn off and the dull gray primer had become their principal color—were also lying dead in the grass and weeds. All were unmarked and David McCarter reasoned that these had belonged to private citizens before being pressed into service by one of the PSOF rebel factions.

The men of Phoenix Force had each thrown on an *abat*—the traditional Arab robe common throughout the Middle East—over their blacksuits, and *kafiyyehs* covered their heads and necks. Led by Abdul Ali, who now carried an AK-47 that rested just beneath his long black-and-gray beard, they slowly made their way through the wrecks and weeds alongside what passed for a highway.

Hawkins had been able to clean enough of the cow manure off his boots to make them wearable again and, for the most part, the snide remarks and needling from the men who had been fortunate enough not to land inside the corral had ceased.

The men from Stony Man Farm and their Radestani guide walked in silence, only speaking when some small anomaly needed to be pointed out, and then in small, hushed voices. In several of the vehicles they passed, corpses still sat behind the steering wheels and in the shotgun and rear seats. Many were upright, their heads partially blown off by enemy gunfire. Those that still had eyes stared blankly into the distance, their souls long gone from their earthly housings. Other bodies were almost headless, while still more appeared to have been burned alive, their blackened arms clawing at the handles inside the vehicles in vain attempts to escape their fiery coffins.

The corpses in the vehicles, and the semi-burned vegetation growing up around them, gave the area an eerie, otherworldly ambience.

While the ground upon which they tread was flat, across the blacktop in the distance stood a high mountain range. Around McCarter's neck hung a pair of binoculars, which the Phoenix Force leader lifted occasionally to scan those mountains and the terrain in front of them.

The group was roughly a mile from the city when a glint of sunlight flashed from the mountains. The reflected glow lasted only a split second. But McCarter had seen such flashes of light far too many times in the past to not immediately identify its origin.

The reflection had come from the front lens of a scope. A scope mounted atop a rifle held in the hands of a shooter too inexperienced to know that he should keep the scope covered until the last few seconds before firing.

Or a rifleman who *did* know his business. And actually *was* only seconds away from squeezing the trigger. The Phoenix Force leader called for an immediate halt. "Sniper," he said in a quiet voice because sounds, he knew, traveled far in such terrain. Raising the binoculars again, he zeroed in on the spot where he'd seen the flash. The field glasses included an automatic range finger, and they measured the distance at 642 feet. Not a long shot by any means. Even for a slip-shod Radestan regular or a semitrained rebel.

Through the lenses, McCarter could just make out the outline of a man. The sniper's hide had been set up behind a boulder at the foot of the mountain. It was crude but sufficient to disguise the man in the distance from all but the most highly trained eye.

As he watched the still figure, the Phoenix Force leader thanked God that he was one of those highly trained eyes.

Quickly swinging the binoculars away from the sniper, McCarter moved them downrange to make it appear as though he had not spotted the enemy. With the eyepieces still pressed to his forehead, he said, "Act busy with your equipment." Then he quickly dropped the binoculars to the end of their strap. "I don't want him to know I've spotted him." Then, to no one in particular, he added, "Can you see him?"

Calvin James had pulled the twelve-inch blade of his Crossada fighting knife from the Concealex sheath he wore on his left hip. The Crossada was a spear-pointed blend of Bowie knife and Arkansas Toothpick, and one well-placed thrust could drop a man at close range faster than a 12-gauge slug through the middle of the chest. But as McCarter watched, James began pretending to cut away some of the brush in front of him. "I can see something up there," the former Navy SEAL said in a hushed voice. "What do you want to do?"

McCarter had swung his Rock River LAR-15 Hunter from his shoulder and pretended to be checking the magazine. The weapon sported a unique anodized finish to the aluminum hand guard, upper and lower receivers, trigger guard and charging handle. Referred to as a WYL-Ehide camo finish, from a distance it appeared to be a bronze color. But looking at it closely, the Phoenix Force leader had to smile at its furlike appearance.

The special camouflage had been digitally adopted from an actual photo of a real coyote's hide.

Designed originally for coyote hunting, McCarter knew the RRA LAR-15 and its 5.56 mm NATO rounds worked equally well when hunting *men*. And it was far more accurate than the common AR-15/M-16 rifles on the market.

Especially after John "Cowboy" Kissinger finished his own tune-up.

McCarter glanced over to where James was still cutting brush. "I want you to get ready," he said, finally answering the knife fighter's question. "I don't know if he's government or rebel. But he's definitely got us in his sights and could start pulling the trigger on us anytime." Extending the LAR-15's six-position stock, he kept the barrel aimed at the ground as he pressed it into his shoulder. "I'm going to take him out. But I've got a feeling he's not alone."

"Affirmative," James said, transferring the Crossada to his left hand and continuing to swing it at the tall grass. Casually, his right hand moved to the Beretta 92-SB 9 mm on his other hip.

McCarter watched as the others silently nodded their acknowledgment of the order.

"Do you want—?" Rafael Encizo started to say.

McCarter knew there was no time for manners. "Quiet," he said bluntly.

Encizo was a professional, too. He immediately stopped speaking.

Abdul Ali was the only man not covered by an *abat*. He didn't need one to blend in. Still wearing his khaki pants, woodland cammo BDU blouse and checkered kaffiyeh, he came hurrying up from McCarter's rear. "If he is with the resistance," said the man with the long gray-streaked beard, "he will recognize me."

"And if he's *not* on our side and he recognizes you?" McCarter said.

Ali shrugged. "It is a chance I must take," he said.

It was one heck of a risk, McCarter knew. Every second that passed was another second during which the sniper might fire and kill one of them. But the Phoenix Force leader knew it was a risk they had to take. He waited another full second, using the time to take in a deep breath and let half of it out again.

This could not be a common countersniper shot,

the Phoenix Force leader thought as he prepared to act. They were lucky that the man in the mountain had created such a bad hide to begin with, and even luckier that he hadn't caught the Phoenix Force leader staring back at him through the binoculars. If he had, he'd have already fired at least once, then moved. And if he saw McCarter's LAR-15 Hunter barrel aimed his way, it would tip him off just as readily.

Taking too much time after he'd aimed the rifle would definitely cause the sniper to change positions.

Slowly, McCarter adjusted the red-dot scope on the top of the LAR's Picatinny rail. Ali's presence had not resulted in action by the sniper so the Phoenix Force leader waited no longer. Suddenly and without further ado, he swung his rifle barrel up and toward the mountain 642 yards away. He could see only the blurry outline of the would-be sniper's head, shoulders and whatever rifle he held in his hands. Sighting in on the middle of the dark figure, he squeezed the trigger and felt the Hunter jump slightly in his hands.

Through the scope, McCarter saw the sniper's head explode like a watermelon dropped from a ten-story building.

But a second later an explosion of a different type took place.

As if from out of nowhere, men bearing a variety of assault rifles, sawed-off shotguns and handguns suddenly shot up fifty feet farther down the line of brush and wrecked vehicles. And, unlike McCarter, they had no reason to hesitate.

The first dozen rounds or so seemed to come at exactly the same time, sounding like one gigantic explosion.

"Down!" McCarter yelled. It was an unnecessary order. The men of Phoenix Force and Ali had all dropped into the grass behind vehicles of their own accord.

McCarter felt his elbows sink into the damp earth just behind what had once been a Radestani army jeep. He'd had no time for an actual head count of the enemy, but a quick skim caused him to estimate roughly two dozen.

Those were the adversaries he could *see*. There could be more—many more, in fact—that had simply been a little slower rising and showing themselves.

In any case, Phoenix Force and their companion were outnumbered. *Greatly*.

But that was hardly a new situation for the men from Stony Man Farm.

John "Cowboy" Kissinger had performed his weapon-smithing magic on the Rock River LAR-15 and given it the capacity to shoot semiauto, 3-round burst or fully automatic fire. McCarter switched the selector to the latter mode as he rose briefly and held the trigger back, spraying the men farther down the roadway with a hail-storm of 5.56 mm rounds. It was not the wild firing act of panic or frustration to which less-seasoned warriors might have resorted. McCarter simply wanted to open the show with a bang. Or, more precisely, with a *lot* of bangs. And to make sure the enemy knew they were in for a fight.

Two of them died learning that fact as the Hunter's barrel swept across the mass of men.

McCarter ducked into the weeds, his shoulder against the rear of a jeep as return fire flew over his head. Around him he could hear the roar of the other men's rifles as they, too, maintained their assault on the enemy. For a brief moment his mind traveled back to the firing range at the Farm where the men of Phoenix Force had tested and evaluated dozens of rifles and add-on combinations before choosing what they liked best. All of the test weapons had been variants of the AR-15 that had been made by different companies and tailored to fit specific needs, likes and dislikes. Each had its own subtle—and sometimes not-so-subtle—differences from the others.

A short lull came to the firefight, and McCarter recalled each of his team's favorite rifle. Manning had liked the Bushmaster. Encizo had stuck with his tried-and-true Colt. James had fallen in love with the titanium Nemo—a rifle that cost one hundred thousand dollars on the open market and was worth every penny. And Hawkins had cast his vote for a Spike's Tactical.

But McCarter had known they would be on their own, and Murphy's Law always applied: things would go wrong. Equipment, no matter how well made, sometimes broke down and carrying spare parts for five different weapons was out of the question. So he had chosen the LAR-15 for all of them. And none of the Phoenix Force warriors had objected very much. After all, they knew that it was a case of men fighting men—not specific weapons fighting other weapons. And the men of Phoenix Force were more than capable with any rifle placed in their hands.

So now the coyote-hide-camo rifles began throwing massive amounts of jacketed hollowpoints down the road toward the men who had sprung the sudden attack.

But were they hitting anyone? McCarter wondered.

And if they were, were they killing government soldiers or People's Secular Opposition Forces rebels?

There was only one way to find out. Keep fighting. And do your best to stay alive. And in the end, it really made little difference. While there was an attempt being made to train and unite the scattered PSOF factions, at the moment some of them were every bit as much the enemy as the Radestani regulars. Each faction had its own selfish agenda. And if any of them actually took over the government, they would immediately begin a campaign of genocide directed at the other factions.

McCarter had seen similar situations in other parts of the world. And he knew they could not allow that to happen here.

Rising again, the Phoenix Force leader aimed his new weapon over the jeep and peered above the scope. Phoenix Force's war in Radestan was, and promised to continue being, an extremely confusing situation. But then *all wars* were confusing, McCarter reminded himself. And as he fired at the attackers, one man near the front finally gave away their identity by screaming out, "*Allahu Akbar!*" McCarter was slightly surprised but hardly shocked. The men attacking them were not government soldiers. But they weren't one of the rebel factions, either. The men trying to kill the warriors of Phoenix Force and Abdul Ali were part of the al Qaeda terrorist faction Phoenix Force had been warned was waiting in the wings, preparing to take over the country as soon as the regulars and rebels had killed each other off.

McCarter cut loose with a 3-round burst from the Hunter, secure now that he was shooting at a faction of "bad guys" in this strange three-way war. Yes, all wars were confusing. This one just happened to be more so.

It was totally, one hundred percent, completely screwed up.

The Phoenix Force leader fired again and a trio of rounds ripped into the chest of the man who had yelled. A terrorist wearing a brown cloth safari-style hat took all three of the Phoenix Force leader's rounds in the face, all but eliminating his head. For a second, the hat seemed to hover above the neck in midair. Then it fell straight down to land on the man's shoulders before the body slumped out of sight and into the tall grass.

Around him, in the grass and behind the trashed vehicles, McCarter could hear the return fire from the rest of his team and Abdul Ali. Phoenix Force's RRA LAR-15 Hunter rounds were easy enough to distinguish from the AK-47 explosions from both Ali and the al Qaeda shooters opposing them.

McCarter fired another burst, then dropped to his knee again behind the abandoned jeep. Following the time-proven strategy that you never showed yourself to the enemy more than once in the same place, he knee-walked his way to the right bumper. Leaning his face around the edge, he kept the rest of his body behind the vehicle and extended the LAR-15 at arm's length. His body still completely covered, he risked only his hands and arms as he used his thumb on the trigger, firing a long full-auto burst blindly in the general direction of the enemy.

McCarter jerked his arms and the rifle back out of sight, immediately edging his face around the jeep's bumper. His blind assault had done the job he'd wanted it to do, causing the enemy combatants to shrink back into hiding long enough for him to make a quick survey of the situation.

One man, however, had not been intimidated by the full-auto blast. He had dark skin and wore a bright red shirt that looked as if the sleeves had been chopped off at the shoulders with a machete. McCarter switched the selector on his LAR-15 to 3-round burst and squeezed the trigger again, this time with his eyes fixed on the center of the man's chest.

Black holes appeared in the red cloth of his shirt as the man danced like a marionette on the end of the strings of a mad puppeteer. As he fell to the ground, another attacker—this one wearing blue jeans and a white T-shirt—caught more rounds from one of the other Phoenix Force men. The AK-47 in the man's hands flew up into the air as one of the hollowpoints apparently hit a nerve, causing his arm to rise. Red blotches appeared on the white shirt—two in the chest and one in the shoulder—as he joined his red-clad comrade in death.

Blood seeping from the bullet wounds in the red shirt had made black splotches. In the white shirt, the holes had turned red. But white or red, either way, someone needed to teach these attackers something about camouflage. Red and white did little for concealment in an environment made up of green-and-brown vegetation and rusted-out vehicles.

McCarter took a deep breath as the firing around him continued. As safe as could be expected behind the old jeep's engine block, his eyes flashed 180 degrees through the tall grass in the vacant spaces of this automobile graveyard. As was the case in so many Third World countries, vehicles so old or used that no

American would have them anymore had been shipped to Radestan. Here, locals had brought them back to life using everything from home-manufactured replacement parts to bailing wire in an effort that was, ironically, called "Yankee Ingenuity." But even the work of such desperate mechanics had its limits, and eventually the scraps had been abandoned.

McCarter caught himself shaking his head in dismay. It seemed that everywhere he looked he saw a make and model of automobile he had not seen since he'd been a child. Other vehicles had ceased being produced before he had even been born.

As he prepared to lean around the jeep and fire again, the Phoenix Force leader saw James rise slightly behind the remnants of a 1965 Dodge Dart GT. A few spots of gold paint could still be seen on the old car's body but ninety percent of the vehicle now sported nothing but gray primer. James's big Crossada was back in the sheath on his hip, and the former Navy SEAL was leaning over the GT's hood with his LAR-15. Sputtering 5.56 mm rounds through the barrel, the Hunter danced slightly in his hands as he fired a full-auto stream across the car at some target that was out of McCarter's vision.

Dave McCarter's attention was focused so intently on the enemies in the tall grass in front of him that he almost missed the crunching sound of footsteps to his rear. But instinct and training took over, and before he even realized what he was doing he had whirled around. Still on his knees, McCarter caught a glimmer of blue through the brown-and-yellow stalks behind him. And in less time than it would have taken to write it up in a report, he knew that no one on his team, nor Abdul Ali, had been clad in anything blue.

His finger pulled back on the trigger.

McCarter's Rock River rifle choked out rounds and a trio of hollowpoints disappeared into the grass. He heard a low, guttural grunting sound, then the fleck of blue descended beneath the dead foliage. As the explosions from the AK-47s and Phoenix Force's LAR-15s died down, the former British SAS man slung his rifle across his back, drew his Browning Hi-Power and crawled forward.

By the time he reached the body with the blue T-shirt, the gunfire had stopped completely. Behind him now, McCarter could hear the quiet chatter of his own men. They were moving slowly through the grass and around the abandoned vehicles, checking to make sure there were no survivors to "pop back to life" and kill them.

The man in blue who had crept toward the Phoenix Force leader from the rear had been gut-shot, then fallen facedown in the mud. McCarter had to have passed by him to the side as he'd moved forward. But the shooter had gone unseen in the underbrush. At some point, he'd regained enough strength to rise and attack from the rear.

The Phoenix Force leader knelt and checked him out closer now. An exit hole the size of a softball gaped upward from between the man's shoulder blades. Multicolored masses of flesh, blood and bone had exited and some of it still lay on the man's back as if dumped there. The Phoenix Force leader reached down, grabbed the shooter's shoulder and rolled him over onto his back. He frowned slightly as he saw that two of the three rounds he had fired at the grass-hidden blue seemed to have missed.

But that didn't matter much. One bullet had found its mark dead center in the middle of the T-shirt. It was far smaller than the one in the dead man's back, as was to be expected for an entry wound. But between the two holes in the man's body, the 5.56 mm hollowpoint had done its job.

The heart had to have been mangled beyond recognition.

The roar of the rifles on both sides of the skirmish was now a thing of the past. McCarter rose, turned around and walked back to join the rest of the men who had regrouped around an ancient Dodge Charger. "Everybody okay?" he asked.

Everyone nodded.

"Good," said the Phoenix Force leader. "Then let's get on in to Ramesh." He paused and wiped the sweat off his brow with the back of his sleeve. "The *real* fighting's about to begin."

CHAPTER FOUR

Charlie Mott, Stony Man Farm's second pilot, was almost as good with wings as Jack Grimaldi. At least he was good enough to get the men of Able Team from Stony Man Farm to Colorado Springs, Colorado, in what might well have been record time—even for a Learjet.

If the flight had been official. But of course it wasn't. There would be no record of the trip since as far as the vast majority of the world knew it had never taken place. To everyone outside the Stony Man Farm family, except for the President of the United States, there wasn't even an Able Team in existence. Just as there was no Mack Bolan or Phoenix Force or Stony Man Farm in general.

Carl "Ironman" Lyons, Able Team's former LAPD detective, felt himself smile inwardly. In a weird way, the whole Stony Man Farm crew—Mack Bolan, the teams, the blacksuits and the specialized computer, forensic and other support staff—reminded Lyons a bit of J. Edgar Hoover's attempt to convince the public that there was no such thing as the Mafia. Of course there were three major differences.First, the now deceased FBI director's nonexistent Mafia had bootlegged countless gallons of illegal liquor, then billions of dollars of illegal narcotics throughout the country.

And they'd been responsible for more murders than could be counted. But Hoover's propaganda had been put out over a half century earlier—at a time when the general public still had at least a little faith that some politicians were honest. Faith in politicians—be they Democrat or Republican, conservative or liberal—had all but vanished in recent years.

The second difference was that keeping Stony Man Farm a secret had actually worked.

Third—and most important of all—was that unlike the Mafia, the crew at Stony Man Farm worked for the good of mankind rather than conscienceless monetary profit.

Lyons glanced over his shoulder at the two men behind him in the jet. Like the Able Team leader himself, the men wore dark business suits. Blancanales was decked out in a deep navy-blue. Schwarz wore his usual gray. Lyons himself had chosen a black suit with gray pinstripes. He had never been high on bling. Nor was the Able Team leader the type to laugh out loud very often. Even his smiles were few and far between. But the sight of his fellow warriors masquerading as FBI agents instead of wearing blacksuits or BDUs made the corners of his mouth curl up slightly.

As the jet's wheels hit the tarmac Lyons's thoughts turned to Hal Brognola. As the Director of the Sensitive Operations Group, the covert operations arm of the U.S. Justice Department, Brognola worked as Stony Man's liaison to conventional law enforcement. So, wearing his DOJ hat, he had called ahead to make sure that two *real* FBI agents out of the Colorado Springs field office would be waiting for them when they landed.

Now Lyons saw them off to the side of the runway,

both leaning against the doors of two near-identical Chevrolet sedans.

The Learjet rolled almost to a halt before making a sharp left turn and taxiing onto a concrete access road. A moment later Mott stopped the plane just in front of the waiting men and cars.

Lyons, Blancanales and Schwarz said goodbye to Mott as they dropped down from the jet. Lyons moved forward toward a man who might have been the poster boy for an FBI recruitment ad. He had short, blond, brush-cut hair and broad shoulders. Even more telling was the way he moved, combining the balance of a tiger on the prowl with the apparent strength of a grizzly as he stepped up and extended his hand.

The Able Team leader gripped the man's hand and immediately noticed two things. First, the man was a weight-lifter. FBI work could be dangerous and sometimes strenuous. But it didn't put calluses on a man's hands like the ones Lyons felt as they shook hands.

The second thing of which he took note was the lining of the man's suit coat as it briefly appeared when the man extended his arm. As soon as he saw the striped material Lyons remembered that somewhere, sometime, someone had told him that striped lining inside a man's suit meant *expensive*. Not being particularly interested in such things, he'd forgotten who and when. After all, he wasn't a model for *Gentleman's Quarterly* or James Bond on his way to a Monte Carlo casino. Able Team was not here to pose for men's clothing photos or to play cards.

They had come to find out what had happened to a pair of nuclear bombs. And to kill anybody who got in their way.

"Special Agent Arthaud," the broad-shouldered man said as he let loose of Lyons's hand.

"Taylor," said the other agent. He was taller and thinner. The fact was he looked more like a marathon runner than the wrestler, power-lifter or body-builder that Arthaud appeared to be. He wore an olive-green sport coat and khaki slacks.

"We have orders to supply you with a car," said Arthaud. "Then to stay out of your way." His smile looked genuine and it didn't appear that he resented not knowing anything more about the men who had just arrived via Learjet.

"Thanks," Lyons said simply. He pulled open the door of the plane's cargo hold and he and the other men of Able Team unload their equipment bags. Their new Yankee Hill Machine Company 6.8 mm sound-suppressed rifles were in obvious padded gun cases complete with extra magazine pockets on the outside of the main compartment. When Arthaud saw them, he said, "Looks like you're expecting something serious."

"We always expect something serious," Lyons said as he hefted a duffel bag in one hand and a rifle case in the other before carrying them both to the trunk of one of the Chevy sedans.

"You guys Hostage Rescue?" Taylor asked.

"Sometimes," said Lyons, which left a quizzical look on the face of the man who had asked the question. A moment later they had finished transferring the equipment and closed the trunk. Lyons turned back to Arthaud. "Can you give us directions to the storage facility?" he asked.

Arthaud smiled again. And again it seemed genuine. "I can do better than that," he said. "I've already set your GPS to take you there."

"Ugh," Blancanales said. "That means we've got to listen to that computer-generated female robot all the way there." His voice climbed two octaves and he mimicked, "Turn right in one quarter mile. Proceed ten miles to intersection." Then, shaking his head, he said, "And if we don't follow directions we hear, 'You have left the route—'" Hermann Schwarz hadn't been nicknamed "Gadgets" for nothing. He loved, and seemed to understand instinctively, every new bit of technology that came along in a computer world that progressed at lightning speed. "Don't worry," he said, grinning at his partner. "I'll dumb it down to your level and explain it to you as we go."

Arthaud laughed and then said, "Tell you what. We'll lead you there. Sound okay?"

"Sounds fine," said Lyons. "But I'm afraid the front door is as far as you get. Nothing personal."

Arthaud shrugged his big shoulders. "No problem," he said. "It's pretty obvious that whatever you're here to do is highly sensitive. I mean, after all, we know the kind of stuff they've got stored at that facility."

"Thanks for understanding," Lyons said.

Arthaud chuckled. "I'm not being completely altruistic," he said. "The bottom line is what we don't know won't hurt us. Meaning that if we know what you're doing, and you screw something up, we'll be tied up for days, maybe weeks, being interrogated ourselves as if we were criminals or terrorists."

"Good thinking," Lyons said. And typically bureaucratic, he thought but didn't voice. Arthaud and Taylor both seemed like nice guys. But as happened with so many in government jobs, they had lost much of the ambition they had probably had when they'd first signed on with the FBI. They had come to know that promotions were more likely to go to agents who never made waves and had no complaints in their personnel files rather than those who worked hard, took chances and cracked major cases. And the best way to stay out of trouble was to avoid as much knowledge and work as possible.

The men of Able Team piled into the Chevy where they'd stored their gear and followed the other FBI car toward a gate in the fence that surrounded the airport. Lyons was behind the wheel. Blancanales had taken the backseat. From the shotgun seat next to the Able Team leader, Schwarz said, "Did anybody catch the other Fed's name?"

"Taylor," said Blancanales. "He seemed like the quiet type. Might help you to listen a little closer, old buddy, instead of always drifting off into that computer world of annoying beeps and buzzes and flashing lights."

Behind the wheel, Lyons silently shook his head. He loved Schwarz and Blancanales like brothers, and had faced death by their sides far too many times to remember. And he knew their jabs at each other were all good-natured. When it came right down to it, any one of the three men of Able Team would lay down his life for the others. Without a thought. But sometimes the frequent friendly bickering got on his nerves.

"You could both learn something from Special Agent Taylor," Lyons said as he pulled the Chevy through the gate and onto the highway.

"How's that?" Schwarz said.

"Talk less and listen more," Lyons said. "Pol had a

point, too. Every once in a while you could pull your head out of that world of gadgets that earned you your nickname and take a quick look around at the real world." He paused, then glanced up into the rearview mirror to catch Blancanales's eyes in the reflection. "And it wouldn't hurt you, Pol, to take a little bigger step into the twenty-first century. A lot of useful electronics have been invented since the pinball machines you played as a kid."

Blancanales laughed. "Hey," he said, "I played 'Pong' when I was a kid."

Schwarz laughed out loud. "Pol, you *do* realize that saying you played 'Pong' is paramount to saying you played football in the days of leather helmets with no face masks, don't you?"

He got no answer.

The Able Team leader drove on, keeping a close eye on the FBI car ahead of him and following the directions of the robotic voice of the GPS.

The highway had begun to climb upward and the Able Team leader could already note the difference in the amount of oxygen in the air. The lead FBI car took an exit, came to a four-way stop, and then turned onto an asphalt road. Now the gradual climb upward became even steeper. In the distance, Lyons could see the snowcapped tip of Pike's Peak. They passed a sign pointing them back down the mountain where they'd find the Garden of the Gods and drove on, at first passing aspen trees, which grew at the lowest altitude that would sustain them, then encountering thicker groves as they continued to rise.

Fifteen minutes later the car carrying Arthaud and Taylor slowed, then turned onto a gravel road. Dust blew from the rear tires, rising into the air in a steady cloud as Arthaud led them around a sharp curve. Almost as soon as Lyons had made the curve in the second vehicle, he saw the gate.

Armed and uniformed men stood immediately in front of it. And through the window of the guard shack in the middle of the road they could see the heads of more guards.

Arthaud brought his Chevy to a halt and Lyons pulled in behind him as one of the guards moved forward toward the driver's window. From a distance, it appeared to Lyons that he wore a standard flak jacket in woodland camo with front-mounted ammo pouches. On his head was a black beret but the insignia was on the far side of the slanted hat and all but invisible. He carried a clipboard in one hand, a ballpoint pen in the other, with his M-4 slung over his shoulder. The carry was more comfortable than the assault position, but took longer to bring into play. But the man's hands were busy with a clipboard and a ballpoint pen anyway, and he was relying on the other guards to keep them covered until their identities had been established.

And keep the men in the Chevys covered, they did. At least a half dozen 5.56 mm carbines were pointing directly toward the two vehicles. The Able Team leader knew that in less than half a second they could be blasted into more pieces than the *Titanic* when it finally sank.

The conversation between Arthaud and the guard was brief. A second later Arthaud exited his car and walked back to Lyons.

The Able Team leader pushed the button, lowering the window at his side.

"Looks like you were right earlier when you said this is as far as we go," the burly man in the high-dollar suit said. "They've got orders to let you guys in. But not us."

"Thanks for leading the way here," Lyons said.

"No problem," said Arthaud. "Nice change from pushing paper." His smile still looked as if he meant every word he said.

Lyons waited as Arthaud got back in his car and pulled through the gate. As the automobile that had brought them here to this first line of defense made a U-turn, he pulled up to the guard house. The same man in the black beret stepped forward as Arthaud and Taylor drove out on the other side of the guard shack.

Now, as the uniformed man leaned down toward the open driver's side window, Lyons could see the patch of the U.S. 75th Ranger Regiment on his beret.

That slightly surprised the Able Team leader. The 75th had seen its share of action during World War II, Korea, Vietnam and other, smaller wars. But it had been redesigned in 1973 to be a highly mobile light infantry unit capable of operating in any part of the world at a moment's notice. They'd been active most recently in Bosnia, then Iraq and Afghanistan.

Guard duty, it seemed to Lyons, even at a nuclear storage facility, was a waste of talent and training. It was like putting an NFL coach who'd won the Super Bowl in charge of training a junior high football team.

Carl Lyons might have been less loquacious than his fellow Able Team warriors but he had never been the timid sort. As he held up the FBI credentials supplied by Brognola, he said bluntly, "That patch tells me you're 75th. So I've gotta ask. Why are you guys even here? You're pulling guard duty any rent-a-cop could manage."

The Ranger had taken Lyons's credentials and was studying them. But the comment made him laugh. "We just got here yesterday," he said. "All we know is that something extraordinary has happened. We're on high alert. And my guess is it's the same thing that brings you guys here, Special Agent Coffman." He handed the credential wallet back through the window. "Care to share that intel with me?"

"Sorry," Lyons said as he replaced the black leather case inside his suit coat. "I hate to sound like the typical, pompous FBI jerk-off who wants everything *you know,* then answers all of your questions with, 'We're not at liberty to disclose that information.' But I'm afraid that's what I've got to do." He waited for a re-action, remembering how badly he'd wanted to punch out several arrogant FBI agents when he'd still been a LAPD detective. There had been one Fed whose face he actually *had* smashed in. That had bought him a seemingly endless stream of interrogation by both the FBI and the LAPD Internal Affairs goons, and almost made him wish he'd just knocked himself out instead of enduring the tedium brought on by the cops who go after cops.The Ranger nodded. "No problem," he said. "That's pretty much the answer I was expecting," he said, grinning. "And you're right."

Lyons returned the facial expression with one of his own rare smiles. But he was soon to find out that he'd misinterpreted the other man's words. "Thanks for understanding," he said.

"Oh, I didn't say I *understood,*" the Army Ranger

said. "I was just agreeing that you're a typical pompous FBI jerk-off."

Lyons didn't feel the rush of anger he might have expected to overcome him. Instead he felt sympathy—no, empathy—for the Ranger at the gate. He had walked in that man's combat boots and knew how they felt.

"Okay, then," said the Ranger. "You've still got retina and facial recognition to go through at the front door of the main offices. But I'll have a man lead you there." He straightened and Lyons rolled up his window. The Able Team leader pulled through the gate as a green Army jeep, driven by another man wearing Ranger regalia, pulled out in front of him. Next to him, he could see Schwarz. In the rearview mirror, Blancanales's face stared back at him. Both looked as if they were doing their best not to laugh.

"Ever think about switching to the diplomatic corps, Ironman?" Schwarz asked. "You'd be a natural. If I was President, I'd like, make you ambassador to North Korea or Iran or someplace where your smooth and disarming charm would end the world's problems."

"I thought he controlled himself pretty well," said Blancanales. "Considering what we both know was going through his mind."

Lyons shook his head as he followed the jeep. "That's enough," he said. "We've got a mission ahead of us. Let's get our minds on *that*."

The dirt road took a sharp curve and suddenly the front of a structure built into the side of a mountain appeared.

CHAPTER FIVE

It was hardly a five-star hotel.

The bedspread was frayed, the walls dirty and in need of paint, and the shag carpet, which had to have been at least thirty years old, was full of holes and unrecognizable stains. The whole room smelled of stale urine, and the box spring and mattress were both roughly an inch too large for the bed frame.

As far as he could tell, the cheap motel room held only one decent feature: the large window just to the side of the bed looked out over a small pond. "Miller's Pond," the desk clerk had told Mani Mussawi when he'd checked in. But he hadn't told him how the small body of water had gotten its name. In any case now, through the glass, Mussawi saw ducks and geese swimming both in groups and singly across the water. Several trees lined the shoreline, and birds and squirrels jumped from branch to branch without a care in the world.

For a few seconds Mussawi watched them, slightly envious of their freedom to run to and fro without thought to any bigger picture of life.

Mussawi finally turned his attention to the box spring, pushing with all his might in an attempt to smash it down inside the wooden frame. It proved impossible. The mattress had been made for some other bed, it wasn't going to fit, and the al Qaeda mole finally gave up. He would have to sleep at a slant. The only thing he had actually accomplished was to pull the sheets farther away from the mattress to expose the faded stripes of the covering. Both the sheets and mattress bore even more stains than the carpet, and Mussawi didn't really want to know the origins of these discolorations.Turning, he walked swiftly to the corner of the room where the blue hard-sided suitcase containing his clothes and toiletries rested next to a large black-leather upright bass case and two black nylon bags. The suitcase and musical instrument case had come from his home; the two nylon bags from the nuclear storage facility.

Grabbing the black leather bass case, Mussawi lugged it over to the bed, dropped it on the mattress and stared down at it. It had been specially made to do its job but to look nonlethal, and it came through in superior fashion in both areas. Flipping the latches, he opened the lid to expose a worn Indian blanket he had purchased in Manitou Springs, Colorado, several years earlier. For almost a decade it had graced the wall in his living room but now, as he began to unwrap it, the obvious shape of an AK-47 appeared and the faint odors of cleaning solvent and gun oil rose to his nostrils. Also wrapped within the blanket were six 7.62 mm magazines. All were fully loaded. And as he unrolled the final fold the Makarov pistol appeared. It, too, was filled with rounds—9 mms in this case— and two extra magazines held together next to it with a thick rubber band.

Removing the Makarov and extra mags from the blanket, Mussawi slipped the pistol into the waistband of his jeans, over his kidney on the strong side. He left the rubber band on the two magazines for the time being and slid them into his left front pocket.

Mussawi looked down at the AK-47 for a moment before rewrapping it and snapping the big case closed once more. The musical instrument carrier idea had come from an old American gangster movie he had seen. In the movie, Italian Mafia hit men had carried Thompson submachine guns in violin cases. The AK-47 had been too big for a violin case. But the string bass—better known as the bass fiddle—size had been perfect for the rifle, pistol and extra magazines.

As he set the case next to the bed, Mussawi's eyes drifted back to the mattress and sheets and the stains on both. They were old and dried, but he didn't intend to sleep on them no matter how ancient they might be. Grabbing the top of the bedspread, he jerked it all the way off the foot of the bed not unlike a magician pulling a table cloth out from beneath a fully set dining table. The sheets below the bedspread looked relatively clean. But just because he could see no germs or bodily secretions didn't mean they weren't there. A moment of dread crept through his heart as he thought about spending the night on those linens.

The naturalized U.S. citizen sat in a stuffed armchair as ragged as the rest of the room, wondering briefly what nauseating fluids might have dried invisibly on the darker material. His eyes returned to the corner and the two black cases next to his suitcase. Without thinking, he shook his head in disbelief. It was hard to fathom the extent of destruction posed within those two bags; difficult to fully imagine the power with which God had entrusted him right here within this dirty motel room in Colorado Springs.

Mussawi took a deep breath, his eyes still on the bags. God worked in strange ways. For a moment he wondered at the destruction he could cause by activating the backpack nukes right here and now. He might not be able to destroy all of Colorado. But he could certainly come close. And the radiation that lingered after the blast would kill anyone who escaped the explosions. The state would be rendered uninhabitable for years to come.

The man who had stolen the nukes from the storage facility crossed his legs and the rubbing of his pants against the chair's frazzled fabric caused yet another strange, unpleasant and unnamable odor to rise to his nostrils. He forced his mind away from the foolish thought of destroying Colorado. That was not why he'd taken possession of the bombs.

Mussawi smiled. His twin backpack nukes were meant for Radestan. And he took pleasure in the knowledge that they would not be used to hurt anyone there, either. He reminded himself of Emad Nosiar's promise that they would serve only as threats. Yes, the first bomb would be detonated—but in the Radestani desert, far away from any people. And when the Radestani government realized that al Qaeda possessed the ability to destroy Ramesh and the surrounding areas, they would give in to Nosiar's demands. The reins of government would be turned over to al Qaeda in a bloodless coup.

Radestan would become the true theocracy that its very name implied. The people would live under the laws of Islam as told through the prophet, Mohammed.

For a brief second uneasiness swept over Mani Mussawi. What if detonating the first nuke in a remote location just for show, then using the second as a nuclear "bargaining chip" was not what Nosiar really had planned? If he chose to hit Ramesh first, it would make an even bigger statement to the world than a detonation in an uninhabited desert. Millions of human beings—most of them fellow Muslims—would die.

Mussawi rubbed a hand over his face and shook his head back and forth at the same time. That was ridiculous. Nosiar would never do such a thing. And Mussawi knew it had to be Satan himself attacking him with such ridiculous thoughts. The hand brushing his face also brushed away the demonic idea.

Mussawi glanced at his wristwatch. It was time to call. His eyes turned toward the ancient black rotary phone on the nightstand and he almost laughed. The contrast between the technology of the phone and the bombs in the black bags was like the difference between a Stone Age ax and the most modern assault rifle.

Mussawi reached for the receiver, still taking in the rotting appearance of the room. He had chosen this motel because of its age and the fact that it was well off the beaten path. If the long shot happened to come through, and someone at the nuclear storage facility noticed that the two bombs were missing before Monday, they would be looking for him. For that reason he had not gone home. And tomorrow he would be staying with his al Qaeda handler in America, and waiting for orders about where to meet Nosiar. He did not yet know where he would be when he handed over the two nukes. But he had picked up a dozen different maps of Colorado, and planned to take county back roads and avoid interstates and other more modern highways, paying cash for gasoline and covering his tracks as best he could.

But his choice of motels for this night had more downsides than just its filth. Mussawi knew, for instance, that using the archaic phone would mean his call went through a switchboard system at the front desk. That, in turn, meant the manager or anyone else could listen in if they wanted to do so. And there would be a phone company record of the call.

Mussawi wasn't worried about the motel staff listening to his call for security reasons. But if they were bored enough—and working in such a dilapidated and depressing environment could make anyone want to cut their own wrists—they might decide that a little eavesdropping would stave off that boredom. Of course he and Nosiar would be speaking in Arabic, and the chances that the desk clerk understood that language were a million to one. But just recognizing the language could be dangerous to his mission. With the *Patriot Act* in place, a quick call from the front desk to the FBI might end up with dozens of agents suddenly kicking in his door.

So, returning the receiver to its cradle, Mussawi rose from the chair. And rising with him was the strange odor he had noted ever since he had sat down. Doing his best to ignore it, he strode swiftly to his suitcase, unsnapped the latches and pulled out a satellite phone. He started to return to the chair, remembered the smell, and changed course toward the bed. But halfway there, he remembered the stains on the bedspread, and turned back to the chair again.

The zigzagging back and forth, the indecision on where to sit, how to call, and everything else going on in his scrambled brain made Mussawi stop and take a deep breath. The pressure was getting to him. He had always had a slight phobia about germs. But now he was becoming obsessed with the dirty room. He had to relax. Had to quit letting his imagination run away with him. Had to think clearly when he spoke to Nosiar.

Standing in the center of the room, Mussawi forced himself to think logically. Okay, whatever the smell from the chair might be, it had not killed him. So it probably wouldn't if he sat in it again. An expression he had picked up from Americans during his long years as a sleeper agent in Colorado came to mind, and he whispered out loud, "Better the devil you know than the devil you don't." He sat in the musty, padded armchair.

As soon as he was seated, Mani's mind returned to germs. Again, he had to push such thoughts from his brain. They were not only torturous, but they also distracted his concentration. Surely God would protect him from germs and diseases every bit as well as he protected him from the bullets and blades of the nonbelievers.

Making sure the scrambling device was activated on the phone, Mussawi tapped in the number to Nosiar. The call, he knew, would be picked up by the closest satellite and transferred around the world to Radestan. But it would also be transferred to a dozen "dead end" numbers on various continents and become virtually untraceable.

As he waited for the call to connect, Mussawi caught himself grinning. For decades now, Americans had worried themselves sick that someone—first the Russians and the Chinese, then various organizations they deemed terrorists—would smuggle a nuclear bomb *into* the United States. But what was happening now—and what would be every bit as destructive to the U.S. as destroying one of its cities—was that two of America's own nukes were to be smuggled *out* of the country and detonated elsewhere.

The smile on Mussawi's face widened. Not a soul would die when the device went off in the Radestani desert. Yet again, he found himself obsessing on that fact. Why? he wondered. Why did he keep coming back to that? Was it possible that subconsciously he didn't believe his old friend?

No. Nosiar had promised. He was taking al Qaeda in a new direction—one that avoided killing people regardless of race, nationality or religion. Al Qaeda's new goal was to *convert* the infidels of the world, not destroy them. And to Mussawi, the plan appeared to be perfect. Soon after the desert explosion, scientists from the United Nations, protected by hazmat suits, would enter the area to investigate. And it would not take long for them to determine that the device had come from the U.S. Every country in the world possessing nuclear weapons had their own small differences in how they were assembled. And the United States' "signature" would be all over the remnants of the bomb that had sent the mushroom cloud up over the Radestani desert.

Smiling slightly now, Mussawi crossed his legs. At first, the United States would be held at fault by the world. That was never a bad thing. But as soon as the dust cleared—and the pun in Mani's brain did not go unnoticed—al Qaeda would announce that *they* had been behind the massive explosion. And the U.S. would still be blamed for being careless enough to allow the group to get its hands on a nuke in the first place. Then, when the world learned that the Muslim freedom fight-ers possessed a *second* device, and were ready to detonate it in Ramesh, the Radestani government would cave in like the walls of an abandoned gold mine during an earthquake.

There would be no need to actually decimate Ramesh. Nosiar had assured Mussawi of that, and Mussawi believed his old friend.

So quit being paranoid, said a voice in the back of his head.

The call connected and Mussawi heard his friend say, "Praise God, my brother. It is good to speak with you."

"Allahu Akbar," Mussawi returned. "It is for him, and him alone, that we live and work."

"And how is life among the pagans and infidels?" Nosiar asked with a short laugh.

Mussawi's mind immediately skipped from germs to the long blond hair above the soft skin of Catherine's face, then traveled to her ocean-blue eyes, to her perfect breasts and down the rest of her naked body. He knew he had been given a special dispensation to sleep with infidel women, drink alcohol and commit other sins that furthered the jihad.

And as he had thought before, he was going to miss some of those sins.

Then Mussawi's brain reminded him that he and Catherine had exchanged bodily fluids four times the night before and a sick feeling invaded his stomach.

"Are you still there, old friend?" Nosiar's voice broke Mussawi out of his reverie.

Nosiar had switched from English to Arabic, so Mussawii did, too. "I will be glad to return to the realm of God," he said, and the contradictory emotions of desire and fear made him wonder if what he'd just said was the truth or a lie.

"Excellent," said Nosiar. "Is everything going as scheduled?"

"Yes," replied Mussawi. "So far, so good, as the Satanic Americans say." But as the word "Satanic" rolled off his tongue, it felt far more out of place than it had when he'd first come to the U.S. His hatred of Americans had faded over the years, and he had actually come to like many of the people with whom he'd become acquainted. And as he'd just thought a moment earlier, he'd come to truly enjoy some of the vices in which he was allowed to indulge for the jihad. He took a deep breath and glanced toward the nightstand by the bed where the unopened bottle of Jack Daniel's bourbon stood. He had picked it up at a liquor store right before checking into the dilapidated motel, and now he pictured pouring a drink of the dark brown liquid as soon as this conversation was over. His eyes moved to the plastic water glasses across the room by the sink. They were covered in paper to prove they were clean. That was good, he thought.

Doing his best to force both the blonde, the bourbon, and the chance that germs might have somehow worked themselves up under the unbroken seal of the Jack Daniel's bottle from his thoughts, Mussawi started to say, "I am in a horribly cheap motel in—"

Nosiar cut him off. "Do not tell me where you are!" The al Qaeda man was practically shouting into the phone. "Not even in Arabic! The infidels have ways of listening. Especially these days when our jihad has caused the NSA and other agencies to spy on their own citizens." Now his anger turned into a laugh. "That, in itself, is a victory. America no longer trusts its own government, and their weak and self-serving President has become a world-wide joke."

Mussawi had been momentarily taken aback by his friend's sudden sternness. But he answered with, "Our American enemies have no reason to suspect me yet. I will be moving every night. By tomorrow, I will not even be in a motel room. I will stay with a friend—"

"I told you not to tell me these things!" This time, Nosiar did shout into the phone. "There is no need to take chances when they are not necessary." He paused and cleared his throat. But when he spoke again, the angry edge still filled his words. "Besides, I know exactly where you are from the GPS unit in your phone. There is no need to broadcast it."

"Understood," Mussawi said. But he was slightly stunned. He had known Emad Nosiar since they had been children. And the only time he had heard his old friend speak with such venom had been in the old days when he had spoken of killing Christians and Jews. Nosiar's tone seemed out of place within his new policy of converting the infidels to Islam and avoiding unnecessary collateral damage.

For a brief moment Mussawi watched a "mental slide show" run through his brain. It started with Catherine, flashed to Jason Hilderbrand, then went on to include several of the other people with whom he had become friends at the nuclear storage facility. Yes, his years in the United States had taken a toll on him, and the fire within his heart to kill all of the people who did not believe in Mohammed had died down to a mere flicker, if not extinguished itself altogether.

The man with the stolen nuclear bombs took a deep

breath and realized that he should be happy that Nosiar no longer planned to kill indiscriminately, either. So why did joy not fill his heart now? He could not pinpoint it exactly. But there was something about Emad's voice—his attitude—that had changed since their earlier talks.

Something that confused, and frightened, Mussawi.

"Is something wrong?" Nosiar asked bluntly. "You are obviously distracted."

"The pressure is great," said Mussawi. "But I will be all right."

"Then continue with the plan," Nosiar said. "I am about to start making my way toward you. I will not tell you where we will meet until the last minute. Again, there is no sense in taking the chance of being overheard."

"Are you sure, Emad, that it would not be easier for me to just transport the—" Mussawi caught himself before he could finish the sentence and changed it to, "Are you sure I should not just come to you? I know you are quite busy where you are."

"No," said Nosiar. "It will be safer for me to come to you. Besides, I have a trusted and capable second in command who can handle things during the very few days I am gone."

"Do I know this man?" asked Mussawi.

"No," said Nosiar. "But let that be the end of the discussion. I will come to you for what you have."

"It will be done, my friend," said Mussawi.

"Then there is no reason to speak further," said Nosiar. "Contact me again tomorrow." Without further words, he hung up.

Mussawi pressed the button, ending the call on his

end. A moment later he had ripped the paper from one of the plastic water glasses, broken the seal on the Jack Daniel's bottle, and begun pouring the whiskey into the plastic glass.

Mussawi took a large gulp and let it burn his mouth, then his throat, then warm his stomach before rising to calm the confusion in his brain. He forced himself to think positively. Alcohol killed germs. No innocents would be killed. He had not picked up any sexually transmitted diseases from Catherine. The police and FBI would not catch him.

Mussawi emptied the glass of the bourbon, then filled it again. He suddenly felt sleepy, but the thought of lying on the soiled mattress repulsed him. So, returning to the chair, he scooted it across the carpet until it faced the window. Sitting, he held the whiskey in his lap with both hands.

The ducks and geese continued their synchronized swimming, and the squirrels and birds began a very low-level competition for the seeds that had obviously been placed in, and around, a bird feeder atop of a six-foot pole. A cloud drifted across the sun and suddenly Mussawi felt sleepy. He took another sip of bourbon and realized that he was probably going to sleep right where he was tonight—in the relatively safe armchair rather than atop the filthy God-knew-what-stained bed.

His eyes already half closed, and drifting in the half-asleep, half-awake twilight of semi-consciousness, Mussawi stared at the pond.

Suddenly a figure wearing a white robe and sandals appeared in the middle of the water and began walking toward him.

On the water.

The ducks and geese seemed oblivious to the man who somehow passed through them without disturbing their formations. As the figure grew closer, Mussawi could see that he wore a beard, and his dark brown hair fell to his shoulders. The skin of the man's face was weathered but his eyes were bright and crystal clear, and if Mussawi had been ordered to describe them in one word, that word would have had to be *loving*. A chill ran through the al Qaeda mole's body as the figure stepped off the water and onto the land, continuing toward the window through which Mussawi watched. Mussawi looked down at the bourbon in his glass. He was exhausted. Surely the whiskey was combining with that exhaustion to create this hallucination. Another drink or two—that was what he needed. A little more whiskey would change his level of inebriation and drive this ghostly image from his imagination.

Mussawi drained the second glass of alcohol.

But the figure outside the window continued to walk toward him.

Jumping up, the al Qaeda mole grabbed the bottle from the cabinet and returned to his chair. But the man in the white robe was still there, coming ever closer to the window. Lifting the bottle to his lips, Mussawi closed his eyes and chugged down several more ounces. Now, he thought. Now this unwanted apparition would surely be gone.

But it wasn't. When he opened his eyes again, Mussawi's shoulders jerked convulsively. The man in the white robe had reached the window and was staring at him through the glass. A wide smile now accompanied the kind and loving eyes. A white sleeve reached out and the man's fist tapped lightly on the glass.

Fear shot through Mussawi's veins like heroin mainlined by a junkie. He stood, the bottle grasped in both hands. "Who are you?" he said out loud, almost shouting. "What do you want from me?"

I want to come in, said the gentle voice through the window. *But I can only come in if you want me to.*

Mussawi could take no more. He tilted the bottle back and drained the remaining whiskey. Then he sat back in the chair.

The man in white stood there. Slowly the smile on his face faded and a sadness so extreme it made Mussawi want to cry himself covered his face.

He's going to kill millions of people, you know, said the man just outside the window.

Mussawii tipped the bottle up again. But it was empty. He stared out the window at the pain on the face of the man in the robe and started to speak. But no words would come out.

A second later the alcohol hit his brain and he was out.

CHAPTER SIX

It was hardly the first time David McCarter had donned the traditional Arabic robe to blend in with a crowd. And he had worn all varieties of Middle East head covers from turbans to the kaffiyeh on his head today. He preferred the kaffiyeh because its long tails, held in place by the *agal* encircling his forehead, further disguised his Caucasian features.

But he had never quite gotten used to such clothing.

McCarter had always been an up-front fighter, preferring to face the enemy toe-to-toe whether it be with firearms, knives, sticks or fists. Undercover work did not come naturally to him. But being the pragmatic warrior that he was he had long ago realized that such deception would often be called for, and had sought out the help of Leo Turrin, Stony Man Farm's top undercover operative.

Turrin was a true master of the disguised persona and could look like the winner of the latest Mr. Olympia body-building contest one moment and turn into a bookish and bespectacled librarian a second later. He had worked with McCarter, and while the former British SAS man knew that undercover work would never become his strong suit, he had reached a level that Turrin had finally smiled and called "passable."

Besides, McCarter thought as he led the way into the

Radestani capital city of Ramesh, they weren't really doing serious undercover work here. All he needed to do was to look the part, not act it. His current goal—and the goal of the other members of Phoenix Force and Abdul Ali—was to blend in and go unnoticed among the people on the streets and sidewalks. Ironically, Ali looked the least traditional of them all in his camo BDU blouse and work khakis. Yet he—being the real deal—seemed more invisible within the crowds than any of them.

McCarter pressed his elbow a little tighter against his side, feeling the hard steel of the RRA LAR-15 Coyote Semi Auto Rifle slung under his *abat*. That was one good thing about wearing traditional Islamic apparel, he thought. The loose and bulky robe could practically hide a Sherman tank.

The smell of spicy food hit the Brit's olfactory glands as he stepped up onto a sidewalk outside a small café. Ali was leading the way. McCarter and his men were right behind. And, like McCarter, their long guns were slung over their shoulders beneath their robes.

Great for concealment, the Phoenix Force leader thought. But all but impossible to access if a sudden firefight erupted. That, however, was always one of the problems when it came to carrying concealed weapons. The more deeply you concealed them, the harder they were to get to when you needed them. In a broader sense, the dilemma was representative of all combat: the safer you made yourself from yourself, the more danger you risked from others.

McCarter unconsciously tucked his right elbow into his side as he'd done with the left a moment earlier. This time, his elbow pressed against the grips of the Browning Hi-Power he had carried since his days in the British Special Air Service. The rest of his men carried Berettas. But McCarter had chosen to stick with the weapon that had served him so well for so long. And if he needed a firearm now, fast, he knew he'd be better off going for the handgun. At least until he could take cover and get to the Rock River assault rifle encumbered inside the robe.

Ali—unable to conceal his own assault rifle—had hidden it in one of the last burned-out vehicles they'd passed before leaving the heavy foliage lining the road into Ramesh. The man still carried a Tokarev pistol, which McCarter assumed must have made its way to Radestan from Afghanistan after the Soviet Union had pulled out. In any case, McCarter and the others followed the Radestani native, passing more cafés, shops and stands selling everything from fresh fish to hand-carved, olive-wood candleholders. The street was as crowded as the sidewalk, with as many camels, donkeys and horses as motorcycles and automobiles.

And the noise was indescribable.

While the motorized vehicles honked incessantly, the animals whinnied and brayed. Each sound that came out of a camel's mouth was accompanied by an obnoxious glob of phlegm and saliva that sometimes dribbled down the beast's face and other times shot like a rocket at any available target.

As in so many Arab countries, the men on the streets seemed to think the louder one yelled the more serious they'd be taken, and the sounds of words he couldn't understand filled McCarter's ears.

The Phoenix Force leader realized—much in the same way he had realized that undercover work would never be his forte as it was Turrin's—that he would not only never understand the words but would also never quite get a grasp on the culture. As he walked, he watched women in burkas, their faces hidden by veils, hurrying past. They were never unaccompanied; always with men McCarter assumed to be their husbands, or in a group of identically dressed women chattering away to each other and making the cloths covering their mouths move in and out, back and forth.

Men at the sidewalk stands—merchants and customers—screamed into each other's faces, their noses almost touching and their eyebrows lowered in anger. Then, as if on cue, both parties would suddenly smile, shake hands or even embrace each other, and conclude whatever business they had been arguing about. To the Phoenix Force leader it looked as if one or the other must have accidentally spoken some magic word. The abrupt 180-degree switch in attitude was unfamiliar to him as it was to most Westerners, and McCarter couldn't help but wonder if most of the yelling and screaming hadn't just been part of an age-old custom rather than a portrayal of truly felt anger or resentment.

Ali suddenly stopped next to one of the sidewalk stands and McCarter was surprised to look to the man's side and see what appeared to be a Radestani version of an ICEE machine. Men were lined up three deep, awaiting the slushed-ice cola-flavored beverage. As was so often the case in the Middle East, the word ICEE appeared nowhere on the cups, the wooden stand itself, or anywhere else. McCarter was hardly surprised. Once again like many of the surrounding countries, Radestan was more than happy to steal Western technology but cared nothing about patent infringements or royalties. And if the locals didn't use the same name as the company that had originated a product, they could not be accused by fellow Muslims of doing business with the Great Satan.

It was the epitome of hypocrisy in the Briton's opinion.

Most businesses in America and Europe that had been ripped off had resigned themselves to ignoring these blatant violations of international patent laws. Such litigation had to be filed in the country in which the violation occurred, and for that reason were rarely won by the Western plaintiffs. Even when the long shot came through and the law sided with the Westerners, the cost of the legal action turned out to be higher than the loss brought on by the "idea theft."

It was a losing battle no matter who won. And just as happened so often, in so many ways, in so many countries under Sharia law, the people of Radestan considered ignoring the payment of royalties to be a legitimate act against a more commercially successful nation like the United States.

McCarter saw Ali turn to quickly glance behind him. The Phoenix Force leader stopped, too. The men had become too strung out behind them, and while they didn't want to make it obvious that they were together, neither did they want to lose each other in the crowd. McCarter's attention focused on Ali. It had become apparent now that the man with the checkered headdress, camo blouse and khaki pants had not stopped at this stand *only* to grab a quick pirated ICEE drink and let the rest of the men catch up. When his turn came, he leaned over the plywood counter, across the brown stains left by overflowing cola slush and whispered softly to the man inside the stand.

The man listened intently. Then, casually, as if just bored with Ali's face and needing to look away for a moment, he glanced at McCarter, then behind the Phoenix Force leader. He made the action look natural. But McCarter could tell he was scoping out the disguised warriors.

It was clear that Ali must have just confided the fact that he was moving along the sidewalks accompanied by armed men. Which meant Ali trusted this man.

Did that mean that McCarter could trust him, too?

The Phoenix Force leader didn't know.

There was nothing to be done, however, but wait and see. McCarter knew that to most people on the sidewalk and street, the way the man had glanced down the sidewalk to view the other men trailing behind him and Ali would have looked trivial. But in its own way—at least to David McCarter—this small gesture was the most encouraging thing that had happened since they'd parachuted into the country. The smoothness in the way this contact had checked them out told McCarter they were dealing with a professional. The counterfeit ICEE man had at least some experience in the art of war and espionage.

After a few more exchanges, Ali turned away from the patent-infringed ICEE stand and stepped backward a few steps to face McCarter. Although the men from Stony Man Farm had not made the fact that they were together obvious, their traditional Islamic attire had been about the greatest length to which they'd gone. But now, Ali looked up into McCarter's eyes and said, "We must break into smaller units. The house to which

I was taking you was compromised. The PSOF men have been forced to move."

"The government forces found it?" McCarter asked.

"No," said Ali. "At least not that we know of, and if so, not before the freedom fighters staying there and all incriminating papers, computers and the like had been removed." He stopped and sucked in a deep breath. "But one of their men was captured. And it's likely that he gave the location away under duress."

"By duress," said McCarter, "I assume you mean torture?"

"Yes," said Ali. "The government is famous for it." He paused a moment and his eyebrows furrowed in thought. "Of course the PSOF and al Qaeda are famous for torture, too."

McCarter saw no need to inquire further. Every man had his breaking point, and the former SAS man knew the Radestani government would have pushed their prisoner to his and beyond. The PSOF faction occupying the safehouse had been wise to move rather than run the risk of being surrounded and trapped inside.

"So where have they gone now?" McCarter asked.

"To another house," said Ali. "It is still within walking distance. But it will require taking several less-traveled pathways where we are more likely to be noticed."

"Whatever you say," said McCarter. He turned to Gary Manning, who was almost directly behind him and repeated Ali's words, ending the dialogue with, "Pass the word on. Tell the men to break off from one another but to stay in sight of Ali and me."

The muscular Phoenix Force man nodded, then turned and did as he was told.

McCarter and Ali turned sideways, appearing to

continue a conversation as they watched the message travel down the line of Phoenix Force warriors. When the word had reached the last man—who happened to be Encizo—the wiry little Cuban lifted his eyes toward McCarter and nodded slowly.

A quick glance around told the Phoenix Force leader that no one on the crowded downtown Ramesh sidewalk had paid them any attention. At least not yet. But it was time to move on. If they stayed in one place too long one of them would unconsciously do something un-Arabic and attract the suspicion of any of the Radestanis who saw it.

"Lead the way," McCarter whispered to Ali.

The two men started threading their way through the masses on the sidewalk once more.

McCarter and Ali walked side-by-side, moving swiftly through the crowd. The Phoenix Force leader resisted the impulse to turn around and check on his men. He would need to do that eventually just to make sure none had lost sight of their leader. But if he twisted and turned too often, that in itself would attract attention.

Three blocks later they came to a small wooden stand selling fruits of every size, shape and variety. "Stop here and buy something," McCarter said out of the corner of his mouth to Ali. "I need to make sure no one's gotten lost."

Ali nodded slightly, then stopped and began perusing an open plywood container filled with raisins. At the same time, he struck up a conversation with the man inside the small stand.

To McCarter, it sounded as if they were arguing. But most conversations he heard between Middle Eastern men sounded like arguments to a Westerner whether they were or not.

Turning casually, the Phoenix Force leader looked out over the crop of men and women on the sidewalk. Although there were other men of obvious African decent moving along the pathway, Calvin James's black skin was easy to spot. He had moved off the curb to the street and was waiting silently. Farther back, Gary Manning was checking out another wooden stand that featured cheap jewelry. Manning kept quiet. But occasionally he glanced up and down the sidewalk toward McCarter and Ali.

Rafael Encizo was still at the rear—a foot or so behind Hawkins, who had turned to face him. Encizo was adjusting the *agal* that held his kaffiyeh in place, and the two men appeared to be talking to each other while pedestrians going both ways on the concrete changed course to walk around them.

In the U.S. or England, McCarter thought, this might attract the unwanted attention they were trying so hard to avoid. But here in Ramesh, where everyone got in everyone else's way without apology, it brought only a few loud yells and what he suspected were curses in the unfamiliar language.

Everyone was blending in nicely, and no one had gotten lost. McCarter smiled. So far, so good.

"Let's go," the Phoenix Force leader whispered to Ali. But before they could move, an ancient blue Ford pickup turned the corner a few feet away from them. McCarter heard a loud and frightened bray, and turned toward the street to see a rickety cart being pulled by a lone donkey. Just in front of the animal walked a man holding a bridle. The pickup's sudden turn had frightened the donkey, and it reared up on its hind legs, braying even louder. The man leading the terrified beast dove to the sidewalk next to the fruit stand.

The man driving the pickup stomped on the brakes. But it was too late. The vehicle hit the donkey while its front legs were still in the air. The animal's loud bray turned into a painful shriek that threatened to burst the eardrums of everyone in the area. The cart turned over, and suddenly boxes bearing the pictures of dates and figs flew out of the bed, smashing into the fruit stand as well as hitting men and women walking by. Several of the boxes burst upon impact, and the dates and figs flew out.

The fruit rained down over the crowd, accompanied by a torrent of blood from the unfortunate donkey.

The cart skidded up over the curb on its side, striking Hawkins on the back of the thighs as Phoenix Force's youngest member tried to jump out of the way. He fell to the concrete, apparently unhurt, because a second later he jumped back to his feet.

Most of the crowd had moved back and away from the accident and no one but the donkey appeared to be injured. But suddenly the Middle East seemed to turn into the West as dozens of hands disappeared beneath *abats* and came out holding cell phones.

For a brief moment McCarter wondered if one of the famous flying-block attacks had just begun and his hand started to reach inside his *abat*. But soon enough, he realized that what had occurred was simply a traffic accident. His eyes flickered across the area, then stopped on Hawkins. The young man's robe had come untied and gaped open, exposing the LAR-15 Hunter beneath it. Hawkins had noticed it himself and immediately cinched it back together, covering the weapon.

The rifle had been exposed for only a second or so. But a second could be a long time, and McCarter knew the weapon had been visible far longer than necessary to burn them and their whole charade. It was time for a lightning-fast assessment and whatever damage control was called for.

The Phoenix Force leader's eyes skirted the crowd right to left, then back left to right. Almost all of the people in the vicinity of the accident were still staring at the overturned cart as they tapped numbers into their cell phones. The donkey's screams of pain and fear died down. But the men in the robes, and the women wearing burkas, still stared at the unfortunate animal as it took its last breath.

One man, however, who looked to be in his late seventies, stood to the side, his mouth open as he gaped toothlessly at Hawkins long after the young Phoenix Force warrior had closed his robe. The old man seemed to hold no interest in the donkey or the cart. His saggy eyes were glued to the American hiding the rifle.

McCarter turned to Ali.

Their guide had noticed the old man, too.

"We've got to grab him and get him out of here," McCarter said quietly to Ali. "Could you tell if he was with anyone else?"

"He appeared to be alone," said Ali.

Without further words, they moved swiftly across the pavement to where the old man stood. Ali moved in on the man's right while McCarter did the same on his left. Reaching him, McCarter drew his Browning Hi-Power with his right hand. Reaching across his body, he let the loose cloth of his left sleeve fall to cover the weapon from any eyes that might tear themselves away from the dead donkey. Then he jammed the muzzle into the old man's ribs.

At the same time Ali began whispering into the old man's ear. And the old man began shaking with fear.

"Does he know that the object poking him in the side is a gun?" McCarter asked Ali.

"Oh, he knows, all right," said Ali.

The old man sputtered out a string of stuttering words.

"Let me just summarize instead of translate," Ali said. "He's perfectly willing to come with us or do anything else we want him to do."

"Good," said McCarter. "Be sure he knows we'll kill him if he tries to get away or does anything else to draw attention to us." The Phoenix Force leader would never follow through with such a threat. Killing an unarmed, helpless and innocent old man would never be a real option. But it wouldn't hurt the horrified Arab to think it was for a little while. And McCarter could tell by the old man's face that he believed the lie as Ali whispered into his ear once more.

By now the driver of the pickup, the man with the dead donkey and the vendor of the smashed fruit stand had begun shouting at the top of their lungs at one another. Suddenly the man transporting the figs and dates threw a punch at the man from the pickup and a three-way brawl broke out. A few of the bystanders joined in, and in the distance the wail of a police siren sounded.

"I can't think of a better time to make an exit," McCarter told Ali. Glancing briefly around to make sure no one else was watching, he kept the Browning in his right hand but stuck it into the loose sleeve on his left arm. With his arms across his body, he walked next to the old man. Ali took the arm on the old man's other side and began leading him away from the accident.

Six blocks later the sidewalks were all but deserted. The police siren could still be heard in the distance. But the old man was exhausted by both the walk and the terror he'd experienced.

Ali stopped just outside an alley between two buildings. "We are only a few blocks from our destination," he told McCarter as the rest of Phoenix Force caught up to them. Drawing the Tokarev with his right hand, he stopped to think for a moment, then returned it beneath his camo BDU blouse. But when his hand came back out it was hardly empty.

A wickedly curved *jambiya* was clutched in his fist, the cold steel reflecting the sunlight like a mirror. "Shall I kill him now?" Ali asked, nodding sideways at the old man.

McCarter was reminded of how cheaply life was regarded in the constantly warring nations of the Middle East. "No," he said emphatically. "We're not going to kill him."

"But he is very likely to go back and report this to the police," Ali said. "And there is no telling who their sympathies will be with—the government or the PSOF rebels. But it will certainly *not* be with us."

"Yes," said McCarter. "He *is* likely to report this. But we're still not going to kill him. We'll buy ourselves a little time another way." With no prying eyes now, the Phoenix Force leader pulled his Browning out of his sleeve and pressed it into the old man's ribs once more.

With his free hand he took the man's arm and began guiding him down the alley.

The old man was crying now, convinced he was about to die. McCarter couldn't help but feel sorry for him. "Tell him we aren't going to kill him," he instructed Ali.

Ali spoke in Arabic. The tearful man answered.

Ali looked across the age-worn body to McCarter. "He said that's what murderers always say to keep their victims from resisting."

The answer almost caused a smile to cut through the pity McCarter felt for the old man. They hardly needed tricks to get this man to comply. He simply wasn't strong enough to resist anyone hardier than a three-year-old girl.

The others had followed them down the alley, and when they reached a back entrance to the building, McCarter stopped. Half turning, he looked over his shoulder, caught James's attention and motioned him over with a nod of his head.

The former Navy SEAL had also trained as a hospital corpsman and acted as Phoenix Force's medic. He knew what McCarter was about to do without being told, and had already dug under his *abat* for his first-aid kit by the time he reached the doorway. Pulling out a syringe and a small vial of liquid Valium, he stuck the needle into the tiny bottle and pulled back the plunger.

The old man was trying to get loose now, doing his best to kick with wobbly legs and jerking his shoulders in a vain attempt to break loose from McCarter and Ali's grasp.

"Tell him he's just going to sleep a little while," McCarter said.

Ali spoke again. And was answered again.

"He's afraid we're going to give him an overdose," Ali translated.

"Well, he'll have a pleasant surprise waiting for him when he wakes up," James said. Pushing the plunger gently with his thumb, he squirted a tiny bit of the Valium out of the needle, tapped out a few bubbles with the middle finger of his other hand, then reached out and pulled up the sleeve of the old man's robe.

"Sleep tight," said the Phoenix Force medic and a moment later the needle was in the bony arm. The weak man's struggling ended and he fell into McCarter's arms.

McCarter lifted him into the air. "I've picked up babies who weighed more than this," he said to no one in particular.

"Well," said James. "The old boy was a fighter to the end. We've got to give him that. He was just old and worn out."

McCarter laid the old man gently down in the entrance to the doorway. "Like we'll all be one of these days."

"And at the pace we're going it won't take long," James said. Then, without further words, he returned his hypodermic gear to the kit beneath his robe.

Gary Manning had moved in closer now. He was standing by in case he was needed for anything. But upon seeing that no action would be necessary, he looked down at the old man sleeping peacefully on the ground and said, "Who says any of us are going to even live long enough to get like that?"

"Good point," said James, turning his attention to Ali.

Phoenix Force's Radestani guide still held the *jambiya* he had drawn earlier.

"Nice blade," James said.

Ali twirled it around and extended it with the handle out. "Would you like to have it?" he asked. "I have many others."

James smiled as he shook his head. "Thanks, but I think I'll stick with my Crossada for now," he said. "And I have several of them, too." He paused and grinned broadly, recognizing a fellow blade aficionado. "Tell you what, Ali," he said. "When this is all over, I'll trade you one of mine for one of yours."

Ali smiled. "Assuming we are both still alive at that point," he said.

"That's *always* a caveat in this business," said James.

McCarter smiled, happy they had been able to neutralize the threat posed by the old man without having to hurt him. Turning to Ali, he said, "Let's go, mate. You guys can play with your knives later. Right now, our work is still just beginning."

CHAPTER SEVEN

Their Army Ranger guide didn't even bother getting out of his jeep as Carl Lyons pulled up directly in front of the entrance to the mountain office complex. The man from the 75th watched all three Able Team warriors get out and walk to the steel door, then pulled away again.

Lyons pushed a button on an intercom panel next to the door and waited. "Name?" a voice said.

"Coffman, Vogt and Kiethley," Lyons replied, using the names on the credentials Brognola had provided them. "Justice Department." He cleared his throat. "Our superiors should have called ahead."

"Indeed they did," said the voice. "We'll still need to see your faces and right eyes."

Lyons watched a metal cover roll up next to the door and moved to stand facing the screen that appeared behind it. He could see his own reflection. Five seconds later the voice said, "Facial ID recognized. Step forward and look directly into the spot you're about to see."

A tiny red spot appeared on the screen and Lyons did as instructed. Almost immediately the voice said, "Recognized," and then, "Next."

Blancanales and Schwarz went through the same procedures, before a loud click, followed by a buzzer, sounded from the door. Lyons reached forward, grabbed the stainless-steel handle and opened the door.

The men of Able Team were met in the doorway by a beautiful raven-haired woman in her mid-twenties. She wore a short black skirt that made her legs appear to reach all the way up to her shoulders, and the pheromones exuding from her body almost bounced off the walls. In her hands were three plastic-coated, pin-on badges that read Guest. "Hello," she said. "I'm Sheila, and I'll be escorting you to Mr. Williams's office." She handed each man one of the badges, then turned away.

The young woman's tone of voice and body language led Lyons to believe that she liked what she had just seen—either in him or perhaps all of them. He wasn't particularly surprised. The good-looking young lady was probably caged in for eight hours a day with overweight civil service types wearing pop-bottle eyeglasses. And even in this day and age—when the average man was almost constantly pressured to be docile and downright wimpy—many women were still attracted to men who acted like men.

But the Able Team leader sensed even more during this brief encounter. Sheila definitely acted as if she had no idea who they were or why they were here. That was good. The fewer people who knew what was going on, the fewer individuals they'd have to weed through to track down the missing nuclear weapons. It would save time. And when you were dealing with stolen nukes, time was definitely *not* on your side.

Lyons saw Schwarz and Blancanales pin their badges to their lapels as he turned to follow the woman. Then, behind him, he heard Schwarz whisper, "You got to hand it to bureaucracy. They might lose track of a couple of bombs that could take out millions of people but they make sure three guys who just passed through facial and retina recognition are ID'd as semi-trespassers."

"Yeah," said Blancanales. "But you've got to admit, the guide inside the building is a lot better than the one who just drove off in the jeep."

"You'll get no argument out of me," said Schwarz.

Lyons was just to the side of the woman and a half step back. He watched the corners of her lipstick-red lips curl up slightly as she pretended not to hear. The comment had sunk in, and she appreciated it. But she settled back into a more deadpan expression as she led them down a long hall.

The Able Team leader's thoughts turned toward the "Mr. Williams" he was about to meet. One thing he had learned as a top LAPD detective was that the adage "Too many cooks spoiled the broth" was especially true during both interviews and interrogations. So as he listened to the young lady's high heels click against the tiled floor and echo off the walls, he began to formulate his plan of psychological attack.

He needed to speak with the director of this nuclear storage facility alone. Although Schwarz and Blancanales were also skilled in the art of extracting information, if all three warriors confronted the man he was likely to become so intimidated that he'd tell them whatever he thought they wanted to hear rather than stick to the simple truth. Or he might even "lawyer up," as the saying went, refusing to speak until he had legal representation present. That would do nothing but delay things even further.

So the Able Team leader reached forward, dropping a hand lightly onto Sheila's shoulder, which stopped her high-heeled-clicking in midstride. "Excuse me," he said. "But is there a lobby or someplace where my friends here could wait? I'd like to speak with Mr. Williams alone if I could."

Lyons glanced back at Schwarz and Blancanales. Both men nodded. This was hardly their first rodeo and they knew why their leader had chosen this strategy. The fact that Sheila was one stupendous-looking lady hadn't passed them by, either. They were *men* after all. But good-looking as she might be, Lyons knew neither man would allow that fact to distract them from their mission any more than he would.

Sheila turned toward Lyons as they continued walking. Her smile this time was wider and showed off a row of perfectly formed teeth as white as the snow Lyons had seen earlier atop Pike's Peak. "Why, certainly," she said. "We'll be passing a waiting room in just a second. It's right on our way." She turned away once more and the clicks began again.

Three more turns through the labyrinth of halls and offices and they came to a glassed-in area outfitted with chairs, couches and end tables topped by stacks of well-worn magazines.

"I guess this is where we go?" Blancanales said as the clicking stopped in front of the doorway. He nodded through the glass. "I sure hope you've got *Cosmopolitan* and *Vanity Fair*."

The statement bought him a laugh from the good-looking young woman. "Somehow, none of you seem quite the type to read those magazines," she said. "But you might find something in there that would interest you."

"I'll be looking for the *National Enquirer*," said

Schwarz. "I haven't been keeping up with the Incredible Frog Boy the way I should have."

That got him another white-toothed laugh.

Lyons's teammates entered the waiting area as he continued down the hallway, walking side-by-side with Sheila. Now that they were alone, she reached out and took his arm. She slowed as they neared a closed door at the end of a hallway, and looked up at the Able Team leader. "Could I bother you for the time?" she asked. "I'm afraid my watch battery's run down."

Lyons could see the small, feminine gold watch on her wrist. He lifted his own arm to his eyes, then said, "Almost three o'clock."

The white teeth flashed again. But this time the eyes above them looked sultry rather than friendly. "Oh, good," she said, still holding her stare. "That means I get off in an hour."

They stopped in front of the closed door but Sheila made no attempt to open it. "Do you suppose you'll need more than an hour to speak with Mr. Williams?" she asked, a hint of coyness in her words.

"I hope not," Lyons said.

Sheila wasn't about to break eye contact. "Well, there's a little bar at the end of the dirt road that leads here," she said. "Right where you get off the highway. My friends and I sometimes stop there for a drink after work." She tossed her long silky black hair and her smile grew even bigger. "You'd be welcome to join us if you'd like."

"Darling," Carl Lyons said, "you don't know how much I wish I could. But I've got a sneaking suspicion that as soon as I've spoken to Mr. Williams we'll have to be out of here and gone."

The smile slowly faded, then returned, looking a little disappointed this time. "Okay," the beautiful woman said. "But you know where I work. Don't forget how you can get in touch with me."

Lyons finally returned the smile with a rare one of his own. "I'm not likely to," he said.

Then he reached out and twisted the doorknob, forcing his mind to switch to what he *needed* to do and away from what he *wanted* to do.

The Able Team leader opened the door and stepped inside, finding himself in an outer office with an older yet still attractive woman busily typing on a computer keypad. She looked up and smiled as he entered, then said, "Mr. Williams has been expecting you." Her eyes shot toward a door just behind her right shoulder. "Go right in."

Lyons nodded his thanks, walked to the door and twisted that doorknob. A moment later he was standing in Gerald Williams's office, shaking hands with the man across his desk. The Able Team leader sized him up quickly.

Another thing he had learned over the years was that people could be divided into two groups. The first group did everything they were supposed to do, the way they were told to do it, and never made waves of any sort. They revered the policy manual of whatever agency they worked for as the *Third Testament of the Bible*.

The second group would have been right at home in Sam Peckinpah's classic movie *The Wild Bunch*. They took chances that sometimes worked out and other times fell flat. Given the chance, they would have re-titled the policy manual *The Big Book of Suggestions*.

As he dropped Gerald Williams's hand, Lyons settled into the stuffed armchair in front of the man's desk.

Williams had been in the process of shrugging into the jacket of his navy-blue suit as Lyons entered. He'd had one arm inside the sleeve when he'd shaken Lyons's hand, and now he slid the other arm in and buttoned the top button. As he sat, Lyons's eyes skirted the top of his desk. It was devoid of anything except a telephone, a small lamp on the upper right corner and a clear plastic cube that held a variety of photographs. The picture facing outward was of a boy, around ten years of age, wearing a team-logo polo shirt and shorts. The boy's rubber-cleated foot rested on top of a soccer ball.

The Able Team leader knew that Williams's workload must consist primarily of paperwork. But no papers were in view and Lyons suspected that whatever documents he'd been involved with when the Able Team leader arrived were now inside a manila file and secreted away in one of his desk drawers.

A small table adjacent to the left side of the man's desk held a computer. Glancing around, Lyons noted that the walls had been decorated with framed pictures and certificates—all carefully nailed at eye-level height. Predominant—in the middle of the pictures that circled the entire office—was a photo of Williams shaking hands with the current President of the United States.

Lyons resisted the urge to frown or to comment. He was dealing with a member of the first group he'd just conjured up in his mind; a man who followed the rules regardless of whether or not they produced real results, and worried about promotions and his pension. This Williams character lived for order, repetition and a clear chain of command. He covered his butt carefully in every action he undertook and every word he spoke.

In other words, he was Carl Lyons's direct opposite. But the Able Team leader knew exactly how to deal with such a man.

"Please, Special Agent Coffman," the man behind the desk finally said, his voice squeaking slightly with nerves, "would you like some coffee?"

Lyons shook his head.

Williams sat as erect and stiff as a military academy cadet awaiting dinner. "Then how may I help you?" he asked.

Lyons already knew this man's primary concern would not be finding the missing nukes. It would be covering his bureaucratic ass. So there was only one way to get the complete truth out of him.

Throw him off balance. Then scare the hell out of him.

Lyons crossed his legs and let his coat fall open to expose the Beretta 92-SB under his arm and the Colt Python on his hip. Just as the Able Team leader had known they would, Williams's eyes darted directly to the pistols. His was not a gun-carrying job, and the big semiauto and revolver impressed, and frightened him.

The process of throwing the bureaucrat off balance—mentally and emotionally—had begun. And Carl Lyons had no intention of changing the direction in which the atmosphere was heading. The office he had just entered might belong to Gerald Williams most of the time.

But for the rest of the time the Able Team leader spent in the room, it would belong to *him*.

"The first thing I'll need out of you, Mr. Williams,"

Lyons said in a stern monotone, "are your weekly activity reports for the past five years."

Williams's eyes widened and his mouth fell open.
Weekly activity reports were one of the banes of the
federal bureaucrat's existence. Each week men and
women like Williams had to spend most of their Monday mornings putting coded numbers into little boxes
on the forms, and accounting for exactly how they had
spent every hour of the previous week.

Complete accuracy, of course, was impossible.

"I'm not sure I have all—" Williams started to say.

Lyons leaned forward as he interrupted the man.
"Oh, Mr. Williams," he said. "You aren't about to tell
me you haven't kept your weekly activity reports up
to date, are you? That would be a serious infraction
of policy."

"No, no," said Williams, his voice threatening to
crack like a pubescent boy's. "I have them all. I'll just
have to gather them up and—"

"Good," Lyons interrupted again. "I'll take them
with me when I leave so I can go over them."

The skin on Williams's face paled almost white.

Lyons worked hard to keep a smile off his own face.
The rumor was that J. Edgar Hoover had come up with
the idea of weekly activity reports, and that the concept
had spread from the FBI to other agencies. The reason was simple. No one could remember exactly what
they'd done or exactly when, which meant if Hoover
wanted to fire someone he could easily prove that their
activity reports were not accurate, and therefore the
agent had lied about where he'd been and what he'd
been doing. A simple mistake could be made to look

like an international conspiracy if the FBI director had wanted it that way.

Carl Lyons didn't know how much of that rumor was actually true. But even if it was a complete fabrication it provided frightening and powerful motivation to a tight-ass like Williams.

The director of the nuclear storage site had stood behind his desk and turned toward a row of huge filing cabinets behind him. Lyons presumed he intended to look for his activity reports. "Sit back down, Mr. Williams," the Able Team leader told him. "I already told you I won't need the reports until I leave." He stopped speaking for a few seconds, then added, "And we may be here awhile."

Williams turned back around, nervously undid the coat button he had just buttoned, and dropped back down into his chair. His face had taken on an ashen look, and Lyons would have bet what little Williams had in his bank account that he was thinking about how much longer he had until he could resign and collect his retirement.

"Let's cut right to the chase," Lyons said, keeping the sternness in his voice. "You received orders to ship twelve small backpack nukes to Florida. Only ten arrived. And you don't have the other two in your inventory here. Am I correct?"

Williams nodded. His hands shook as he adjusted the knot in his tie.

"Well, then," Lyons said, "this breaks down very much like a grade-school arithmetic 'thought problem' doesn't it? If Johnny has twelve oranges, and he gives ten to Sally, how many oranges does Johnny have left?" He didn't wait for an answer. "The correct answer is two, Mr. Williams," Lyons said, with just a touch of sarcasm in his voice. "Unfortunately, unlike Johnny, you don't have the correct answer."

A lump formed for a moment in Williams's throat, then slid on down out of sight like a small animal being swallowed by a boa constrictor.

"So," Lyons continued. "Right now you've got an F on your math test. But I'm a very generous and kind teacher. I'm going to let you retake the test." Suddenly, and completely without warning, the former ace interrogator jumped to his feet and brought a big fist down on Williams's desk in what karate practitioners call a "hammer hand" blow. The force of the strike made the photo cube jump into the air, then fall over onto its side and display another picture of Williams's soccer-playing son. It also rattled the lamp in the corner and made the telephone receiver jump out of its cradle.

The pictures and other framed documents on the wall shook for a moment, then everything settled back into place and the office fell into silence except for the dial tone emanating from the displaced phone.

Williams was taken completely by surprise. He sat there, his mouth wide open like a child encountering his first circus clown. Lyons leaned in closer to make the man even more uncomfortable. "Hang up your phone, Gerald," he said in a low, menacing voice.

Williams's trembling hand followed the order and the dial tone disappeared.

"Where are they, Gerald?" Lyons demanded.

The bureaucrat's voice resembled that of a cartoon mouse when he spoke. "I don't know," he said.

"You must have some suspicion," the Able Team leader said.

"No, really…" the terrified man said. "I can't imag-ine…who…where—"

"You evidently don't keep a tight enough rein on your employees," Lyons said. "How many nukes do you have in all here?"

"I…I'd have to…check," Williams sputtered.

"Quit stammering and answer me like a man," Lyons said. His sudden anger had begun as an act, but now he was genuinely disgusted with this career bureaucrat who was as frightened as a child at a zombie movie. "What do you mean, you'd have to check?" Lyons felt his face frown. "You've got enough nuclear weapons in your charge to take out Russia and China and still have enough left for Iran and North Korea. And you don't know that number off the top of your head?"

"Well…no…not without checking my records." Wil-liams turned to look down at his computer, and Lyons would have almost sworn he saw *love* for the machine in the man's eyes. The computer was something with which he was familiar; something within his comfort zone. A refuge from the raging Justice Department agent who was all but physically assaulting him from across the desk.

"I can check the total number and the sizes of each one," the man said, still staring at the computer. He reached out and placed his hands on the keyboard.

It reminded Lyons of a toddler clutching his teddy bear during a thunderstorm.

"It's only two of the little ones that are missing," Williams said as he began to type.

Lyons reached across the desk and grabbed one of the man's forearms, jerking it away from the keyboard. "Did I hear you right, Gerald?" he said, and this time his words were full of sarcasm. "Just two *little* ones? Allow me to let you in on a secret I'd have thought someone in your position would already know." His eyes drilled holes through the other man's, and Williams couldn't sustain the gaze. He looked down at his desk. Then Lyons said very slowly and clearly, "There is no such thing as a *little* nuclear weapon!"

Williams slithered back down in his seat. He looked as if he might fall asleep out of sheer emotional exhaustion.

"Get back on your beloved little computer," Lyons said. "Find out who had clearance to access the inventory list. I want every name. And then I want you to cross-check those names with employees who didn't come to work today. You understand?"

"Yes…" Williams breathed. "Yes…that makes sense. I—"

"I didn't ask for your approval, Gerald," Lyons growled. "I asked for names. Just shut up and do it."

Williams's fingers began to move across the keys. But his hands were shaking, and he kept making mistakes that had to be corrected before he moved on. Lyons waited, the adage "You can't have your cake and eat it, too" crossing his mind. It had been necessary to frighten the man half out of his wits to cut through Williams's meandering around the truth to cover his own bureaucratic ineptitude and laziness. It would be nice if that fear would now go away and allow the man's hands to work competently. But that was going to take a while.

Gerald Williams wasn't likely to settle down until long after Lyons had gone.

Five minutes later the bureaucrat finally looked up. "There are two men and one woman—absent from work today—who also had clearance to access the inventory file," he said. He stopped speaking long enough to take a breath so deep it made his chest shake. "One of the men and the woman called in absent. The other man went home sick early last Friday."

"Did he call in still sick today?" the former LAPD interrogator asked.

Williams tapped a few more keys. "No," he said. "He probably just assumed we'd know he was still—"

Carl "Ironman" Lyons gave Williams his best disgusted look. *"Probably,"* he said. *"Just assumed."* He shook his head. "For a man trusted with enough explosives to blow up half the world, you don't run a very tight ship, Gerald. I think I maybe have to speak to your superiors when I get back to D.C."

Williams opened his mouth to speak but no words came out. So Lyons went on. "How about *you,* Gerald?" Lyons said, interrupting. "You have the right codes to get to inventory, don't you?" The Able Team leader held no suspicion that Williams himself had stolen the nukes. The statement was made simply to continue keeping him scared and off balance.

"Why…yes, of course I do," Williams mumbled. "But—"

"Never mind that last question," Lyons said. "As evil and self-serving as it might be, trying to pull something like this off would take a certain amount of courage. And courage is a trait in which I find you sadly lacking, Gerald."

The Able Team leader had never seen a man so delighted to be called a coward.

"Give me the names and addresses of the three people you mentioned," Lyons practically barked.

"Wilber Dickerson, Marie Schneider and Mani Mussawi," Williams breathed.

Lyons had been leaning down, watching the screen as Williams worked. Now he straightened and tapped the printer next to the computer. "I want their home addresses and phone numbers. Run me a hard copy of all that. In fact, just run me a hard copy of their whole personnel files."

By now Williams's face had almost completely drained of blood. "Really, Special Agent Coffman," he said. "I can't do that without going through proper chann—"

Lyons slammed his fist down on the desk again, even harder than before. "I don't have time to play your stupid protocol games," he thundered into the man's face. "If those two nukes are in the wrong hands, every second counts. So do it, Gerald. Run me a copy of their personnel files and *do it now*."

Two minutes later Carl Lyons had three manila files filled with information about the absent nuclear storage facility employees. As he tucked the files under his arm, he stared Williams in the eyes. "Here's the rest of the deal. You don't talk to anybody about my visit or anything we've discussed. My gut instinct is that one of these people is on the run and that's the real reason he, or she, isn't here today. But once in a great while, my gut's wrong. Which means it could be all three of them behind this." He paused for emphasis, then went on. "Or I might even have made a mistake about *you*. Maybe you've got more intestinal fortitude than I imagine. So give me your cell phone number."

The hands behind the desk shook as if Williams was a palsy victim as he wrote down the number on a piece of white printer paper. Lyons stuck the sheet inside one of the files.

"Do you still want my activity reports?" Williams asked.

"No," said Lyons. "I might later. But not now." He suppressed a smile, knowing that as soon as he was gone this ultimate-bureaucrat would pull out his activity reports for the past five years and start going over them with the temperament of a cat on a high wire.

"You stay within reach," he ordered. "Either here, or at the end of that cell phone. If I need to call you again and can't reach you, the entire Department of Justice will make your life a living hell."

Williams didn't speak. But his facial expression told Lyons that he understood.

The Able Team leader pivoted on the balls of his feet and headed toward the door. As he grasped the knob, he heard a desk drawer slide open.

Lyons threw a quick glance over his shoulder in time to see Gerald Williams pull a bottle of Maalox out of his desk.

The Able Team leader passed the waiting room where he'd left Schwarz and Blancanales and found it empty. He dropped his Guest badge at the desk of the Ranger just inside the front door and hurried out of the building to the car. Schwarz and Blancanales had grown bored reading *People* magazines and were both sitting on the trunk of the sedan.

"Let's go," Lyons said. As soon as he was behind the wheel, the Able Team leader twisted halfway around and handed the personnel files to Schwarz. Then he and Blancanales waited as their electronics expert entered the three names of the absent employees into his laptop computer.

Schwarz tapped a few more keys, and the small portable printer resting on the seat next to him hummed to life with a combination of clicks, clacks and beeps. A moment later Schwarz pulled a map of the Colorado Springs area from the machine and handed it over the seat to the Able Team leader.

The full-color map bore three tiny stars, marking the addresses of Wilber Dickerson, Marie Schneider and Mani Mussawi. And bright red lines indicated the quickest route to each site.

Lyons twisted the key and started the engine. "One of these people is a traitor," he said. "So let's go."

CHAPTER EIGHT

Emad Nosiar took a seat behind his solid oak desk and looked at the phone. Although the inside of the instrument was covered in the same plastic as all telephones, it bore a special feature that Nosiar had never seen anywhere else: The cradle and receiver were both covered with a thin layer of wood straight from the Cedars of Lebanon. The wood had been stolen from what was now a Lebanese national park, smuggled into Radestan, and the cover hand-made by an expert wood-crafter.

Then the woodworker had been killed. For two reasons. First, Nosiar did not want word of his extravagances to become known among his al Qaeda minions. Second, he simply wanted the phone to remain one of a kind. It provided the most pleasing odor of cedar when he held the receiver to the side of his head, and he did not care to have it copied and enjoyed by others.

The phone, Nosiar realized as he settled into the leather chair, was symbolic of his entire attitude toward al Qaeda and the rest of the Islamic world. Al Qaeda was at the top of the food chain when it came to what the Satanic West called "terrorists" and the followers of Islam referred to as "freedom fighters" and "jihadists." Everything in Nosiar's office, from the phone and oak desk to the Persian carpet on the floor and the Moroccan-leather lounge and matching chairs in front of the desk, was of the finest quality. It was necessary, Nosiar told himself, to keep up the cover image that was represented by the sign on the outer door. The sign read Ramesh Import and Export, Ltd. But unless you counted the illegal cedar coming out of Lebanon, the company did no business importing or exporting whatsoever.

In the next couple of days, however, that was going to change. Ramesh Import and Export was going to import two very rare and valuable items: a pair of nuclear bombs manufactured and, until recently, stored in the United States of America.

Nosiar opened the lid to a cigar box on his desk—made from the same smuggled cedar as the phone cover. Inside were a dozen thick, eight-inch-long cigars from Cuba. A box of fifty such cigars was sent to him each month by his friends in the Cuban government. Now he pulled two of them out and extended one across the desk.

Harun Bartovi, wearing a white turban with his *abat*, leaned forward and took the smoke. "Thank you," he said and sat back again.

Nosiar looked at the man. Bartovi wore a carefully trimmed beard and hair that was all but hidden from sight under the turban. The shorter beard allowed him to be more flexible; he could change from his robes to a business suit and present a completely different persona in seconds. Such a talent, in addition to the organizational skills he demonstrated in setting up the flying blocks, had made him invaluable to Nosiar and the al Qaeda faction operating in Radestan.

Nosiar lifted a large and heavy marble lighter from the desk and rolled the wheel with his thumb. A few seconds later, both his and Bartovi's cigars were sending blue trails of smoke to the ceiling.

Bartovi smiled. "It is a shame the prophet forbade the use of tobacco," he said as he took a deep drag.

Nosiar chuckled. "Yes, but it is fortunate that he makes exceptions to the rules when they further our cause."

"Are we furthering our cause smoking cigars here, by ourselves, where no infidels can see us?" asked Bartovi.

Nosiar laughed and took in another mouthful of the aromatic smoke. "Of course we are," he said. "We are *practicing* for when the infidels *are* looking on."

The comment brought more laughter to both men.

"When do you begin your journey?" asked Bartovi.

"In less than an hour," said Nosiar. "The airplane is being readied even as we speak."

Bartovi stuck the cigar between his teeth and nodded his head. "And have you decided where you will meet Mussawi?" he asked.

"Yes," said Nosiar. "But I cannot even tell you yet. I will give you my destination right before I leave." He leaned forward and shook his head. "Do not take that as a personal insult, Harun. It is simply my policy that no one knows such things who does not need to know such things."

"I am not offended," said Bartovi as he pulled the thick cigar out of his mouth. He glanced quickly around the room. "It is a wise policy. Very wise."

Nosiar looked at his watch and stood. "It is time that I pack my clothing and ready myself for the trip. It will be the most important trip of my life."

Bartovi stood on the other side of the desk. The cigar

was in his right hand but he transferred it to his left. Extending his right hand, he took Nosiar's. "Go with God," he said. "And do not worry. I will take care of things here while you are gone."

"I know you will," said Nosiar.

The two men walked out of the office together.

THE NEW SAFEHOUSE didn't look all that safe to David McCarter. Constructed centuries ago using a clay-and-mud process not unlike that used by the Pueblo Indians in the Southwestern United States, it was the end unit on a block of four separate dwellings that shared common walls.

"Very nice," T. J. Hawkins said to no one in particular as they made their way toward the front door. "Sort of ancient town houses, if you will."

A queasy feeling made its way from McCarter's abdomen up to his throat. It wasn't fear, exactly—he had overcome that years ago. It was more of a metabolic warning system that went off inside his body sometimes when things weren't quite right. And it was going off loud and clear within him right now.

The Phoenix Force leader scanned the area as he and Abdul Ali led the rest of Phoenix Force toward the structure. They had entered what was usually referred to as Old Ramesh and the whole area was filled by similar town houses, as Hawkins had called them. The packed-mud structures were centuries old, and more than one had collapsed in upon itself. Most had been abandoned. But what bothered McCarter the most was that while the two archaic homes in the middle of the block appeared to be empty, the one on the far end did not. On top of the hard dry dirt in front of the door he saw two children playing.

And that he didn't like.

McCarter turned to Ali as they neared the front door. "The PSOF don't have any better safehouses than this?" he asked.

"They do," said Ali, reaching up and tugging on his long beard. "But none that they could transfer to as quickly." Smoothing out his chin hair, he added, "They had short notice that they might have been compromised. They had to get somewhere *fast*."

The two men led the rest on to the front door. "The man the government captured," he said. "Did he know about this place?"

"I am not sure," said Ali. "But I suspect he did."

"If you aren't sure, then we have to operate on the assumption that he did," said McCarter. "Which, in turn, means we have to assume they've tortured this location out of him, too. We're going to have to vacate this place as soon as possible." The Phoenix Force leader took another look around before entering the open front door. There were five men in his company including himself. And they stuck out like a burka in a synagogue.

There were roughly fifteen to twenty men inside the house as they entered, and most automatically reached for weapons as they crossed the threshold. Then they recognized Ali, and the AK-47s, a smattering of CAR-15s and a variety of pistols were returned to leaning against the walls or reholstered.

McCarter turned to Ali. "I don't like this place," he said. "I don't like it at all. It's a death trap."

Ali nodded. "I don't like it, either," he said. "It is far too obvious. Any fool walking down the street would recognize it for exactly what it is." He paused and ran his fingers through his beard again. "And it is dangerous for the children at the other end of the block. Let us prepare to move on immediately."

The words had barely left his mouth when a man wearing a striped *abat* appeared from one of the other rooms. McCarter was half surprised to see a Heckler & Koch 91 slung over the man's back. The German .308—or 7.62 mm if you wanted to measure in metric standards—was a pricey assault rifle, and fired a round the same circumference as an AK-47. But the similarity stopped there. The brass boattail casing for the H&K was 7.62 x 51 mm instead of the shorter 7.62 x 39 mm employed in the Kalashnikov and other Russian-based rifles. And longer meant room for more gunpowder, and more gunpowder meant the Heckler & Koch packed a much fiercer "punch."

McCarter gave the weapon a quick visual inspection. Like Ali's Tokarev pistol, most of the rebels' weapons, be they assault rifles, pistols or even shotguns, had drifted into Radestan from Afghanistan. And there were an impressive number of American CAR-15/M-16 designs that had undoubtedly been seized in both Afghanistan and Iraq. But the H&K was fairly unique, and McCarter guessed it must have originally been brought into Radestan by some outside mercenary.

Both the government and the PSOF had employed mercenaries, and which side of the war the merc had fought for was anybody's guess. But McCarter couldn't help wondering how the man in the striped robe obtained the scarce ammo for the rifle.

Ali stood next to McCarter as the Phoenix Force leader looked over the undisciplined men sitting and lying on the hard-packed dirt floor. "You've been training these blokes?" he asked.

Ali nodded. "I have been trying."

"Where are the Special Forces men who were helping you?" asked McCarter.

"Probably with another faction of the PSOF," Ali answered. "As I told you, it is all very disorganized."

"And you were correct," said the Phoenix Force leader. The man in the striped robe stepped up to them. He stuck out his hand and said, "My name is Jabbar. And these are my men."

McCarter grasped his hand and shook it firmly. "Can't help asking," he said, "where'd you come up with the H&K?" Although he was facing the man in the striped robe, the Phoenix Force leader could see Ali in his peripheral vision. And he noted a thin smile curling the corner of the Radestani's mouth.

Ali answered the Phoenix Force leader's question for Jabbar. "These guys are both sinners and saints," he said. "We employ our own version of 'Don't ask, don't tell,' on things like that."

McCarter nodded. What Ali meant was that the disorganized rebel factions in Radestan, who were fighting alongside each other right now, were a mixed group of both Shi'ite and Sunni Muslims. That, in turn, meant they had probably fought each other in the past and would likely do the same in the future.

The high-dollar German rifle had come from some dead fellow Muslim. It was one of those things best left unmentioned.

"I am the leader of this faction of the PSOF," Jabbar said. "We are freedom fighters who are in the process of overthrowing the evil government under which we now suffer." He paused and adjusted the sling over his shoulder to allow the H&K 91 to point directly downward. Then he said, "You are the new Americans we were told would come?"

McCarter had taken note of the man's near-perfect grasp of the English language. He might have learned much of it from books. But no one spoke a foreign language that well unless they had actually lived in, and mixed with, people who spoke it on a regular basis.

What surprised the Phoenix Force leader even more, however, was Jabbar's accent when he spoke English. He didn't sound at all like the Cuban-born Encizo, of course, or South Side Chicago's Calvin James, or Canada's Gary Manning. And his voice certainly bore no resemblance at all to Hawkins's Texas drawl.

The fact was Jabbar sounded more like McCarter himself.

"We're based out of America," the Phoenix Force leader said, answering Jabbar's question. "But we're comprised of a variety of men. What we've all got in common, however, is that we stand for, and we fight for, freedom and democracy."

As he spoke, the former SAS operative noted in his peripheral vision that James and Hawkins had slightly suspicious expressions on their faces. And Jabbar didn't look as if he was going to roll out the red carpet and trust his life to five formerly unseen faces, either. None of that particularly surprised McCarter. Battle trust was something that had to be earned. A warrior might have earned the United States' Congressional Medal of Honor somewhere, sometime, away from the men he was about to join. But until he had proved himself at their side, he was not one of them.

The men of Phoenix Force all shook hands with Jabbar—which meant absolutely nothing. And the Phoenix Force leader saw by the look on the Radestani rebel's black-bearded face that the gesture was nothing more than a formality to him, too.

Each man would still have to prove himself to the other side.

When they were finished, Jabbar looked back to McCarter and said, "You are from England by your accent."

"I am," McCarter agreed. "Born in London." He stared at Jabbar. "And I can tell by your accent that you studied in England. Where, exactly, may I ask?"

Jabbar's chest puffed out—but only slightly. "Oxford," he said. "Nuffield College."

"Graduate or undergraduate?" McCarter asked, although he could have predicted the answer.

"Both," said Jabbar. "I have a graduate degree in social sciences."

"Well, you've certainly chosen a good area and environment for further study," McCarter said.

"I also played football," said Jabbar. Then, looking at the other men of Phoenix Force, he added, "*Real* football. What you call soccer. Not the kind of American football where you armor yourself with head-to toe padding like a bunch of 'nancies.'"

Manning, who had played the slightly different version north of the U.S. border, couldn't suppress a laugh. "Come over to our side of the world sometime, Jabbar," the big Canadian said. "We'll deck you out in all those pads you're making fun of and let you go helmet-to-helmet with a 350-pound offensive tackle. Then you can see just how 'nancy' the game is."

For a brief moment the air was filled with tension. Then Jabbar gave out his first smile since meeting the men from Stony Man Farm and said, "I am certain that you are correct."

It was time for McCarter to bring the conversation back to their present situation. "I'm sure we could argue football, soccer and probably baseball and cricket all day," he said. "But we have more immediate problems to solve. For instance, this is probably the worst safe-house I've ever seen in my life. The block is empty except for an innocent family that is bound to get hurt if the Radestani government takes note of it. And sooner or later they're *going* to take note." He stopped speaking long enough to take in a deep breath. "I'm surprised they haven't found you already."

"We were forced to evacuate our former base of operations," said Jabbar. "And this was the best we could come up with considering the short notice. But we have made plans to move again as soon as possible."

"Do you already have a place in mind?" asked Mc-Carter. "Because we might as well be flying a flag atop this house that says, 'PSOF Inside—Shoot Us.'" He looked the Oxford-schooled Arab directly in the eye. "The simple fact is, you should have moved out of here already."

Jabbar nodded and opened his mouth to speak. But the words never had a chance to come out.

As if someone outside had heard McCarter's last string of dialogue, a bombardment of rifle fire suddenly came blasting through the windows and forced the men of Phoenix Force and the rebels inside the ancient dwelling to the floor.

Colorado Springs

MAYBE IT WAS cop's intuition. Or it might have been pure dumb luck.

Carl Lyons even considered the possibility of divine intervention, for he believed in a God who helped the good men and women of the world in their fight against evil. But whatever it was, the feeling the Able Team leader got inside his chest made him drive past the second address on Schwarz's map and scrutinize the structure as he turned the corner.

Lyons felt himself nodding slightly as he circled the block. There was *something* going on at the one-story ranch-style home owned by one of the men absent from work at the storage facility. Unless, of course, that man also owned all four cars parked on his circular drive-way out front. And Lyons didn't think that was the case. Which meant the "sick" man had company. And unless the house was filled with doctors and nurses and aunts who'd brought over chicken soup, there was something else going on inside.

And the odds that whatever it was, was good, were not good in the Able Team leader's estimation.

Blancanales had read from the man's file as they'd driven to the ranch house. He was single and had no living relatives. The only car he appeared to own was a Buick LeSabre—one of the cars parked out front. Had a friend come over to look after him during his illness? That would explain one of the other three vehi-cles. But three friends in three cars? Not likely. Which led Lyons to throw the whole "really sick" idea right out the window.

No, this man wasn't really sick. What was going on inside the house could be anything from a poker game among friends to meeting three other terrorists to de-cide what to do with the two nuclear bombs he'd stolen from the facility.

"Terrorist reps from different groups all meeting here to bid on the nukes?" Blancanales said as if he'd just read Lyons's mind. Then he answered his own question. "Doesn't seem likely they'd do that this close to home, if you know what I mean."

"Doesn't make sense to me, either," Schwarz agreed. "But it doesn't look like this guy's sick in bed, either."

Lyons turned the next corner as he said, "No, it doesn't. There are maybe a hundred different reasons all those vehicles might be parked out there. But not very many of them add up to anything lawful or moral. Somehow, I can't believe this clown called in sick to host a Sunday School board meeting at his house."

"Whatever it is," said Schwarz, "we've got to check it out. And I don't think just waltzing up to the front door like we did at Marie Schneider's condo is a particularly good idea."

Lyons's mind traveled back to the condominium building they had left twenty minutes earlier after speaking with Marie Schneider. The woman had been wearing a quilted bathrobe when she answered the door and readily welcomed them inside. Then she had sniffed and sneezed during the entire three minutes it had taken the men of Able Team to determine that she wasn't the nuke thief they were after. Schneider had told them she had only eight months left before retirement, and had seemed disappointed when they had all turned down her offer of coffee and sweet rolls.

Lyons pulled the Chevy over to the curb on the street. "We can cut through the backyard of this house, then see if we can get a look through the windows," he said. "The only problem is it's broad daylight, and we're dressed like FBI agents on some cheap TV reality show."

"If anybody's watching, we're going to draw attention as soon as we get out of the vehicle," Blancanales agreed. "So I suggest we just get out and do it. Walk casually until we get out of sight on this side of the block and act like we know exactly what we're doing and where we're going and why."

Schwarz nodded. "There's a good chance nobody on this side of the block even knows our suspect," he said. "People don't even know their next-door neighbors anymore."

"Okay," said Lyons. "Let's do it. Handguns only. And keep them covered until we're out of sight between the houses."

As can be found in so many cities, there was a definite economical line that ran directly through the center of this block of residential sites. Carl Lyons took note of it as he closed his car door and started up the driveway between two houses. The two sides of the block were uniquely different, and had obviously been developed years apart.

With the other members of Able Team trailing a step behind him, Lyons headed toward a run-down garage—unattached to either of the houses to its sides. The one-car building was definitely in need of paint. Worn gray wood stuck out all over the small structure, with a few chips of paint hanging courageously on before the inevitable happened and they fell to join the other white spots on the ground.

The ranch house—and the houses on both sides of it—that the men of Able Team saw as they neared the alley had been built of brick. They contrasted drastically with the wood-framed homes they had just passed.

By now, all three warriors had drawn their Beretta 92-SBs but kept them low-profile, pressed to the sides of their thighs. Each weapon held fifteen rounds of semijacketed hollowpoint ammo in the magazine, with one extra cartridge already chambered. In addition, all three men had two extra fifteen-round mags in leather holders on their belts.

Lyons turned sideways as he stepped over a low wire fence and came down in an alley that looked as if it had recently seen a light rain. He walked quickly but carefully across the damp ground, doing his best to keep his shoes from sinking.

Lyons wasn't afraid to get his shoes muddy. But the Able Team leader knew that if this turned out to be the place where the nuke thief lived, there was every chance in the world that he'd have to move quickly. And an extra pound or so of wet dirt clinging to the soles of his shoes wasn't going to help that.

He couldn't see them. But as he stepped up out of the alley onto the grass again, Lyons felt Schwarz and Blancanales a step behind him.

The backyard of the house toward which they were headed was far more carefully tended. And this time, he saw a waist-high chain-link fence. But a gate stood to the right of the fence, making it unnecessary to climb over it and attract any more attention. Not that he was worried about prying eyes at this point. No one appeared to be looking out of the rear windows on either side of the block. And if they were, they didn't appear to care what three men dressed in suits and carrying pistols were doing.

Lyons guessed that there was at least a hundred thousand dollars' difference in property values between the two sides of the block as he opened the gate and ushered Schwarz and Blancanales past him. Without needing

to be told, Blancanales took off to the right side of the
sprawling ranch house and Schwarz started walking
left. Lyons took a path directly toward the patio at the
rear of the house. He noted that the blinds were down
and the curtains closed in all of the rear windows even
though the sun was high overhead and would not be
shining directly through the glass.

Another feeling hit Lyons in the gut. While there
were exceptions, most people raised their blinds and
pulled back the curtains to let in light until the sun
rose or fell directly in line with the windows. Then it
became too hot or too irritating to the eyes and they
closed them.

That was not the case here. And it made Lyons wonder exactly what the occupants of all the automobiles
parked out front were trying to hide. These blinds and
curtains were not covering the windows to block out the
sun. They were there to block out prying eyes.

As soon as he reached the patio, the Able Team
leader stepped up off the grass onto the concrete, noting
that while the lawn had been carefully mowed—both
front and back—the patio was littered with a broken
wooden swing, stacked white plastic chairs and several
steel tables that were as badly in need of more green
paint as the garage they had just passed was of white.
And the concrete was covered with a thin coating of
dirt that would have taken months or years to accumu-
late in the fashion it had.

Lyons frowned. Yet another clue that things weren't
quite right at this house. With a patio like this, he would
have expected to see people keep it up so they could
come out in the evenings and enjoy the cool Colorado
Springs night air. He still didn't know exactly what it

was. But Able Team leader and former LAPD detective Carl Lyons knew *something* here was just flat wrong.

Moving cautiously on, Lyons reached the window and noted a small gap between the shade and the bottom left corner of the glass. He knelt quietly, pressing an eye to the screen covering the glass and wondering if that eye might just take a bullet that would kill him before he even realized what had happened. He shrugged the possibility off. Such risks were just part of the job when you worked out of Stony Man Farm.

He could see nothing through the gap. But he did hear the murmur of voices inside.

Pulling back from the window, Lyons stood as he sensed movement on both of his sides. Schwarz and Blancanales appeared almost like two halves of the same entity. Schwarz was the first to whisper, "Couldn't see a thing, Ironman. They're covered up tighter than a spinster's knees."

Blancanales nodded. "Same on my side," he said quietly.

Lyons was about to speak when the sound of several gunshots exploded inside the house. They were muffled by the walls. But there was no doubting for whom the bullets were meant.

The window in front of the three Able Team men suddenly shattered in a hailstorm of flying glass.

Lyons, Schwarz and Blancanales all dived to the sides of the window, falling belly-down on the dirty concrete.

"Anybody hit?" Lyons asked as the unexpected assault suddenly halted.

"I'm fine," said Blancanales.

"Me, too," said Schwarz.

Lyons was already rising from the patio. Inside the house, more gunshots roared. But the glass he heard breaking now was on the side of the structure that Schwarz had scoped out earlier. What had happened was clear. One of them—maybe all of them—had been spotted a few seconds earlier as they'd tried to catch a glimpse of what was going on behind the windows. It had taken a few moments for whoever was in command inside the house to make the decision to open fire.

Lyons had missed catching that bullet in the eye, he'd thought about by less than five seconds.

"How do you want to handle this, Ironman?" Schwarz asked as new gunfire erupted—now on the side of the house that Blancanales had reconned.

By now, the Able Team leader was on his feet. Without looking to either side, he said, "Head-on." And then, the Beretta grasped in his right hand and his left arm up to protect his face, he dived straight through the already crumbled glass in the window in front of him.

Again, Carl "Ironman" Lyons couldn't see them. But he knew without looking that his teammates were right behind him.

CHAPTER NINE

David McCarter jerked off the kaffiyeh and *agal*. Next came the *abat*, which exposed the Rock River LAW-15 Hunter with the coyote-camo "furniture." Rounds from AK-47s—the Russian weapons had their own distinctive sounds—continued to fly over his head like swarms of raging hornets. Twisting back and forth, he made his way across the room to the front window through which the majority of the gunfire was coming.

Long, towel-like cloths hung over the opening, making it impossible to see outside without reaching up and pulling them aside. And doing that, of course, would be paramount to suicide, more or less painting bull's-eyes on the heads and chests inside the safehouse.

McCarter shook his head silently. Whoever it was— maybe Jabbar himself—who had picked this archaic mud house as a hideout deserved to be hanged.

Waiting for a brief lull in the attack, the Phoenix Force leader rose just far enough to get an eye over the packed clay window sill. Then, the Rock River LAW-15 in his right hand, he rested the barrel on the quickly disintegrating windowsill and used his left hand to pull the curtain back at the corner.

What he saw wouldn't have bred much confidence in the average man. There were at least twenty uniformed Radestani regulars in front of the house, all firing AK-

47s or in the process of changing magazines to reenter the foray. Back-crawling a few feet from the window, he turned his head around and saw that Manning and Encizo had taken up similar positions at the back of the large room. "What've you got?" the Phoenix Force leader shouted over the explosions.

"Fifteen—maybe twenty back here," Manning yelled back.

James and Hawkins had taken refuge on both flanks of a side window in the ancient building. "About the same here," James yelled as he pulled off his own head-gear and robe.

Jabbar and some of his men had disappeared into other parts of the house. Others were still on the floor in the main room. McCarter glanced at them. Several had taken rounds and were wounded. One looked dead.

None of them looked very anxious to head toward the windows and return fire.

Jabbar came back out into the main room and dived to the floor next to McCarter, his H&K 91 grasped in both hands. "I have some of my men covering bed-room windows," he breathed. "We are surrounded on all three sides."

McCarter knew that the fourth side was the shared wall with the next vacant clay-and-mud house in the block. It had appeared to be vacant when they'd arrived. But on the end of the connected structures, he remembered the children playing outside in the front yard. The Briton sent a silent prayer skyward for the safety of those children.

Bullets from the Radestani government troops continued to fly through the windows. Others drilled

straight through the clay walls, making dust rise into
the air and creating nature-made smoke grenades. Mc-
Carter began to hear coughing behind him. At first, it
was just one or two rasps. Then the sounds of many
men trying to clear their throats of the dust met his ears.

Two consecutive "taps" struck the Phoenix Force
leader in the side. It felt as though someone had cocked
his middle finger to his thumb, then flicked him twice
in the ribs. But the former SAS officer knew what it
really was without even having to look down.

AK-47 rifle rounds: 7.62 mm to be exact. They had
missed the window but hit the front wall next to it,
and while the thick mud had slowed them to nonlethal power it had not stopped them completely. The
Phoenix Force leader was thankful the rounds had not
come from a rifle like Jabbar's. The more powerful
7.62 mms in the rifle held by the man at his side would
have blasted all the way through the wall and into his
body, crippling, if not killing, him.

What the bullets really did was make the former
SAS man realize that they had to get out of this house
as quickly as possible. The ancient walls were undoubtedly thinner in some areas than others. Regardless of
thickness, they were old and made of dirt, and would
eventually crack and then fall to enough ongoing gunfire. When that happened, all cover and concealment
would evaporate like water in the desert.

By now, McCarter himself was coughing in the dust
storm that pervaded the room. And so was every other
man inside the quickly disintegrating house. The chok-
ing sounds blended together until the room began to

sound like the tuberculosis ward of some nineteenth-century hospital.

The bullets from the government troops continued to blow through the windows and walls. McCarter heard a full-auto blast from outside and watched the window-sill he had just hidden behind explode in dust and tiny chunks of dried clay.

McCarter knew they had only minutes before the entire house came tumbling down on top of them. The lulls in the attack from outside were becoming fewer and farther between, meaning the occasions when the men of Phoenix Force and Jabbar's men were able to rise up and fire back through the windows were diminishing in direct proportion.

Even then they were firing blindly—unable to see their targets. "Spraying and praying" as the old saying went.

Squinting through the dust in his eyes, McCarter looked out between the ragged cloth strips and saw the blurred outline of one of the government soldiers. The man had become overconfident and was striding toward the window. The Phoenix Force leader shifted his rifle barrel slightly and lined the sights up on the man. A quick semiautomatic round from the WYL-Ehide Camo Finish LAR-15 blew out the left side of the government trooper's face and sent him sinking to the ground. But the Phoenix Force leader's shot did not go unnoticed, and he was forced to duck back to the floor as a furious onslaught of return fire came his way.

David McCarter lay flat on the floor, watching the rounds tear the cloths covering the windows to shredded rags. A quick glance around the room told him the same thing was happening to the side and rear of the large living room. And while his men were doing their best to pick off soldiers at every opportunity, their efforts would never be effective enough to win this battle.

They were trapped and vastly outnumbered. There was no way they were going to come out on top. Or even alive if they stayed where they were. All they could hope for was survival, and that meant somehow getting out of this death-trap "safehouse" before the whole place crumbled and left them in the open with bull's-eyes painted on their heads and chests.

McCarter felt himself frowning in concentration. The adage "Never change horses in midstream" didn't apply here. The best leaders knew that they often had to change strategy in the midst of gunfire. And when they did, they had to do so quickly and decisively under extreme pressure.

This was one of those times.

Rolling to his side, McCarter reached behind him and unzipped the main compartment of his backpack. Blind fingers fumbled through his gear until he felt the familiar steel of the folded entrenching tool near the bottom. Pulling it out, he turned toward the back of the room and caught Gary Manning's eye.

Speech was unintelligible over the gunfire and screams coming from some of Jabbar's semi-trained, semi-trustworthy men. But Phoenix Force had worked together for so long that Manning knew instinctively what McCarter wanted as soon as he saw the folded shovel. Like the members of Able Team, all of the men of Phoenix Force were leaders who could take over and formulate their own battle strategies at a moment's notice if called upon to do so. Jerking his own entrenching tool out of his pack, Manning nodded to McCarter before speaking quickly to Encizo at his side. Then, reaching down to retrieve a small clod of dried clay that had blown from the wall to the floor, he cocked his arm like a major league pitcher on the mound and threw it across the room at Hawkins.

The clod had the desired effect, hitting the man called Hawk in the back and calling his attention away from the window and toward Manning. The big Canadian lifted his entrenching tool much as McCarter had just done, and Hawkins nodded before speaking more words the Phoenix Force leader couldn't hear to James.

As Manning and Hawkins rose and sprinted out of the main room, McCarter, James and Encizo doubled their efforts of firing through the ragged strips of cloth hanging from the windows. The makeshift curtains were in such shreds, they could actually get visuals on their targets, and the uniformed Radestani government troops began to fall one by one.

But so did the ancient house as the enemy soldiers continued to bombard it with automatic fire. Each single bullet that struck the age-old structure did little to it. But collectively, they were well on their way to bringing down the walls.

McCarter continued to pull the trigger on his LAR-15 Hunter. They were in a race for time. Would Manning and Hawkins dig them an escape route into the empty house next to them before the walls came tumbling down around them? And what would they do then? They'd find no more than a temporary respite from more walls caving in.

The Phoenix Force leader didn't know exactly what they'd do next. But at least he'd buy a little time to come up with a new plan.

Firing a final full-auto blast through the window, McCarter saw two more of the uniformed men fall to the ground. But he could hear what sounded like jeep engines above the other turmoil. That meant more Radestani soldiers were arriving to take the places of those who had fallen.

His eyes focused on the window, McCarter didn't hear or see Encizo until he dived to the ground next to him. The man had disappeared into the back room but had now returned and seemed to have appeared out of nowhere.

McCarter squeezed the trigger again and another Radestani soldier dropped outside. "How's it going back there?" he shouted.

Encizo was on his stomach, his Hunter barrel aimed out the window. "About like in here," he said, as he sent a volley of rounds out through the rags. He glanced around at the thick fissures that were beginning to appear in the walls. "I'm afraid Joshua's playing his trumpet and the walls are a-tumblin' down."

"What are Jabbar and his men doing?" McCarter asked as he ejected the magazine from his LAR-15 and inserted a full load.

An expression of disgust came over Encizo's face. "A few of them," he said, "including Jabbar, are doing okay. Fact is, that dude's pretty fancy with his Heckler & Koch. But a lot of them are curled up in corners. One's even crying."

The Phoenix Force leader suspected his own expression mirrored Encizo's disdain. "If they didn't want to fight, they shouldn't have signed up," he said as he fired anew through the strips of cloth hanging over the window.

Encizo rose high enough to position his rifle over the quickly crumbling windowsill. "About half of them are okay fighters," he said, then fired another volley of rounds. "But when I say 'okay' that's just what I mean—*just okay*. The rest are completely worthless." His bullets hit their mark and another uniformed Radestani trooper bit the dirt outside.

"Not a Bolan in the bunch, huh?" McCarter said without thinking as he fired again himself.

Encizo knew exactly what he meant and laughed out loud. "There's only one Mack Bolan, David," he said.

Even under such extreme and deadly conditions, McCarter couldn't help but laugh along with him. Mack Bolan was the solo warrior around which Stony Man Farm had originally been built. The man known as the Executioner was the very heart and soul of the installation.

Encizo pulled his trigger again, sending a full-auto stream of fire out of what remained of the window. "Manning and Hawk looked like they were about halfway through the wall into the next prehistoric condominium," he said.

"Good," said McCarter. "Think you and James can hold the fort down while I go help dig?"

"I'm not sure *anyone* can," said Encizo. "But I'll give it my best shot." Then, as if to prove it, he pulled the trigger back and sent another 3-round burst out of the disintegrating house.

"Then I'm gone," said McCarter, rising to his feet but staying low in a crouch. "I'll get word to you when we've got an opening made."

Then, with his rifle in one hand, the entrenching tool in the other, the Phoenix Force leader raced out of the room to help Manning and Hawkins.

Colorado Springs

CARL LYONS'S SHOULDERS caught the shards of glass still sticking to the sides of the window as he dived into the living room of the ranch house. The sharp edges tore through his jacket. But he could tell they barely scratched his skin.

He'd been lucky, and he hoped his teammates would have the same kind of luck as they followed him into the house. But as soon as that thought had passed, another one took its place.

The house was all wrong, just as his instincts had told him earlier. But it wasn't wrong in the way he'd expected. The first thing that told him that was the sweet smell of growing marijuana plants that hit him as he dived under more gunfire and shoulder-rolled across the carpet.

Lyons came up on one knee, the Beretta gripped in both hands at shoulder level, his eyes taking in the entire room in one glance. The living room looked like a jungle, with marijuana plants growing in carefully tended rows all over what had been built to serve as a living room. Hydroponic grow lights were suspended from the ceiling and hung atop poles, beaming down onto the plants. Most of them appeared to be in the vegetative state during which the grower made sure they got eighteen to twenty-four hours of light a day. But toward the other end of the room—the front of the house—the plants were taller and had started to flower into buds. The lights above these plants were off. Lyons had worked narcotics in Los Angeles long enough to know that they had reached the stage where they needed twelve hours of light and twelve of darkness.

The marijuana plants answered another question that had perplexed Lyons, as well. Just as the Able Team leader had suspected, Wilber Dickerson wasn't sick and he was up to no good. It just wasn't the kind of nuclear-no-good Lyons had expected.

Between the stalks and leaves of the marijuana jungle Lyons saw a burly man in a blue tank top raise a 1911 Government Model .45 and begin firing. The big slugs clipped five-pointed leaves from their stalks and cut one plant almost in two.

Lyons returned fire, sending a double-tap of 9 mm semijacketed hollowpoints into the shooter's forehead—one above each eye. The man in the tank top fell backward to the carpet.

Automatic sprinklers were attached to many of the plants, and the Able Team leader knew that the water would contain nutrients with a pH solution of around 5.5 to 6.0. White hairs covered the plants still growing, proving they were female cannabis—the kind containing the THC chemical that produced the pothead's beloved "high." But haphazardly thrown to the carpet, along the side of the walls of this grow house living room, were other plants that had begun producing grapelike balls. Some of the balls had already started turning into pollen sacs.

Male plants, Lyons knew. No THC. No "high." Good

for little more than producing rope, and certainly not cost-productive enough to risk attracting the attention of law enforcement by trying to sell them for such purposes.

All of this flashed through Lyons's brain as he began to squeeze the trigger again. His first shot into the man wearing the blue tank top had come from the long double-action trigger pull. The second, however, had been light since the hammer had remained cocked after the slide slid back closed. Now another light touch of the trigger sent a third 9 mm drilling through the brain of a man who looked like a throwback to the Age of Aquarius. Long hair fell far down his back, covering the shirtless shoulders beneath his faded blue denim overalls. His face was covered with a long full beard straight out of ZZ Top, and embroidered on the bib of the overalls was a peace sign.

Two details, however, contradicted his Summer of Love appearance. The first was the fact that both his hair and beard were solid white. And the second thing, which clashed loudly with the peace sign, was the double-barreled shotgun in his hands.

Lyons felt the Beretta jump slightly in his hand as yet another hollowpoint flew from the barrel to the center of the old hippie's forehead. The man stood in place for a moment. Then the shotgun rose toward the ceiling and both 12-gauge barrels exploded as the man fell to the floor into what looked like some twisted and contorted yoga position.

The double blast shattered one of the grow lights suspended above him, and the brightly lit room darkened slightly as more glass rained down.

But the fight was hardly over.

Suddenly men bearing a variety of arms emerged from doorways to the grow room like cockroaches scurrying away when a light switch is turned on. And cockroaches was exactly the way the Able Team leader thought of them as he detected the 9 mm pop of two rounds from his rear. Either Schwarz or Blancanales had just taken out another armed grass-grower wearing a black T-shirt and OD green BDU pants. But while he couldn't see the shooter, the Able Team leader saw the results. Both rounds hit the man squarely in the chest, sending small explosions out the front of the black shirt and larger ones flying out the back. The man in the BDU pants had been wielding a pump-action Mossberg scattergun. But it fell to the carpet next to one of the taller plants before he could pull the trigger.

Yet again, Lyons *felt* rather than *saw* his men fan out behind him. Years of working together negated the need for formal orders. They had practiced taking down rooms a thousand times. More importantly, they had actually done it in real time far more times than that.

So while he didn't know exactly which of his fellow Able Team men would take the left side of the room, he knew one of them would. And the other would concentrate on the right. Lyons, as pointman within this relatively small battleground, would divide his duties between dealing with any threat that came from the center of the room and acting as "cleanup hitter" by backing up both Schwarz and Blancanales for extra insurance.

The front room was devoid of furniture or anything else one would expect to find there. This meant there was no cover. And the marijuana plants offered little concealment. Staying alive in this down-and-dirty gunfight was going to amount to shooting and moving, accurately and fast. Like the famous Shootout at the O.K. Corral, the winners would be determined simply by whose gun was quicker but still on target.

A young man in his early twenties, with a shaved head and rings in both ears and both nostrils, tried to raise a Taurus .45 into the fight. Lyons pulled the trigger of his Beretta again. At almost the same time, he heard a similar roar behind him as one of his teammates fired.

The man with the shaved head wore no shirt—he just *looked* like he did. His torso, both arms and neck were covered in a variety of merging tattoos. In the center of his chest was a dragon breathing fire, and it was the dragon's neck at which Lyons fired.

It was impossible to see where his double-tap of rounds actually hit through the dark ink.

But that didn't bother the Able Team leader. As the man fell backward in death, he knew that the actual fire had ended the dragon's red, orange and yellow breath for all eternity.

Two more grass farmers came out of a hallway to Lyons's left, stupidly exposing themselves to the fire from the men of Able Team. The first wore designer blue jeans speckled with sparkling rhinestone designs on the front pockets. They looked more befitting for a woman than a man, Lyons thought as his next round burrowed through a T-shirt paying homage to some band he'd never heard of. The rhinestones sparkled in the remaining overhead lights as the man did a backward jackknife and slammed against the wall behind him. In the process, he dropped a replica of a huge ball-and-cap Walker Colt single-action revolver. But the gun didn't fall until he'd convulsively squeezed the trigger, allowing the cocked hammer to fall and send a round lead ball harmlessly into the carpet. Burned black powder spewed from the barrel and the cylinder, filling the area with clouds of smoke and the stench from the ancient load.

Lyons wasted only a second wondering why the man had utilized such an archaic weapon. Then he reminded himself that the invention of new technology never meant that old technology quit working. And many men had died from the round lead that blew out of ball-and-cap pistols. In any case, the man's choice was irrelevant to the situation at this point.

The Able Team leader heard Schwarz and Blancanales open up on the second man. It sounded as if both men had decided on what was sometimes called the Mozambique Technique—two shots to the chest, then one to the head. That, in this case, meant four 9 mm hollowpoints actually blasted into the grass-farmer's heart, and another pair practically took off his head just above the neck.

Suddenly the house went deadly quiet. All of the men in the living-room slash grow-room lay dead on the carpet. But the cloud of black smoke from the Walker Colt continued to spread across the room, thinning and dissipating as it went.

The Able Team leader finally turned to his comrades. Waving his Beretta toward the hallway from which the last two men had emerged, he nodded at Schwarz, who took off to check whatever rooms he'd find that way.

Pointing toward the kitchen, which they could see through another doorway, another nod sent Blancanales off on his own search-and-destroy mission. Lyons himself strode his way through the marijuana plants to the front door. With the Beretta hidden behind his back in case anyone was watching, he twisted the knob, opened the door and stepped out onto the front porch. Looking outward, he saw the same four cars and the same upper-middle-class neighborhood he'd driven past before parking on the other side of the block. He took a few steps out into the yard and turned back.

The grow house looked no different than the other homes in the neighborhood. It blended in perfectly with the rest of the houses. The pot cultivators had even hung a bench swing from the roof over the porch to make it look more "homey."

The Able Team leader seriously doubted that anyone else in the neighborhood had harbored suspicions as to the ranch house's true role. If they followed the usual procedures when hiding marijuana in plain sight, three of the men—one driving each of the three vehicles still parked out front—would have come and gone occasionally, wearing far more conservative attire than they had died in. The rest—particularly the weirder-looking ones—would have entered through the back from the alley.

And that same alley would have been used when the plants were ready to harvest. It would have been a simple enough procedure to cut the stalks, wrap them in sheets or blankets or other cloths, and carry them out to a truck in the middle of the night.

Lyons reentered the house and closed the front door behind him with mixed feelings. Colorado had recently legalized marijuana. But it still violated federal laws, and even the state laws regulating the weed's cultivation, sale, possession and use were still up in the air.

And if the Rocky Mountain State's politicians and bureaucrats were true to form, it could take years for all those things to come together.

In the meantime, Lyons knew that the best thing for him and the other two Able Team warriors to do was to get out of there. He had no doubt that the "wasteoids" they'd just killed—who had been armed with everything from illegally sawed-off shotguns to the ball-and-cap revolver—deserved to die.

He looked down at the face covered in tattoos. Guys like him didn't stop with marijuana.

Blancanales had seemed to be on a mind-reading streak lately. As he came striding back into the main room, he said, "You know the old saying about God looking after drunks and fools, Ironman?" he asked Lyons.

The Able Team leader just waited for him to go on.

"Well, we weren't drunk just now," Blancanales said.

"And your point is?" asked Lyons.

"Three of the other bedrooms are grow rooms just like here," said Blancanales, sweeping the room with the barrel of his Beretta. "But the master bed and bath is set up as a fully functional meth lab."

The Able Team leader took in a deep breath, realizing immediately what Blancanales had meant about God watching over fools. The men of Able Team weren't fools—they'd had no way of knowing there was a meth lab that could blow the whole house sky high if a stray bullet penetrated the wrong component. Even if they had known, they'd have had no choice but to take down the house in the same manner. But Lyons looked upward anyway, feeling a little on the blessed side.

By now Schwarz had joined them in the living room.

"I guess Pol told you we barely escaped being vaporized," he said.

"So I heard," said Lyons. "Here we are looking for nuclear weapons and we almost blow ourselves up with antihistamines and antifreeze concoctions." The dead man with the full-skin tattoos was at his feet and Lyons leaned down, using the muzzle of the Beretta to pull his upper lip up toward his nose. What he saw inside the man's mouth would have sent an oral surgeon to a psychiatrist. The man had lost more than half his teeth to meth. And he looked as though he was well on his way to losing the other half.

"This clown's had his share of crank," the Able Team leader said.

Blancanales stepped over and looked down at the man. "This guy ought to have been shot just for the bad tattoos," he said.

"I checked the closets," said Schwarz. "They're packed with everything from fifty-pound sacks of nutrients and fertilizer to equipment for the manufacture of methamphetamines."

Lyons knew the answer to his next question before he even asked it. But it had to be asked. So he said simply, "But no sign of the backpack nukes?"

"Uh-uh," said Schwarz.

Blancanales shook his head. "That would make things too easy, Ironman."

Lyons's jaw tightened as he walked quickly to the body of the man who'd worn the black T-shirt and BDU pants. Luckily, he had been killed by chest wounds alone, and his face matched the photo in his personnel file. "Wilber Dickerson," said the Able Team leader. "You've been a very, very, very bad boy." Then, turning back to Schwarz and Blancanales, "Did either of you find anything that might lead you to believe this guy was involved with the missing bombs?"

"I hate to say it," said Schwarz. "But no."

Blancanales shook his head silently.

"I think we just stumbled on a government employee who had a little capitalistic side business going on," Schwarz added. "I don't think this place has anything to do with the missing backpacks."

"Neither do I." Lyons walked to the window next to the door, pulled the shade up and looked outside again. None of the neighbors appeared to have heard the gunfire. Or if they had, they weren't interested in checking out its source. At least not in the front.

Blancanales seemed to tap into Lyons's brain again. "They might have heard it, called the police and then stayed safely in their houses."

Lyons turned around and nodded. "In any case, it's time we got out of here." He pulled a satellite phone from inside his shoulder-tattered jacket as he led the way toward the rear of the house. But before he even switched it on, he turned to Schwarz. "You didn't get the nickname Gadgets by chance," he growled. "Get out your phone and take pictures of the faces on the floor." He paused a moment, then said, "Even the ones that don't look like faces anymore." Passing the shattered window through which they'd entered, he reached for the knob on the back door. "Then roll the prints of each thumb and forefinger on the right hand on your screen—we don't have time for a full set of prints on each man and with AFIS that'll be enough. Send the pictures and prints to the Farm. We'll see if Kurtzman can run them down." The Able Team leader had started walking toward the back door but now he stopped and turned around. "But I'm almost as sure they'll turn out to have nothing to do with our current mission."

Schwarz had already started taking pictures with his phone by the time Lyons finished.

Lyons knew he needed to call the local police just in case none of the neighbors had. Someone had to take possession of the marijuana plants and dismantle the dangerous crank lab in the bedroom. Otherwise there would likely be other members of this cultivation cartel who would come back to the house, see what had happened and cut their losses by taking the plants and meth to another location. If the police played it right, they might be able to grab them, too.

As he twisted the doorknob, the cop in him thought again of fingerprints. But this time it wasn't the prints of the dead men on the floor that entered his mind. It was his own. As well as those of Schwarz and Blancanales. They'd probably be leaving partials and even a few full prints on the doorknobs and other surfaces around the house. But that hardly mattered.

The fingerprints of all of the warriors connected to Stony Man Farm had been erased from AFIS and all other databases by computer expert Aaron "Bear" Kurtzman long ago. The local forensic specialists would lift their prints, but they'd hit a stone wall. All three sets would come back marked "Not on File."

Lyons led the way across the yard, over the fence and between the lower-income houses to their vehicle. "Let's move out," he said to Blancanales as he got behind the wheel. "We've still got one address left to check out." He twisted the key and started the engine.

Schwarz had finished at the house and came jogging past the old garage to take the shotgun seat.

"Which one's left?" Blancanales asked from the back seat. "I can't remember."

Lyons lifted one of the files on the seat between him and Schwarz and handed it back. "Mussawi," he said. "Mani Mussawi."

Blancanales took the file, sat back and opened it in his lap. "I've got to say the name sounds more promising than Marie Schneider and Wilber Dickerson."

"There you go, Pol," Schwarz said, shaking his head in mock disgust. "Stereotyping and profiling."

"Nope," said Blancanales. "Just playing the odds. While I'll be the first to say there are more good Arabs than bad, in case you haven't been paying attention, it's mainly men with names like this who've been carrying out the terrorist strikes around the world." The East L.A. native stopped talking for a second and in the rearview mirror Lyons could see him frowning. "Where did Hal say Phoenix Force was?"

"Radestan," said Schwarz. "The civil war over there. Why?"

"No particular reason," said Blancanales. "Something just got me thinking."

"Well," said Lyons, "keep right on thinking and we'll pray that this Mani Mussawi turns out to be the man we're looking for. Because if we don't catch a lead at his place, I don't know *where* we're going from here."

CHAPTER TEN

David McCarter turned his head to the side, then spit out a gritty mouthful of saliva. It hit the floor just to the left of the slowly widening hole in the wall, and was every bit as reddish brown in color as the floor on which he stood. He had already tried to blow his nose on a bandanna he'd had stashed in his pocket. But nasal fluid wasn't the problem. The red dust flying through the air had caused the membranes in his sinuses to swell, blocking a good ninety percent of his breathing.

Taking in air through his mouth wasn't an option; it had become a necessity as the dust swirled thicker through the air with every shovelful of dirt he, Manning and Hawkins displaced in the common wall the safehouse shared with the dwelling adjacent to it.

McCarter resumed digging, striking the wall with his entrenching tool much like a man might lunge with a spear. Slowly but surely, they were making progress. But time was definitely *not* on their side.

Outside, the barrage of gunfire from the Radestani government troops continued. Phoenix Force and the few of Jabbar's PSOF rebels who were not too afraid to raise a rifle, kept returning that fire. But new fissures were appearing in the walls—even the ones in this bedroom where the digging continued. It was only a matter of time before the whole structure came down.

McCarter had taken his turn with the shovel, giving Hawkins a brief rest. Then he'd handed the entrenching tool back to the young warrior and moved to the side of the bedroom window. Next to him, he could hear the steady pounding of a rifle caliber louder than the 5.56 mm and 7.62 mm weapons most of the men inside the dwelling were firing. He glanced over his shoulder and saw that Jabbar had taken up a kneeling position next to another window not ten feet away. It was the roar of his longer 7.62 NATO rounds—referred to as .308s when measured in inches rather than millimeters—causing the racket.

McCarter could only pray that the more powerful rounds were taking out enemies.

T. J. Hawkins had been digging at the wall next to the Phoenix Force leader. Now he stepped back and dropped his arms to his sides. The tip of his folding shovel rested on the ground as he took a brief ten-second rest. "We *would* get saddled with the thickest wall in this whole prehistoric apartment house," he said. "We're trying to dig through this while the other walls are about to come down on our heads." His voice trailed off, his eyes looked upward and his mouth opened slightly. Then his eyes dropped to meet McCarter's.

As for the Phoenix Force leader, he stared back. It was obvious to the two men that the same idea had struck them both at the same time.

"Why didn't we think of this earlier, Hawk?" McCarter said.

Hawkins shrugged as he leaned his entrenching tool against the wall next to the hole.

By now, Gary Manning had tapped into the sudden

inspiration. "Are we sure there aren't any innocents in the room on the other side?" he asked.

"It didn't look like it when we got here," said Hawkins. "And I can't imagine anyone stupid enough to run inside any of these places after the shooting started." The youngest member of Phoenix Force stopped talking long enough to spit out an orange-red mouthful of dirt. "But even if there is someone next to us, by now they should have either found some cubbyhole to crawl into or flown the coop altogether."

"It's a risk we'll have to take," said McCarter. "The fact is, they'll be in less danger from us than the rounds coming in from the government troops. So let's get it on. *Fast*." He dropped his own entrenching tool and stepped back, pulling the partially filled magazine from his LAR-15 and replacing it with a full load. "Give it all thirty rounds," he said. "Then we'll see where we stand."

The three Phoenix Force warriors stepped back and aimed their rifles at the dent in the wall where they'd been digging. McCarter nodded.

They opened fire.

One after another, ninety rounds of 5.56 mm ammo slammed into the caked mud. McCarter couldn't help thinking about how much ammunition they were burning up, and how many enemy soldiers were still outside. But running low on ammo would have to take second place to the problems of here and now, and that meant softening up the packed dirt so their entrenching tools could finish the escape route faster.

As the full-auto fire went on, tiny streaks of light began to appear through the wall. Gradually, the holes got bigger until all three LAR-15s had run dry.

The indentation in the wall looked like a reddish-brown beehive. Then the red dust became so overpoweringly thick in the air that the wall at which they were shooting all but disappeared.

Coughing and sneezing, the three Phoenix Force warriors jerked the empty magazines from their weapons and inserted fresh loads. Gradually the dust began to settle and the wall appeared again. It was riddled with small entryways into the next house, and light streaked through at almost every angle possible.

"Now," said McCarter, picking up his short folding shovel. "If we can just get it big enough to squeeze the men through before the whole wall comes down on top of us...." He didn't bother finishing the sentence. Both Manning and Hawkins knew what would happen if the wall suddenly collapsed. The ceiling was likely to follow, and whoever was going through the short tunnel—and probably everyone in the nearby area—would be buried under the avalanche.

The men with the folding shovels resumed digging. But more gingerly this time as the rapid fire from the various weapons continued to pour into, and be shot out of, the mud dwelling.

Five minutes later Phoenix Force had a crawl hole at the bottom of the wall big enough to get a small-to-medium-size man through. As the gunfire continued, McCarter looked at Manning. There were certain advantages to being big and strong. But the Canadian's size had disadvantages, too. And getting him through the hole as it stood now was going to be a problem.

McCarter decided to keep Manning back until the rest of the men had made it through the opening. He could go right before McCarter himself. Then, if those giant power-lifting shoulders caught the sides of the hole and caused the wall to crumble, at least the majority of the men would already be safe.

The Phoenix Force leader turned to his side and waited for a short break in the gunfire in the other room. As soon as it came, he yelled out for Encizo, who lowered his weapon and turned toward him.

"Get through there," McCarter said, pointing at the hole in the wall with his rifle.

Encizo shook his head. "I'll stay with you guys," he said. "You can get Ali and Jabbar and his men out and—"

"We don't have time to argue," McCarter cut him off. "Jabbar's men are going. But I want someone responsible on the other side before they do. Half of them will freeze up if there's no level head to encourage them. There's no telling how the other half'll freak out." He gingerly rubbed more dust from one of his eyes as he went on. "I need someone who can fit through there and someone who can take the lead once they have," he went on. "You're the only one who fits the bill."

Encizo understood immediately. He dropped to the ground on his chest.

"Make sure no one fires from inside there until I've gotten all of Jabbar's men through," McCarter said to Encizo as he started squirming through the opening. "We don't want to give away our new position until we have to." The Phoenix Force leader turned to his side. "Manning," he said, "go back through the rooms and pick out all the men you think can squeeze through that hole. Hawk and I'll keep digging." He slung the LAR-15 over his shoulder and picked up the entrenching tool once again. Hawkins did the same as Manning raced out of the room.

The room where they were digging the escape route continued to look as if someone had doused it from ceiling to floor with orange talcum powder. McCarter and Hawkins kept coughing, sneezing, and occasionally lapsed into spasms of a short series of chokes as they did their best to capture oxygen through the thick clouds of disturbed dirt. Every so often they were forced to drop their shovels and do their best to rub the filth out of their eyes.

By the time Manning came back, the tunnel into the next house was considerably larger. But a new problem had developed. A few of Jabbar's men who trailed the big Canadian showed discipline. But others dived for the hole in the wall like terrified children, doing their best to be first to squirm through the opening, and looking for all the world like the Three Stooges trying to get through a doorway on their hands and knees.

"Get them under control," McCarter ordered the big Canadian.

Manning didn't hesitate. Stepping forward, he leaned down and grabbed two men blocking each other's progress through the hole by the scruffs of their necks. He jerked them back up to their feet. "All right!" the big Canadian shouted. "All of you! Stand up and form a straight line. Jabbar, you're last. You stick with me."

Jabbar moved in next to the barrel-chested Canadian. "Now," he said to his men, "follow the orders of this man!"

Some of the men remained cool. Others shook like trees in a tornado. But one way or another, they all fell into line and took turns moving forward and crawling into the next apartment. McCarter and Hawkins continued digging at the sides as the men slipped through. But by now they were thrusting their entrenching tools far more gently, and each time they struck the dirt they stopped to look up at the ever-weakening wall above.

The upper wall and the ceiling were beginning to shake. They didn't have much time left. If they didn't get the rest of the men and themselves through the opening soon, they could easily die under the rubble of their own making when the ancient structure came tumbling down.

When all of Jabbar's men had crawled into the next apartment, McCarter sent Abdul Ali through the hole. He called for James and sent him through. Then he looked up at the big Canadian.

"You're next."

The Phoenix Force demolitions expert frowned. "I'd have to be a complete fool not to realize why you saved me until now," he said. "But that hole is still going to be tight for me. You go first. I'll bring up the rear and—"

McCarter shook his head impatiently as he cut his fellow warrior off. "That's the problem with leading other leaders," he said. "Everyone thinks they have a better idea." He spat more slimy orange phlegm to the side. "I know your intentions are good, but we don't have time to discuss it. *Go*."

Along with muscle, Manning had an I.Q. in the 150 range and he snapped to the fact that time really was of the essence. Without further words he slung his LAR-15 Hunter over his back and dropped to all fours. A moment later he had scrambled out of sight.

But he didn't get through the hole quite as "cleanly" as McCarter might have hoped for. The Phoenix Force leader saw the big man's right shoulder barely clear the side of the hole. But the left dragged across the other side and made the whole wall, and the ceiling, shake even harder.

McCarter knew he had only a few more seconds before the wall and roof came tumbling down on top of him. His own coyote-camo Hunter went over his back on the sling and he dropped down on all fours, then to his chest.

The wall in front of him was no longer shaking; it was *swaying* back and forth, ready to come down in huge chunks at any moment. As McCarter moved forward, he watched it lean away from him, then toward him, then away from him again. He was alone now in this original safehouse but behind him he could still hear the gunfire from outside, and the splatter of bullets hitting the clay and mud walls. Round after round after round continued to pound the quickly disintegrating structure as he stuck his head through the opening.

By now, the soldiers outside had figured out what was going on inside and more rounds were slapping against the walls and sailing through the windows of the living quarters into which Phoenix Force had just burrowed.

All McCarter and his men had done was buy themselves a little more time. It was going to be the same story all over again in here. The fact was, the Radestani soldiers had figured out where they were and what they were doing. And McCarter, the other members of Phoenix Force, and Jabbar and his men had little choice but to immediately start digging out a hole into the *third* connected dwelling, hoping against hope, once again, that they could do so before the walls of the second mud-and-clay home disintegrated like the first was doing.

But what would they do then? McCarter wondered as he continued to pull himself across the clods of dirt on the floor of the escape hole. After they entered the third dwelling they would be next to the last home on the block—the one that was occupied; the one outside of which he'd seen the children. The kids would have instinctively taken refuge inside when the shooting started. And in addition to them, at least one innocent civilian adult would presumably be at the location.

McCarter knew he was going to have his hands full just trying to get his own men out of this death trap. But he felt responsible for the kids and adults on the end of this block of ancient houses, too.

How in the world was he going to protect them?

The Briton pulled himself forward, getting his upper chest through the hole. Maybe the children and any adults at the end of the block had fled the scene rather than hide inside the house. He could hope so. But deep in his heart McCarter knew that was unlikely. Normal noncombatant thinking would have sent them scurrying toward the first familiar place. And that meant the end dwelling.

As he dragged himself on through the wall, McCarter knew he would just have to play it by ear and move one step—or, in his current position, one belly-crawl—at a time. And right now there was nothing he could do about it so he pushed that train of thought from the front of his mind to the back. He would deal with the problem of the children when it came up. Right now, he had other obstacles to face. Obstacles that would very likely result in the death of the men from Stony

Man Farm if he didn't overcome them, and overcome them quickly.

McCarter was still half-in, half-out, of the escape hole when he looked up to see the others positioned around the room. Encizo and Manning had done their jobs and done them well, organizing Jabbar's rag-tag band of amateur freedom fighters and positioning them at the window openings as best they could. The loud and steady pounding of the .308 continued to roar above the smaller calibers. And just like had happened in the original dwelling, some of Jabbar's men were fighting. Others were cowering in corners, under furniture, or anyplace else they could find to hide.

McCarter had almost gotten his hips through the opening when he felt, rather than heard, the rumbling to his sides and over his head. He was still half in the old dwelling, half in the new, when the wall finally gave way and came down on top of him. Suddenly it was not only his mouth that seemed full of the dusty powder but his ears and nostrils, as well. A reddish-orange blindness came over his eyes. Then the color suddenly switched to black.

And once he'd entered the darkness, no colors at all existed anymore.

Colorado Springs

Mani Mussawi had lived through his share of hangovers during his years as an al Qaeda mole in America. But this one "took the cake" as his American friends would have said. It was still with him, making his head feel like the inside of a kettle drum and his stomach threaten to send whatever bile was left in it shooting out of his mouth at any moment.

It was all he could do to turn the wheel of the rented Kia Cadenza and glide into Zaid Baharlou's driveway.

Mussawi killed the engine but sat where he was for a few moments, hoping his stomach would settle. It didn't. He twisted his neck slowly back and forth, on the chance that stretching might relieve some of the pain in his head. That didn't happen, either. He sat still and closed his eyes. At first, he saw only blackness. Then the memory of the hallucination he'd had the night before crossed his mind and he saw the gentle man in the white robe standing outside the motel room window, asking if he could come in.

Somehow—Mussawi didn't know exactly how—he knew that the man hadn't just wanted to come inside the filthy room. He'd wanted to actually come inside Mussawi himself. He'd wanted to enter his mind and heart. His very soul.

The man had actually walked on the pond, he remembered.

The al Qaeda mole watched behind his closed eyelids as the man's loving smile turned to a look of sorrow again, and he heard him say the same words he'd heard last night. *He's going to kill millions.* Mussawi opened his eyes and shook his head back and forth, preferring even the pain it caused him to the memory of the hallucination. He'd had slight but controllable hallucinations a couple of times over the years when he had smoked particularly strong marijuana with some American friends. But he had never experienced anything like what had happened the night before. Particularly on alcohol. Mussawi had heard of such things happening to late-stage alcoholics but he knew he didn't fall into that category. At least not yet, and God was getting him out of here before he had time to create such a dependency.

Mussawi shook his head again and let the pain do what it wanted to do. The hallucination had to have been caused by stress and the speed with which he'd consumed the bottle of Jack Daniel's. Never before had he drank an entire quart in less than ten minutes. Most of it he had chugged trying to get rid of the ghostly image coming toward him. And it had all hit his brain at the same time.

Mussawi supposed he was lucky such a shock to his system hadn't killed him outright.

He opened the Cadenza's door and got out. He was about to close it but stopped. His Makarov was tucked into the waistband of the jeans he wore under his dark blue blazer. The two extra magazines were in the left and right pockets of the jacket, balancing it out to avoid the attention that might come with it drooping on one side.

He was well armed. But the bass-fiddle AK-47 case, his personal bag and the black nylon bags containing the nuclear devices were locked in the trunk. Should he leave them there or take them up to the porch with him? He looked around at the neighboring houses and saw well-tended lawns, cleanly swept porches and structures that fell into the upper-middle-class price range. At the end of the block on the other side of the street was a small park with swings, slides and a red merry-go-round.

This was a safe neighborhood. The chances of anyone breaking into the trunk of his car while he checked to make sure Baharlou was home were too minimal to worry about.

Mussawi took a deep breath of the thin, high-altitude Colorado Springs air as he closed the door. Now that he was here—at the second planned stop in his mission— the pain in his head and belly didn't seem so bad. And the activity enabled him to push the frightening hallucination out of his mind, as well. He moved from the driveway to the sidewalk that led to the porch, stepped up and pushed the doorbell.

Inside the house, he heard chimes.

A moment later Baharlou appeared at the door, smiling through the glass. Mussawi smiled back. But at the same time he wondered what the man's real name was. It certainly wasn't Zaid Baharlou.

All Mani Mussawi knew was that Baharlou was his contact back to the world of al Qaeda. The man was not a mole, as he was; Baharlou was an intermediary. A "handler" if his title was translated into CIA-speak. Zaid Baharlou's chief function was to pass encoded messages back and forth between Nosiar and Mussawi without even understanding the codes himself.

Usually, these messages were left at specific drop points; the two men had met face-to-face only a few times. The fact was, Mussawi was not even sure he would have recognized Baharlou now if he saw him on the street—out of context, so to speak. He knew that Baharlou had never been officially notified that Mussawi was a mole but Mussawi knew the man would have to be a fool not to have figured that out for himself over the years.

The main wooden door opened and Baharlou's face smiled through the glass of the storm door. Mussawi remembered his contact as having worn a full beard. But now it had been trimmed into a neat mustache and goatee. The smile grew larger as Baharlou pushed the storm door open, then stepped back to let Mussawi inside. *"Allahu Akbar,"* he said.

Even though his head still throbbed and his stomach churned, Mussawi forced a smile and returned the greeting.

Inside the house now, under the lights, Mussawi could see that Baharlou was essentially bald on the top of his head. The remaining hair on the left side of his head had been purposely grown long and forced into a comb-over. Thick, greasy-looking stripes crossed his pate; in between them his scalp shone like a full moon through thin dark clouds. As he started to speak again, his right hand rose and patted the strands down in what looked to Mussawi like an unconscious gesture.

"So," said Baharlou. "We meet again. And for the final time, as I understand it. It must mean, as the Americans say, you are finally 'coming in from the cold.'"

"Yes." Mussawi laughed. "I read that book myself, I believe. A novel about a spy who 'comes in from the cold'—meaning he finishes his undercover work. American novelists can come up with some of the most ridiculous expressions imaginable. I have never heard anyone outside of fiction use that expression."

Baharlou laughed and patted his hair down again. Then he frowned. "You have no luggage?" he asked.

"I have luggage," said Mussawi. "I just waited to ensure that you were home before lugging it up here and then having to take it back." He paused as a streak of pain hit him behind the eyes and reminded him again of all the whiskey he'd downed the night before. "So, can you help me with it?"

"Of course," said Baharlou. He pushed through the storm door and led the way back to the car. Mussawi followed, popped open the trunk and reached inside. He handed Baharlou his suitcase and the upright bass case.

"I had no idea you were a musician," said Baharlou. "And a player of such a large and heavy instrument."

Mussawi saw the deadpan look on the man's face and couldn't tell if Baharlou actually believed the case contained a stringed bass or was making a joke. Regardless, he decided not to answer. Instead he reached into the trunk and picked up the two small nuclear device bags. He carried them both by the handles, one in each hand, as they made their way back to the front door.

Baharlou glanced over his shoulder twice, eyeing the black ballistic nylon, a slightly puzzled look on his face. But by the time they had reentered the house, his expression had become a smile of understanding. He led Mussawi out of the entryway into a living room, where two large matching sofas faced each other. Carefully setting the bass case and Mussawi's personal bag on one of the sofas, he turned and took a seat at the end of the other.

Mussawi carefully set the two nuke bags down next to his other luggage, then took a seat at the other end of the sofa from Baharlou.

"You look tired, my brother," said Baharlou. "I have no doubt the last few years have been stressful."

"They have," Mussawi conceded. "Especially the past few days."

Baharlou looked across the living room at the bags on the other sofa. "I do not know the entire plan, of course," he said. "But considering where you have worked, and the way you clung to the two black cases yourself, I can guess what they are."

Mussawi didn't respond.

"Would you like a drink?" asked Baharlou. "We are both still under the special dispensation from God concerning alcohol. It furthers the jihad. Right now, to calm you during this time of crisis."

"Do you have bourbon?" asked Mani.

"Of course," said Baharlou, rising to his feet. "Give me one moment, please." He started out of the room, then turned back. "What would you like with it?" he asked. "Coca-Cola? Water? I also have some Seven-Up—"

"Just some ice," said Mussawi. "I am afraid I have developed a taste for whiskey on its own."

Baharlou nodded, then shook his head, as if asking himself a question and then answering it. "I must watch it myself," he said. "I look forward to returning to Radestan someday where the temptation will be gone." He disappeared through a doorway and Mussawi heard the sound of what he assumed was the refrigerator freezer door opening, then the clink of ice cubes falling into a glass. A moment later Baharlou returned to the living room with a glass of ice in each hand and the neck of a half-empty bottle of Rebel Yell bourbon gripped between an index and middle finger. He set all three items down on a marble end table next to Mussawi, twisted the cap off the bottle and poured the brown liquid over the ice in both glasses, making the cubes crackle.

Mussawi waited patiently. But as he did, he remembered what he was supposed to do next during this leg of the mission. And it made his head and stomach hurt even more.

The al Qaeda intermediary handed one of the glasses to Mussawi, then lifted his own into the air. "A toast," he said. "To the success of the mission. And the prompt takeover of Radestan by God through his servants in al Qaeda."

Mussawi lifted his glass and tapped it against Baharlou's, causing a click to drown out the still-crackling ice. He downed the whiskey in on long gulp and felt it chase the hangover away. Within a few seconds, his headache was gone and his stomach had settled.

And when he remembered what he was supposed to do, it did not seem nearly as distasteful as it had only seconds before without the whiskey in his system.

"Another, if you would please, Zaid," Mussawi said as he set his glass on the marble end table.

"Ah, my brother," said Baharlou, who had taken only a small sip of his own whiskey. "You *have* developed a taste for the beverage of the infidels." He poured again into Mussawi's glass but shook his head once more as he did. "You will have to be careful when you return home."

"I will be," said Mussawi as he picked up his glass. "But for now, it is helping clear my head and relaxing me." He took a smaller mouthful this time, swished it around in his mouth, then swallowed it.

And, once more, remembered what he had to do next. He was surprised that it no longer bothered him at all. But then a creeping thought began to infiltrate his brain along with the alcohol. Did what he was about to do no longer trouble him because it furthered the jihad?

Or was it no more than the bourbon dulling his senses to anything and everything?

The thought caused Mussawii to drain his glass again.

Baharlou had obviously been watching him. He said, "My brother, you must stop this. Even with the dispensation you should not—"

"One more," Mussawi interrupted, setting his glass down on the table just a little too hard. "One more drink and I will quit it for good."

Baharlou opened his mouth to speak, but Mussawi kept on talking. "There is no reason anymore for me to do this. Tonight is the last night I will consume alcohol. I will no longer need it either to keep up appearances or to calm my nerves."

Baharlou nodded slowly, then filled Mussawi's glass one more time. As soon as he had, he screwed the cap back onto the bottle and stood, taking the bottle with him and disappearing into the kitchen again. When he returned, he no longer held the bottle.

Mussawi drank half the bourbon in his glass as Baharlou sat. He stared at the man. Then, suddenly, the vision he had seen last night came to him again and instead of Baharlou sitting at the other end of the couch it appeared to be the man in the flowing white robe. The man's face still looked kind and gentle. But, just as he had looked last night, he appeared troubled, as well. And as Mussawi watched, the man slowly shook his head back and forth, over and over again.

Mani knew exactly what the man was saying. *Don't do it.*

The man was telling him not to go through with the next part of his mission.

Mussawi drained the rest of his whiskey with his eyes closed. When he opened them again, it was Baharlou sitting on the sofa. But the man with the long hair and beard and white robe stood in front of them both, looking down at Mani and still shaking his head.

Thou shalt not murder. He knew what he had to do. And he knew he had to do it quickly or he might not do it at all.

Zaid Baharlou was a loose end that had to be gathered up. He knew too much and the best way he could serve the jihad now was by dying, and taking all he knew to the grave and then to paradise with him. There was no other way to handle the situation. God used suicide bombers at times. This was little different than that.

Mussawi took one last look at the man in white and saw the disappointment on his face. So he forced his eyes away from the spirit and stared at Baharlou. His al Qaeda contact bore a peculiar confused look. Could he see the man in white? He didn't act as though he could. At least, he wasn't looking that way.

Mussawi knew he could not afford to wait any longer. If he did, this apparition might trick him into believing what he was about to do was wrong. His hand moved under his jacket.

"Mani?" Baharlou said. "What is—?"

The al Qaeda intermediary never finished the sentence. Mussawi's hand came out from under his coat gripping the Makarov and without hesitation shoved the pistol up under Baharlou's chin. A split second later Mussawi pulled the trigger and sent a 9 mm Makarov round drilling through the man's skull and brain and out of the back of his head.

Blood, tiny bone fragments and gray matter blew back into Mussawi's face. Even more exited the back of Zaid Baharlou's head to splatter the sofa and the lampshade on the end table. Some of it even blew all the way to the living room wall ten feet behind the dead al Qaeda operative.

Mussawi felt the heat of the pistol in his hand. He looked up at the man in white.

The man looked even more sad than before. But he opened his mouth and this time Mussawi actually heard a voice say, *I can still forgive you. But only if you let me.* That sent goose bumps down Mussawi's spine and caused him to vault to his feet in search of the remainder of the bourbon.

CHAPTER ELEVEN

Carl Lyons's suit coat had suffered the most damage during the encounter with the marijuana and metham-phetamine manufacturers. The shoulders had been torn so badly as he'd dived through the broken window that the suit coat was going to call unwanted attention from anyone who saw it. The only backup he had with him was a plaid sport coat. And that would clash terribly with his black pin-striped slacks.

He wasn't going to be offered any best-dressed award, but at least now he just looked like a man with bad taste instead of a man who'd just been in a fight for his life. Okay, Lyons thought as he drove past the building with the giant "C" attached to the bricks. Able Team had done a good service for the world by taking down the dopers at the grow house. Far better was the demise of the meth lab. All that was great.

On the other hand, it wasn't the service they'd set out to provide. And quite frankly the damage the grass and even the crank could do didn't compare to a pair of nuclear weapons. The world wasn't going to change much just because there was one less hydroponic mari-juana grow site, or one more crank lab out of business and unable to distribute its poison or explode and kill innocent neighbors.

But a whole lotta shakin' was gonna go on, Lyons

reasoned, if they didn't get the missing nuclear devices back before whoever had them got a chance to use them.

"Looks like a million other medium-rent apartment buildings to me," Schwarz said from the shotgun seat, breaking into Lyons's thoughts. The Able Team leader glanced at Schwarz, then looked up into the rearview mirror at Blancanales's head nodding in agreement.

"Good place to just fade in the background," the infiltration specialist said. "Go to work, come home, and never even get to know your neighbors. Management probably operates on a six-month lease. Five-hundred to a thousand-dollar security deposit, first and last month's rent paid up front, and the tenants come and go every year or so."

Schwarz had Mani Mussawi's personnel file open in his lap. "Yeah but Mussawi's an exception to the rule," he said. "Been here in this same place for twelve years according to the date on the copy of the lease."

Lyons nodded. "Apartment 4, wasn't it?"

"Yep," he said. "Very appropriate, I'd say. Building C. Apartment 4. C-4."

"An explosive address," said Blancanales from the backseat.

Lyons pulled into the parking lot, which was already three-quarters filled with automobiles of every size, shape, make and model. "Okay," he said, "enough with the bad puns. Let's go see what Mr. Mussawi's story is." He found an open space, parked with the back tires an inch from the curb, and killed the engine. "But let's do this one on the quiet side," he added. Twisting to his side, he handed the car keys over the seat to Blancanales. "Get us some props out of the trunk, will you, Pol?"

"Ah, yes," said Blancanales as he opened the door at

his side. "One of the old cardinal rules of undercover work. Always have a story and a reason to be there."

Lyons and Schwarz sat where they were, waiting as they heard the trunk open, then slam shut again. Blancanales appeared with a thick stack of folded leaflet-looking papers in one hand, a briefcase in the other.

Lyons and Schwarz exited the vehicle, and Blancanales divided the stack of papers in half, handing a bundle to both men. "I'll keep the briefcase," he said.

"What's in it?" Schwarz asked.

"I can't remember," said Blancanales as they started toward the steel steps that led to the second story of Building C. "But it's just for show anyway. Like your papers."

Lyons glanced down at the papers he'd just been given. They were blank white pages folded into thirds. All show in case anyone sinister was watching them head toward Mussawi's place.

"I don't know which we look like more," said Schwarz as they climbed the steps. "Mormon missionaries or vacuum salesmen."

"If we were Mormons there'd only be two of us," said Blancanales. "And we'd be on bicycles."

"And if we were selling vacuums, Ironman would look right at home in his plaid jacket and striped pants," Schwarz chided.

"Yeah," said Blancanales. "But one of us would have to be lugging around a demo vacuum," he said. "So my guess is we look more like civil process servers." They reached the landing at the top of the steps and headed toward a door with a large number four tacked to the front.

Lyons let out a long, slow breath from between his

teeth. "What do you say we get our minds back on the business at hand?" he said. He transferred the blank sheets to his left hand and inched his right toward the .357 Magnum Colt Python on his belt. Although the Beretta 92 was a far more up-to-date handgun, he had begun his career of protecting and serving the public with the wheelgun and it still held a fond place in his heart. And, the Able Team leader reminded himself, the 125-grain .357 Magnum semijacketed hollowpoint was still the best "man stopper" in existence as far as he was concerned. Granted, there were other rounds that came close, and certainly other pistols that held up to three times the amount of ammunition as the Colt six-shooter. But there was a lot to say for familiarity and plain old-fashioned *fondness* when it came to close-quarters combat with weapons. As he wrapped his fingers around the Python's grip it felt like shaking hands with an old friend.

Schwarz was now directly outside the door to apartment C-4 and had turned back toward the steps, waiting for Lyons and Blancanales to catch up. As soon as the other two men from Able Team had reached the concrete landing, Blancanales stepped to the left of the door as Schwarz shuffled silently to the right. Lyons let the index finger of his right hand creep into the trigger guard of his still-holstered Colt but pressed it upward, away from the trigger itself.

The Able Team leader had never subscribed to the philosophy that you should keep your finger outside the guard until you were ready to shoot. That requirement had come into existence so that firing range officers could look up and down the line and *see* that the shooters weren't touching the trigger. In reality, when it came time to shoot under life-and-death pressure, pulling the finger in from outside the guard tended to throw the first shot of a right-handed shooter down and to the left. Not much, maybe. But some. And in the game the men from Stony Man Farm played on a daily basis, even a tiny miscalculation could get you killed.

Lyons drew the Python from his holster but kept it hidden under the tail of his jacket. With his left hand, he pressed the doorbell and heard a short series of musical notes sound inside the apartment. When he got no response, he made a fist and tapped on the wood right below the numeral.

He stared at the peephole in the door, waiting for it to darken, which would tell him someone was looking through it. That didn't happen.

Lyons made a quick 180-degree turn on the balls of his feet. Unless they were hiding behind the curtains and shades on the windows of other apartments and peeking out, no one appeared to be paying them any attention. Lyons looked at Schwarz but didn't have to speak.

Schwarz had already produced the well-worn leather case he always carried and was choosing the correct picks to open the door in front of them.

Lyons stepped to the side and let Schwarz work his magic. A few seconds later he heard a series of clicks and then the door popped open.

He kept his revolver hidden under his coat as he stepped through the doorway into the apartment. Behind him, he heard the soft sound of both Schwarz's and Blancanales's feet on the carpet. Then one of them closed the door.

The stench of rotting food filled his sinuses and

called his attention to the left side of the main room. The kitchen. Lyons lifted the Python now, letting it lead the way as he cut across the living room to the tile. The kitchen floor, the counters, the small dining table—every surface in the kitchen—had been wiped clean and smelled of some ammonia-based cleanser. But when he opened the dishwasher, the Able Team leader saw the origin of the stench.

Dirty dishes—several days' worth if this Mani Mussawi character lived alone—were standing upright within the plastic racks. In the basket above them were glasses and coffee cups awaiting their own cleaning. In the door, two Electrasol Jet-Dry Powerball cakes of dishwashing detergent had been pressed into place. But the trap door that would release them during the wash was still open, and the cycle had yet to be started.

It appeared that Mani Mussawi didn't run his dishwasher every day. Lyons stared at the cheap steel knives, forks and spoons upright in the basket on the right side of the washer. Some were encrusted with the remnants of whatever the man had eaten the past few days. The Able Team leader guessed that he waited until the machine was filled then cleaned them all at once.

Lyons moved to the side of the dishwasher and opened the cabinet doors above it. In one, he found clean plates. In the next, every kind of beverage receptacle imaginable from highball glass to beer stein. In the third, three bottles of Jack Daniel's bourbon, assorted bottles of vodka, gin and other spirits and a steel martini shaker.

Backing out of the kitchen, Lyons saw that Blancanales had moved down the short hallway to the bedroom. In between, he could see an open door and heard the sound of a medicine cabinet opening. That would be Schwarz in the bathroom.

Lyons's eyes searched the living room. He saw a small couch, a desk with a television on top and a wide chair that looked like it folded out into a makeshift bed. A quick search through the desk drawers produced nothing of interest. Just old bills with handwritten dates and the word "Paid" scrawled across them, several carry-out restaurant menus—assorted pizza parlors, Chinese food and barbeque joints—and coupons for the same places. In another drawer, he found credit card receipts in Mani Mussawi's name. It appeared that the man favored using his MasterCard, but there were also receipts from American Express and Visa. The grease-smeared paper on top showed that he'd paid for a full slab of pork ribs cooked and delivered by a restaurant that bore the name of a once-famous Denver Broncos quarterback.

"Uh, oh," came Pol's voice from the bedroom. "Someone's been a naughty, naughty Muslim."

Lyons left the desk and passed the bathroom, where Schwarz was checking out the shower. He found Blancanales standing next to the bed. The bedspread was on the floor at the foot and the sheets were crumpled—as if someone had just gotten out of them. A small bedside table held a reading lamp, a telephone and a copy of the Koran. A chest of drawers was crammed in on the other side of the bed.

The Able Team leader stared down at the Koran that, at first glance, appeared to be resting cover-down on the table. He reached down, lifted it, flipped it open and realized that the book was anything but new. Its well-read pages were in Arabic, and he knew the words went from right to left instead of the left to right style in which Western books and periodicals were printed.

Pol reached down to the crumpled sheets and appeared to pinch something. But when his hand rose again, it still appeared empty.

"What are you doing, Pol?" Schwarz demanded as he entered the room. Blancanales lifted his hand higher and held it next to the window by the bed.

Carl Lyons finally saw what was clenched between his thumb and forefinger. A golden hair—at least ten inches long—glowed in the sunlight.

"Unless Mr. Mussawi has long blond hair," said Blancanales, "he hasn't been reading his book." He nodded his head sideways, indicating the Koran next to the lamp. "Or at least paying attention to it."

"There's a receipt in the front-room desk for barbequed pork ribs, too," said Lyons. "And he's got enough whiskey and other liquor in the kitchen cabinets to stock a Farm Christmas party."

"Assuming, of course," said Schwarz, "that Stony Man ever *had* a Christmas or any other kind of party."

"We make the mistake sometimes," said Blancanales, "of thinking that everyone who says they're a Muslim actually follows the rules. We forget a lot of them are like people of any other religion. They say one thing and do another."

Lyons nodded. "I think it's safe to say, though," he said, "that Mussawi is one of two things. Either he's not a religious man or he's super-religious. And by that I mean jihad-religious and therefore crazy as a loon under a full moon."

"Meaning the gloves have come off," said Schwarz.

"He can drink, eat ribs and fool around with the babes all he wants if it helps get rid of us infidels."

"Exactly," said Lyons.

Blancanales had dropped to his knees and was crawling toward the bed. "Haven't checked under here yet."

"Careful," said Schwarz.

Blancanales lifted the bedskirt and stuck his face beneath it. A second later his arm disappeared for a second, then came back holding a half dozen *Playboy, Penthouse* and *Hustler* magazines. "Ah, what other secrets are we going to find out about you, Mani?" he said, setting the rumpled magazines upon the bedspread.

"I'll remind you to wash your hands at the first opportunity," said Schwarz.

"You won't *have* to remind me," said Blancanales. "I'll remember." His face had disappeared beneath the bed again and his words came out muffled.

"Anything else under there?" Lyons asked.

"Yeah…something…just let me…." Blancanales dropped all the way to the carpet on his chest and stretched his arm farther under the bed. Then he withdrew his arm, rose to his knees and then to his feet. "Look at this," he said, holding up a shining brass, steel and lead firearm cartridge. "The man's got a gun—we at least know that now," he said.

"Still doesn't tell us much," said Schwarz. "It *might* mean he's a terrorist. Or it might mean he's just a normal guy exercising his God-given right to protect himself."

"Well," said Pol, "he's a fan of the 9 mm. At least we know that."

"Him and a few hundred thousand other men and

women in Colorado," Schwarz said. He patted the Beretta 92 holstered on his hip. "Including us."

"I think there's a little more intel to be gained here," Lyons said, his eyebrows lowering in concentration as he stared at the cartridge in Blancanales's hand. "Let me see that a minute."

Blancanales handed him the round.

Lyons held it up and let the overhead light shine on the bright brass cartridge. "It's a 9 mm, all right," he said. Then he handed it back. "But you notice anything else about it?"

Blancanales held the cartridge in the palm of his hand and stared down at it. "Yeah," he said. "I do." He drew his Beretta, ejected the magazine and used his thumb to peel the top cartridge off the box. Then he dropped it into his other hand with the round from under the bed.

Schwarz had moved in next to Lyons and was looking down at the two cartridges himself. "The round from under the bed is a 9 mm Makarov," he said. "Russian 9 mm instead of the 9 Parabellum we use."

"Exactly," said Lyons.

"It's still not definitive," Blancanales said. "A lot of Makarovs hit the American and other markets after the Soviet Union fell. A lot of them went to the Middle East. Along with the appropriate ammo." He paused but continued to stare at the two different, yet similar, rounds. "On the other hand, I haven't seen one of these in a while."

"For lack of a better lead," Lyons said. "I'd say we pursue this one. Let's look at the facts. The man's got the Koran by his bed. And it's well-worn. But he's drinking alcohol, eating pork and fornicating his fool head off with some blond infidel chick."

Blancanales shrugged. Then, with a deadpan expression of fake naiveté on his face, he said, "Sounds like a party to me."

"Yeah," Lyons practically growled, "to you, it would be." He paused and took in a deep breath, his eyes still on the two different versions of 9 mm cartridges. "But you add the fact that this Mani Mussawi also has a gun—of a type *usually* associated with the bad guys— and I think we come to a different conclusion."

"The key to the whole thing," said Blancanales, "is the *condition* of the Koran. It hasn't just been sitting here for twelve years." He reached down, lifted it, and began flipping through the pages. "It's not just for show. It's *worn*. It's not only been *read*, Mussawi *studies* it."

As Blancanles turned the pages, Lyons could see all of the places that had been underlined in ink. Other sections had been marked with an orange or yellow or lime-green highlighting marker.

"He hasn't just read this book," said Schwarz. "It looks like he's tried to memorize it. But his lifestyle contradicts all of its teachings."

"Except for one of those teachings," Lyons said. "And that's that he can break all the rules he wants as long as the end justifies the means."

"And the end is jihad—holy war," said Blancanales.

"When you know that fact," said Schwarz, "all the rest falls right into place."

Carl Lyons reached inside his sport coat and pulled out his sat phone. "I think it's about time we learned a little more about Mani Mussawi," he said. "I'm going to contact Stony Man."

Schwarz and Blancanales both nodded as the Able Team leader speed-dialed the Farm. They knew who he was calling, and what would be done.

"But there's no sense wasting any more time here," Lyons said as he started out of the bedroom. "We can head down to the car while the line connects."

Schwarz and Blancanales followed.

"I think there's one other stop we should make before we go on," said Schwarz as they hurried down the staircase outside the apartment.

"What's that?" Lyons asked.

"The first men's clothing store we see," said Schwarz. "You looked okay when we were out of sight, inside Mussawi's house. But out in the public you're going to draw more attention wearing that plaid sport coat with the striped slacks than some homeless bum who found them both in an alley."

"Yeah," said Blancanales. "You remind me of the cover of one of my great-grandfather's old ragtime 78 records. Spike Jones was his favorite, if I remember right."

Lyons didn't bother answering. He just kept heading for the FBI sedan, waiting for the line to Stony Man Farm to connect.

AARON KURTZMAN rested his elbows on the arms of his wheelchair as the phone to the right of his computer rang. Reaching out, he lifted the receiver and held it to his ear. "Yeah, Ironman?" he said into the instrument.

"Hello, Bear," the Able Team leader said from three-fourths of the way across the nation.

"So how are the Rocky Mountains treating you?" asked Kurtzman.

"Sometimes good, the rest of the time bad," said Lyons. "Is Hal with you?"

"No, but he's on site. I can get him if you need me to."

"Better do it," said Lyons. "We've found our man but hit a dead end. We need a new lead."

"Hang on," said Kurtzman. He pressed a button and put the Able Team leader on hold. A second later he buzzed Hal Brognola's office and had the big Fed on the other end of the line.

"I've got Ironman calling in," the cyber genius told Brognola. "He wants you. Want me to connect you?"

"Negative," said Brognola and Kurtzman could tell by the sound of his voice that the man had one of his well-chewed cigars stuck between his teeth. "I'll come down there." He hung up and Kurtzman was left holding a dead line.

But the man in the wheelchair had barely switched back to Lyons's satellite call when Brognola came striding up the ramp to the bank of computers. "Hal just walked in," Kurtzman said into the receiver. "I'll put you on speakerphone."

A second later both Kurtzman and Brognola heard Lyons say, "Can you hear me?"

"Loud and clear," Brognola answered, the stump of cigar still clamped between his lips. "What's up?"

"We've checked out all three homes of the nuclear storage facility employees who called in sick today," Lyons told him. "The first two were a bust—unless you want to count a hydroponic grass grow with a crank lab in the back. We took them down and got out of there before we got tangled up with the cops."

Kurtzman, watching Brognola, saw the man almost

bite his cigar in two. "I take it this wasn't related to the nukes?" he exhorted around the stogie.

"Uh-uh," said Lyons. "At least we don't think so." There was a pause. "But it tells us that whoever's in charge of security at the storage facility isn't doing their job very well. The occupant of the grow house had quite a little illegal side business going on."

"What did you do with him?" Brognola asked.

"Left him dead on his floor," said Lyons. "As soon as we figured out his house was a detour in our mission, we forgot about him and got out of there."

Brognola nodded his head. "No sense wasting time. The local cops can handle the cleanup."

"That was our thinking," said Lyons. There was another short pause during which Lyons cleared his throat. "It was the third place—an apartment, where I think we may have struck gold."

"What about it?" said Brognola.

The man called Ironman did just that, explaining about the Jack Daniel's whiskey, the long blond hairs, the receipt for barbecued pork, the pornography and 9 mm Makarov round under the bed. "And we found a copy of the Koran on the nightstand next to the bed. It isn't just there for show. It's almost as well-worn as Billy Graham's Bible."

"That tells us more than anything else in my opinion," said Brognola. "Our boy's a radical who thinks anything he does will be excused by his faith."

"Hold on a second," said Kurtzman. Moving to his computer, his fingers flew across the keyboard like those of a concert pianist. In less than twenty seconds he had broken through the program firewall at the Colorado Springs nuclear storage facility, located Mani Mussawi's personnel file and sent it to his printer. "Okay, I'm back," Kurtzman said. "And I've got to agree with you, Ironman. A lot of Muslims have some very strange views on getting nonbelievers to convert to Islam."

"They seem to think they can *force* their beliefs on people," said Brognola, taking what was left of his cigar from his teeth and holding it in his hand. "They think if you hold a gun to someone's head and make them say they believe in Mohammed and the Koran they've converted you. When all they've actually done is force weaker men and women to say what they have to say to keep from getting murdered." He stuck the cigar back into his mouth. "Inside, in their brains and hearts and souls, they still believe whatever they want to believe."

"What it all boils down to," said Lyons, "is that I'm ninety-nine percent sure this Mussawi either has the missing nukes himself or knows where they are. There's evidence here that he hasn't been home in a few days. So he's in the wind. On the run? And I don't have the foggiest idea where to start trying to find him."

Kurtzman had been looking through the sheets that had just come out of his printer. As with all government employees, Mussawi's personnel file included a complete set of fingerprints. "Ironman," Kurtzman said.

"Yeah?"

"You're still at Mussawi's apartment?"

"In the parking lot, getting ready to leave," Lyons said.

"Can you head back inside?"

"Sure. What do you want?"

"I'll tell you once you're back inside." Kurtzman and Brognola listened to the sounds of car doors opening and closing, then feet jogging up what sounded like steel steps.

A few seconds later Lyons said, "We're back inside, Bear. Tell us what you need."

"You said you had a receipt from a barbecue place where he used a credit card?" Kurtzman asked.

"Yeah," said Lyons. "There's a whole stack of credit card receipts for different things."

"Dig through them, will you?" said Kurtzman. "See if you can find one for a rental car."

Through the speaker, it sounded as if Lyons had turned away from his sat phone. Kurtzman could hear the Able Team leader say, "Gadgets, go back to that desk drawer and..." His voice faded away.

There was no reason to waste time during the Able Team electronics expert's search. "Ironman," Kurtzman said, "can you lift me a fingerprint or two? I not only need to double-check to make sure his prints match up with those in his personnel file, I've got an idea on how to find him."

"I don't have a print kit with me, Bear," Lyons said.

"They don't have to be perfect," Kurtzman said. "Did you come across any tape during your search?"

The line went silent for a second, and Kurtzman could practically see the Able Team leader's eyebrows drop in concentration. Finally, Lyons said, "Yeah. There was some in one of the other drawers of the desk. Along with some paper clips, pens, pencils—all that kind of stuff."

"Send Pol after the tape and a couple of pencils," Kurtzman said. "We're going to have to do our forensic work under battlefield conditions."

Schwarz's voice came back on the air. "I've got the

receipt for a rental car—a Kia Cadenza—Mussawi picked up last Thursday," he said. "It's from Hertz. Want the number, Bear?"

"That's why I asked you to find the receipt, my fellow techno-friend," said Kurtzman.

Schwarz read the long receipt number off to him.

All of the men involved in this conference call waited. A few seconds later Lyons said, "Okay, I've got the tape and the pencils, and I've snapped to what you have in mind."

"Then all you need now is your Spyderco and a clean piece of white paper," said Kurtzman.

"No problem," said Lyons, and a split second later Kurtzman heard a click as the Able Team leader used the trademark thumb hole in the Spyderco's blade to open the knife.

"What model are you using?" Kurtzman asked.

"The Schempp Tuff," said Lyons.

"Straight edge or serrated?"

"Straight edge," Lyons returned.

"Good," said Kurtzman. "That'll make for better 'make do' lifting powder." He leaned in closer to the speaker and went on. "Now, scrape off enough of the graphite—which most people still call *lead*—so you can lift a couple of prints. You have the white paper to catch it with?"

"Believe me," Lyons said. "We brought in dozens of leaflets as cover for coming up here. They're all blank white paper."

"Then start whittlin'," said Kurtzman.

Again, seconds that seemed like hours clicked away. But Kurtzman forced himself to be patient. His job, he had learned over the years, was not very different than that of the Farm field agents in many respects. And one of those respects was that the Army adage of "hurry up and wait" rang true. With his computers in the Computer Room—as with Able Team's and Phoenix Force's guns in the field—he was either too busy or being forced to wait to get too busy. Either way, it took mental discipline. And while *doing* was often difficult, *waiting to do* was even harder.

After another eternity, Lyons said, "Okay, Bear. I'm ready."

"You didn't happen to come across a small brush of any kind, did you?" Kurtzman asked. "Like an oil painter might use?"

"Uh-uh," Lyons responded.

The line went quiet and Kurtzman could picture Schwarz and Blancanales shaking their heads at the same question.

"I didn't figure we'd get that lucky," said Kurtzman. "Okay. Again, we'll do the best we can. Tell me. Is there a land line in the apartment?"

"That's affirmative," said Lyons. "Right next to the bed."

"Well, thank the Good Lord for the fact that Mussawi's over thirty years old," said Kurtzman. "Anyone younger would just rely on the cell phone growing out of their ears." He stopped speaking for a moment, then asked, "Have any of you touched that telephone?"

"No," said Lyons, and again Kurtzman pictured the other two members of Able Team shaking their heads.

"Great," said the Stony Man computer wizard. "We're getting lucky again. The most likely place to find a print is the receiver. On the inside, up near the top. You know where I mean?"

"The natural place for your thumb to go when you hold it to your ear," said Lyons.

"Right. Grab the receiver with your thumb and index finger. Down toward the bottom by the mouthpiece where most people don't touch it anyway."

Lyons carefully complied. "Got it, Bear," he said.

"Great. Now lift it out of the cradle and lay it down, right side up."

"Got it again."

"Now," said Kurtzman, "the tricky part. Since you don't have a brush, you'll need to fold the paper and let the powder glide gently down the fold onto the phone. Don't go too fast. Spread it around *gently*. If you start picking up anything that looks like it might be a print, slow down even more. Once the area's covered with the powder, blow gently on it." He stopped talking for a moment then said. "Okay, then. Give it a try."

Again the line went silent except for the gentle rustling of paper. Kurtzman kept his fingers crossed, waiting.

"I'm getting something," said Lyons.

"Take your time," said Kurtzman. "We'll only get one chance at this."

"I used to do this kind of thing for a living," Lyons said, sounding slightly irritated. But, Kurtzman reminded himself, Lyons almost *always* sounded slightly irritated. A few seconds later the Able Team leader added, "I think I've gotten all I can get. It's only a partial."

"It might be enough," said Kurtzman. "Use your phone camera and take a picture of it."

"Don't you want me to lift it with the tape?" Lyons asked.

"Probably," said Kurtzman. "But if we can get the print directly from the phone you can send the photo straight to me and we won't have to chance smearing it with the tape."

"Like I told you, Bear, I've done this—"

"I know you have, Ironman," said Kurtzman. "Humor me."

A rare Carl Lyons's chuckle came over the line. "All right," he said. "But you're going to get a picture of dark brown powder on a black phone receiver."

Kurtzman didn't bother responding. He was preoccupied, accessing the Hertz rental car records in Colorado Springs and entering the receipt number.

The computer connected to Kurtzman's phone clicked to life; a dark blob appearing on the screen, a sheet of white cotton paper rolling out of the printer. Neither the picture on the screen nor the print on the paper was discernible.

"Well," said Kurtzman, "it was worth a try. Go ahead and—"

"Lift it with the tape," said Lyons. "I'm in the process right now. But even though it's only a partial, I'm going to have to do it in two parts. This tape isn't as wide as regular print tape."

"Take your time and be careful, Ironman. Again, you'll only get one shot. I'll be waiting."

Kurtzman could hear breathing over the line and imagined Lyons trying to place the second piece of tape perfectly next to the first to get an accurate print. It would not be easy. And the Able Team leader was far better known for kicking butt and taking names than for precision in delicate matters.

Finally, Lyons's voice came back once again. "Okay,

I've got the partial off the phone. Now I'm going to do my best to get the tape on another sheet of white paper. Hold on."

Kurtzman was tempted to ask the man how the print looked on the tape. But he didn't want to distract Lyons from what was, once again, going to require great care and finesse.

This time, Lyons came back on the line sooner than Kurtzman expected. And the tone of his voice told him the operation had been successful even before the Able Team leader's words did. A few seconds later, a second sheet was churning out of Kurtzman's printer. And this time, even an amateur could have made out the peculiar ridges, islands, bifurcations and part of what Kurtzman suspected was an ulnar loop.

"Perfect, Ironman," Kurtzman said. "Just perfect."

"Well, what did you expect?" said Lyons. "Does it match what you've got in Mussawi's personnel file?"

Kurtzman dug quickly through the pages from Mussawi's personnel file and found his fingerprint card. Laying the page he'd just pulled from the printer next to the left thumb, he stared down at both prints. Although it was at a different angle than the image from the personnel file, the two prints looked identical. "We've got a match," Kurtzman said. "And for what it's worth, this Mussawi holds the phone in his left hand when he talks."

"So, what do you plan to do with it?" Lyons asked.

Before he could answer, Hal Brognola stepped in again. "I'll tell you what we're going to do with it," the director said. "We're going to enter all of the fingerprints from Mussawi's personnel file into a software program Kurtzman's come up with. It's a lot like facial recognition—which we'll also be running, of course. This new program doesn't need fingerprint powder or iodine or any of the agents that have been used in the past to make prints stand out. It zeros in on the natural oil on the fingertips and can spot, identify and photograph these prints from a long distance. Then it runs through AFIS until it gets a hit."

The line went quiet again for a moment, then Lyons said, "By long distance, what do you mean?"

"I mean like from the air," said Brognola. "We're going to position drones overhead that Kurtzman can control from here. They'll be equipped with cameras, which include Bear's new program and will be able to search out fingerprints on steering wheels and dashboards of cars driving down the road."

A long silence followed, and Kurtzman knew Lyons was trying to take all the new information in. "Hal," the Able Team leader finally said, "do you know how many automobiles are on the road within the area Mussawi could have driven since last Thursday when he rented whatever vehicle he rented?"

Kurtzman heard a small buzzing sound and activated an icon near the top of the screen. He tapped the right hand side of the screen and the name of one of the Colorado Springs Hertz car rental establishments popped up.

"Okay," the computer whiz told Lyons. "I just double-checked through Hertz records and confirmed what you found on the car rental receipt. Mussawi rented a Kia Cadenza."

"Gotta hand it to those Islamic terrorists," Brognola said. "When God gives them a green light to break training they sure do it in style. But to answer your question, Ironman, the drones will be programmed to only look for Kia Cadenzas. They'll skip over the rest of the traffic."

"How about license plates?" Lyons asked. "And you mentioned facial recognition."

Brognola chuckled. "The cameras in the drones will be set up for both of those programs, too," he said. He stopped talking long enough to reach inside his sport coat and pull out a fresh cigar, then began unwrapping the cellophane enveloping it. "And you and your side-kicks are going to be in the air with Mott. So just as soon as we get a hit—fingerprint, facial or plate—you'll swoop in and take down the vehicle."

"Well," said Lyons, a faint trace of sarcasm in his voice, "when you put it that way it sounds easy. Let me make sure I've got this clear. Your programs can skip over all vehicles except the Kia Cadenzas?"

"Should be able to," said Kurtzman, then cleared his throat. "But keep in mind that this is the first time I've had a chance to try it out for real, and I'm sure there'll be a few bugs to iron out. Problems like tinted windows. Or the vehicle being holed up out of sight from the air. Actually, we've got no proof that Mussawi's even left the Colorado Springs area. The Cadenza could still be parked in some garage or other covered space we don't know about."

"We just have to do what we can with what we've got," said Brognola.

"If I was Mussawi," Lyons went on, "I'd have switched vehicles at least once by now. Probably more than once."

"I'll keep monitoring the use of the man's credit cards if you'll give me the number and expiration dates," said Kurtzman.

Schwarz had brought the cards into the living room with the receipt and now Lyons read off the numbers. "Great," said Kurtzman. "If he uses one to rent another car, we'll know."

"And if he pays cash?" asked Lyons.

"It'll be harder. But at least he'll have to show several types of identification. And I can track him that way, too."

"I'm sure he'll have plenty of fake IDs," Lyons returned.

Kurtzman turned to look up at Brognola. The big Fed was smiling, trying not to laugh. Kurtzman shook his head, remembering that Carl Lyons could be much like a dog with a bone sometimes. Once he got onto a problem, he refused to let it go until he'd solved it. It could get a little annoying at times—Lyons was an expert at finding the black cloud around every silver lining.

On the other hand, few men could anticipate potential problems as accurately as Lyons. So Kurtzman reminded himself that the ex-cop's occasional negativity just demonstrated his thoroughness.

"All that's true, Ironman," the computer genius finally said. "It's a good program I've written. But I never said it was magic." He cleared his throat. "So let's not borrow trouble, as my father used to say. We'll find ways to work around whatever problems come up."

"Ten-four," said Lyons.

"Charlie's still in the Colorado Springs area, waiting on you," Brognola said. "There's a small landing strip about ten miles from where you are now. He'll meet you there."

"We'll need directions," said Lyons.

Brognola gave them to him. "One more thing," he said.

"What's that?" Lyons asked.

"Good luck. I'm afraid we're going to need some on this one."

CHAPTER TWELVE

He could not have possibly been unconscious more than a few seconds, McCarter reasoned as he opened his eyes. His vision was blinded by the mist of swirling dirt that had broken off as the wall had finally given in to the onslaught of rifle fire combined with the digging.

For all practical purposes, David McCarter was buried alive.

But the crumbling of the wall made it possible for him to move, if ever so slightly. And he could see more movement within the clods and dust particles. Then he heard the sound of a shovel—one of Phoenix Forces entrenching tools, no doubt—and knew his men were digging him out.

It took only a few more shovelfuls to give him room to rise up on his own. And his first sight as he came up out of the dirt was of Calvin James. The black skin of Phoenix Force's knife expert was now the same orange-brown as the dust swirling through the air. James grinned at him, still holding his entrenching tool. "You could use a shower," he told McCarter as he brushed the dirt from his face and neck.

"We all could," said McCarter as he stepped high, climbing over the mound of dried dirt. "But I'm afraid we're both going to have to wait a little while on that."

The gunfire from outside continued to pound the

centuries-old walls around them. "Have you figured that out yet?" James asked as he dropped the shovel and gripped his LAR-15 again.

"Figured out what?" McCarter asked.

"How we're going to get out of here," said James.

"Not yet," McCarter answered.

"Well, I'm not trying to tell you how to do your job," said James, "but you might want to think about it. We've got one more wall we can dig through. After that there's a family."

McCarter nodded. With the majority of the dirt out of his eyes, he was ready to enter the fight once more. "You've already got people digging?"

James nodded.

"Then let's do a little shooting." The Phoenix Force leader hurried to the side of a front window in the new dwelling. This house appeared to be laid out exactly like the one they'd just escaped. Even identical towels—already starting to be blasted into ragged strips by incoming fire—hung in the dirt-surrounded apertures.

James dropped down to a kneeling position on the window's other side.

Sweeping the ragged strips to the side with the barrel of his rifle, McCarter looked out to see that most of the government troops had taken refuge around deserted dwellings similar to the one they were in. Some of the men had even taken refuge inside the empty buildings. Others were crouched behind old cars parked along the dirt road.

One man—braver than smart—stood in the open, directly in front of McCarter's window, less than twenty feet away.

McCarter pulled the trigger and he stood no more.

The Phoenix Force leader saw James tighten his grip on his own Hunter and a second later a full-auto burst of 5.56 mm NATO rounds blew from the coyote-camouflaged weapon. McCarter saw the first two rounds strike the dirt just below a window across the road. James adjusted his aim, walking his rounds upward until a volley struck a soldier in the face and he dropped out of sight.

McCarter saw another head pop up inside an old gray primer-painted Oldsmobile thirty feet to his left. He pressed the trigger of his Hunter back again and sent a 3-round burst that way.

Another head exploded like a ripe watermelon inside the car.

The bolt on McCarter's LAR-15 slid back and locked open, empty. As he dropped the magazine and reached for another 30-round box, he looked past James. On the knife expert's other side was another window in the adobe-like wall. Once again, Gary Manning was on one side. Rafael Encizo was on the other.

Both men were firing their rifles and knocking down uniformed Radestani troops with every burst of fire.

McCarter turned around as he jammed the new magazine into his Hunter. The Phoenix Force leader tripped the bolt and the LAR-15 chambered the first round. He tried to see through the rear window. His vision was blocked by several of Jabbar's cowering men. But he could tell there was resistance coming from that direction. It just didn't seem as intense as from the front. On the other hand, as he turned back around, McCarter reminded himself it only took one well-placed bullet to kill a man.

The mayhem continued, with the larger 7.62 mm

AK-47 rounds taking their toll on this aged mud home just like they had the last. McCarter fired his new magazine in three steady bursts, getting two men with the first, three with the second and three more with the third. The bolt locked back once more, and he was forced to reload.

As had been the case before, a few of Jabbar's men were firing through other windows. But the majority of them were nowhere to be seen. McCarter wondered briefly where they were, then began returning fire through the window again. A 3-round burst took a Radestani soldier in the heart and lungs. Another caught an enemy combatant in the throat, severing the carotid artery and causing him to bleed out almost before he hit the ground.

McCarter took a breather to gather in the facts of the situation as it stood. Turning to Calvin James again, he saw that he appeared to be hitting what he wanted to hit. Every time the Phoenix Force leader heard the man's Rock River roar he also saw an enemy combatant or two fall inside the houses or behind the automobiles.

But even though they had not yet lost even one man, McCarter knew they were losing the battle. There was only so much ammo a man could carry into combat, and Phoenix Force was using theirs up fast. McCarter had only one more 30-round box mag in his blacksuit, and then he'd be down to his Beretta. The 92 held one 15-round magazine and an extra load already chambered. With two more 15-round magazines in a carrier on his belt, that made forty-six 9 mm rounds.

What that meant was that he had eighty-six more shots, plus whatever was left in the magazine he was currently using. It sounded like a lot. Until you considered the fact that he was firing about that many rounds every minute.

The Phoenix Force leader didn't know where the rest of the men on his side of the battle stood on ammo. But they couldn't be much better off than he was. McCarter heard a break in the firing to his side and turned to see James reach to his selector switch on his coyote-imprinted rifle. When he resumed firing, it was evident that he'd thought about the ammo problem, too.

James had switched to semiauto. Now, one squeeze of the trigger sent only one round out the window and across the street. Looking farther down the line, McCarter saw Manning say something to Encizo. Both men pulled their rifle barrels back inside the dirt dwelling and adjusted their selectors.

They knew, too.

McCarter glanced over his shoulder. Jabbar's men were truly half trained as Abdu Ali had warned, and they were blasting away like the frightened amateurs that they were. McCarter had no doubt that far more of their 7.62 mm rounds were missing their intended targets than hitting them.

Earlier in the battle, McCarter had wondered where Hawkins had gone. Now he got his answer. Hawk suddenly came barreling through the doorway that led deeper into the house and hit the ground, rolling under a burst of 7.62 mm fire that further shredded the towel in the window opening. He came to a halt next to McCarter, and with a wry grin on his face said, "Are we having fun yet?"

"Having a blast," said McCarter as he fired out the corner of the window again and saw a uniformed man fall behind a twenty-year-old Buick. "Pun intended. Where have you been?"

"In one of the back rooms," Hawk said, "with the majority of Jabbar's men. Who are, for the most part, useless." He rose to his knees but kept low beneath the window. "I wouldn't trust them to clean out a latrine. They're too afraid to fight so I put them to work digging into the next place."

McCarter nodded as he fired again. "That's fine," he said. "But we're about to run out of two things."

"Ammo's one of them," said Hawkins. "I've been firing from one of the bedrooms and I'm down to my last mag. What's the other?"

"Ancient mud-packed cave-like dwellings to take cover in," said McCarter. He pulled the trigger again and watched another Radestani soldier fall. He turned back to Hawkins and was about to speak when the roar of a large engine cut through the rifle blasts.

Both Phoenix Force men looked through the shredded towel and saw a huge troop carrier come to a halt a half block away. Man after man after man began pouring out of the back of the truck, then sprinting to cover across the street.

"Oh," said Hawkins, "this just keeps getting better and better. Want to just shoot ourselves in the head and get it over with?"

McCarter ignored the remark. "How close are you to getting into the next house?" he asked.

"The hole should be big enough by now," said Hawkins. "Let me check." He dropped to the ground and belly-crawled out of sight into the next room.

The incoming rounds seemed to double now that the Radestani reinforcements had arrived. McCarter shook his head. The walls were again starting to shake. Especially the wall in front of him, which was taking the most fire. It had been connected to, and partially reinforced by, the common wall they'd come through earlier—the wall that had collapsed on top of the Phoenix Force leader. And now it was about to go, too, which would leave the Phoenix Force warriors in the main room suddenly out in the open.

Hawkins returned to the edge of the hallway on his feet, staying out of the line of fire but shouting, "Jabbar's men have started going through!"

McCarter could barely hear him over the gunfire, but he nodded. "Keep firing, everybody!" he ordered. "Until I call you out. Then get through that opening as fast as you can." He could still feel the dirt in his throat. "And when I say fast, I mean *fast*," he said. "I'm going last, and I don't care to get buried alive again." He turned and fired three quick cover shots through the window, then turned back. "Jabbar! You and the rest of your men. Go now!

The Radestani resistance fighter herded his men quickly out of sight.

So many weapons were roaring now that it sounded almost like one giant explosion. McCarter continued to fire, giving Jabbar and his men what he considered to be sufficient time to get through the wall to the next empty living quarters. Then he turned to Manning and Encizo and yelled, "Go!"

The biggest and the smallest members of Phoenix Force took off out of sight.

McCarter turned toward the short hallway. Hawkins had disappeared again into the back. And if he knew Hawk, he knew the young Texan would be waiting there, helping the others get through before going himself.

"You ready to go?" McCarter asked James during a break in the fire.

"Oh, yeah," said James. He held up his rifle. "Runnin' close to E." He tapped the Beretta on his right hip, then the huge fighting knife on his left. "I'm about down to my trusty pistola and pig sticker."

"Well, as good as you are with that giant piece of steel," McCarter said, "I think it's time for us to take our leave. You ready?"

"When you are."

McCarter fired three more rounds through the window and twisted around, letting his LAR-15 fall to the end of its sling. Both he and James crossed the room on all fours like football players during a training drill.

As he'd suspected, Hawkins was the only man left in the back room. When he saw McCarter and James, he dropped to his belly and squirmed through the hole himself.

James went next, holding his rifle in one hand as he pulled himself forward with the other.

McCarter couldn't help but think about the wall that had collapsed on him while pulling this same stunt only minutes earlier. But he'd survived that, and he'd survive another cave-in if need be.

As soon as James was through the hole, the Phoenix Force leader dropped to his chest.

This time, the wall stayed in place while he wiggled through it.

The third clay-and-mud dwelling had the same layout as the first two, and the men had pretty much taken up the same positions they'd had since this gunfight started. McCarter took his place at the window with James. But he didn't fire. "We've got to get out of here," he shouted.

"You have any idea *how*?" asked James. He was shooting slower now, one round at a time. So were the other men of Phoenix Force. Even Jabbar's undisciplined men had paced their rate of fire or run out of ammo and stopped shooting altogether.

Before McCarter could answer, Hawkins appeared on his belly again, sliding over the dirt to a spot below the window. "One thing about slithering around like a lizard," he said in his slow Texas drawl, "you notice things you wouldn't on your feet."

"And," James said, then stopped speaking long enough to pull the trigger on his Hunter and fire another round. "You've noticed what, exactly? That we're almost out of ammo and about to get killed?"

"Not at all," said Hawkins. McCarter saw that his grin had become a wide smile. "Take a look over there." He pointed to a rough-hewn table in the corner of the large front room. Several rounds had hit it, and one leg had been shot off, leaving it to wobble precariously on the remaining three.

McCarter felt himself frowning as he looked at the table. It stood on what looked like an old Persian rug. Bullets had found their way to the carpet just as they had the table, and one corner had curled back upon itself.

"Look lower," Hawkins said.

McCarter did. And what he saw made him smile as widely as Hawkins.

CHAPTER THIRTEEN

Charlie Mott had flown Able Team to Colorado in one
of Stony Man Farm's small Learjets. But for the mission
ahead, he needed maneuverability rather than speed.
And he certainly didn't want an aircraft marked as
Colorado Springs Police, FBI, ATF or any other law-
enforcement agency.

So he had done the only reasonable thing.

Rented an unmarked helicopter.

The chopper's blades had a soothing effect once you
got used to it, Carl Lyons realized after they'd been in
the air a few minutes. And Mott had been flying so
long he seemed to be able to avoid air pockets and other
causes of turbulence by pure instinct. Which was no
mean feat in the Rocky Mountain region.

Lyons rode shotgun in the little SAB chopper, with
Schwarz and Blancanales crammed in behind him.
Each man had a set of binoculars. But so far, they
hadn't proved to be much good. Every so often, they
caught a glimpse of a large Predator drone overhead.
And smaller unmanned flying machines—looking like
strange futuristic robotic insects—fluttered in the air
around and below them.

More out of boredom than necessity, Lyons set the
sat phone across his lap, speed-dialed the Farm, pressing the speakerphone button as it connected. Barbara

Price, Stony Man Farm's Mission Controller, answered the call. "Hello, Ironman," the honey-blonde said. "What can I do for you?"

"Hey, Barb. Can you give me Kurtzman?" Lyons said.

"I was just getting ready to call you," said Aaron Kurtzman a moment later when he picked up his phone. "One of the drones just spotted the Cadenza's license plate."

Lyons fought an ongoing battle within himself. It seemed in his nature to resist technology, and he favored doing things the old fashioned cop-on-the-beat way. But the former LAPD detective was no fool, and he recognized that high-tech was the way of the future. So he forced himself to not only learn what he needed to know to remain effective but also to pretend that he even *liked* it.

Once in a while, however, a semi-sarcastic comment just seemed to slip from between his teeth all on its own. "Was it one of those big predators that spotted it or one of the tiny little mosquito-looking things?" he caught himself saying.

The question made Kurtzman—the ultimate technician—laugh out loud. "One of the big ones caught the fact that it was a Cadenza," the computer genius said. "And it sent one of the mosquitoes down to confirm the license at closer range. But that's not the important thing here. Tell Charlie to fly you over to Manitou Springs. There's a place to land—a vacant lot that looks like it serves the neighborhood kids as a sandlot baseball field—about a half mile from the site where the Kia's parked. I'll have the FBI meet you there with another car."

Mott could hear the conversation and had already whipped the chopper around and headed back to the west. Leaning slightly toward the phone in Lyons's lap, he said, "Send me the coordinates on the vacant lot, Bear."

Kurtzman complied, and five minutes later they were descending next to a makeshift baseball backstop. Chicken wire had been strung between old railroad ties planted in the ground, and a piece of paisley floor tile—set at an angle so that it formed a diamond rather than a square—appeared to serve as home plate. A worn and weathered wooden sign next to the fencing announced in hand-scrawled red paint that they had just arrived at Mechner's Field. "Glad there wasn't a game going on," Schwarz said as they set down.

"And there's our ride," said Blancanales. "Anybody but me getting déjà vous?"

As the chopper touched down Lyons saw the familiar sight of FBI agents Arthaud and Taylor. They stood next to a pair of Chevy sedans. As the men from Able Team exited the helicopter, Mott said, "I'll be waiting on you. Or give me a call if you need me to meet you somewhere else."

"Will do, Charlie," Lyons said. "And thanks."

FBI Special Agent Arthaud walked forward to meet them. "Your ride awaits, gentlemen," he said with a smile. But Lyons noted that while his lips curled upward, his eyes looked cold.

Arthaud had been friendly and eager to help during their first meeting. But being kept out of the loop and used as nothing more than a glorified car jockey seemed to have changed his attitude. Lyons could sense that the man's patience was growing thin.

Carl Lyons could understand Arthaud's frustration. No cop—municipal, county, state or federal—liked being cut out of the action. And while Arthaud and Taylor would have had to be blind, deaf and dumb not to have figured out that some major action was going down here in the Colorado Springs area, all they'd been called upon to do so far was deliver vehicles to three men they didn't even know. *Twice.*

"Care to let us in on what's going on?" Arthaud asked Lyons as Schwarz and Blancanales began unloading their gear bags from the chopper.

"I wish I could," Lyons said as the two men walked toward one of the Chevys. Which was actually a lie. There was always competition between local cops and FBI agents, and like many city and state officers, Lyons believed a lot of the Feds possessed egos just a little too big for what they actually did.

"You could tell me but then you'd have to kill me," Arthaud said, dragging the overused cliché out in a disgusted breath. Then, before Lyons could speak again, he said, "Okay. You know how to reach us if you need us. Or just another car."

Schwarz and Blancanales had stowed most of their gear in the trunk of the sedan. But the cases holding their new Yankee Hill Machine Co. Model 15s had gone into the backseat. Lyons nodded goodbye to Arthaud, took the keys from the FBI agent and slid behind the wheel of the Chevy. A moment later they were pulling away from the sandlot baseball field.

The Able Team leader handed his sat phone to Blancanales, who had taken the shotgun seat. "Get Bear on the line. We need directions to the house," he said.

A moment later Kurtzman's voice came through the

sat phone's speaker. "Take a right at the next corner," he said. "According to last month's city water bill and the electric and gas company bills for that address, you're heading for the home of Zaid Baharlou."

"The name is either Arabic or Persian," Schwarz said from the backseat. "Not particularly Muslim but not Cheyenne or Arapaho, either."

"It sounds promising," said Blancanales.

Kurtzman directed them on. But a half block from the house, he said, "Pull over, Ironman. *Now*. There's something going on."

Lyons did as instructed, parking the Chevy along the curb but leaving the engine running. "You've got an eye in the sky on the house?" he asked.

"Affirmative," said the cyber whiz. "The place has been quiet since we spotted the Kia about fifteen minutes ago. But two carloads of men just arrived. They're heading for the front door right now."

"Cops?" Lyons asked, trying to see from his position. But the street curved, and trees near the curb blocked his sightline.

"I don't think so," said Kurtzman. "But I suppose I could be wrong."

"Just to be sure, ask Barb to check her sources," Lyons suggested. "See if there's any kind of Manitou Springs PD drug raid or similar police action. I don't want to go in and kill a bunch of players on our own team."

"Give me a second," said Kurtzman.

Over the air waves, Lyons could hear him talking to Barb, as well as the tapping of keyboard keys. Then they stopped. But then they started again. When they stopped for the second time, Kurtzman came back on.

"Barb says there's nothing from Manitou Springs. And I checked with the Colorado Bureau, too. Nothing at the state level." The man paused for a moment. "I suppose they could be Feds—they're all wearing business suits. But I can see them on the screen from the drone. They just don't *feel* like cops, you know what I mean?"

"I know *exactly* what you mean," said Lyons. Kurtzman was not only a whiz with the "artificial brains," his instincts were finely honed from years of field work before losing the use of his legs. Which meant a hunch from the man in the wheelchair was well worth listening to.

Lyons strained to see farther down the block. "Your drones provide you with sound as well as picture, Bear?" the Able Team leader asked.

"Yeah, but all I've heard so far are footsteps. *Quiet* footsteps. They aren't talking."

"Keep us informed on everything they do," said Lyons. "I want a blow-by-blow account of every movement."

"Whoever they are," said Kurtzman, "it looks like they want to surprise whoever's in the house…. I count eight of them…okay…wait a minute…one of them is pressing the doorbell…"

The speakerphone went quiet. Then ten of the longest seconds Lyons had ever lived went by.

When Kurtzman came back on he said, "They aren't getting any answer at the door. Four of them are going around to the back. Wait a minute…all right…one of the men on the front porch just stepped back. Looks like he's going to kick in the door."

"Is the Kia still in the driveway?" Lyons asked.

"Right where it's been since the drone spotted it,"

said Kurtzman. "Now it's flanked by the two cars these men came in. One had to park on the grass. Okay, he kicked the front door in. And pistols are coming out from under jackets, Ironman."

"Still no talking?" Lyons asked.

"Oh yeah, they're talking up a storm now," said Kurtzman. "And I think what they're saying just answered your question about whether or not they're cops."

"Tell me what they're saying, Bear," said Lyons.

"I can't," said Kurtzman. "I can't understand a word of it."

Lyons heard the computer man blow air out of his mouth.

"But I can recognize Arabic when I hear it," said Kurtzman.

"That's good enough for me," said the Able Team leader, throwing the sedan into drive. "We're going in. Whoever they are, my guess is they're looking for the nukes just like we are."

"My thinking, as well," Kurtzman confirmed. "The men at the back just kicked their way in. Keep in mind that they've all got guns and there're eight of them and three of you, Ironman. That doesn't make for very even odds."

Carl Lyons pressed his foot down on the accelerator and the sedan shot down the street. "No, the odds aren't fair, Bear," he said. "But we don't have time to let them bring in more men."

His statement got him a short, hard laugh from Kurtzman.

Hal Brognola, who had been silently listening for most of their exchange, came on the line. "We've got an

Arabic-speaking blacksuit on the grounds right now," he said. "I've sent for him. But they're on a training drill. It'll take him at least half an hour to get here."

"If the nukes are in that house, we don't have time for that, either," said Lyons. "Whoever these guys are, they're up to no good and we're going after them. Now."

"You're the man on scene, Ironman," Brognola said. "It's your call."

The Chevy sedan rounded the curve and the three men from Able Team could see the Kia Cadenza and the two vehicles parked on both sides. As Kurtzman had said, one of the automobiles—a Dodge Ram van— had pulled onto the grass in the front yard. Behind him, Lyons heard the sounds of zippers opening and turned to see that Schwarz had unzipped the cases and pulled out all three YHM-15s. The titanium suppressors were still in the cases. Schwarz leaned slightly forward. "Want to go in loud or quiet, Ironman?"

"As outnumbered as we are, I think we can use all the confusion we can muster," Lyons said. "Leave the shush sticks off. But we'll take them along in case we need them."

Schwarz nodded and handed two of the weapons, along with the screw-on titanium suppressors Cowboy John Kissinger had tooled for them, over the seat. Blancanales kept one weapon for himself and shoved the suppressor into his belt. The other ten-inch-barreled YHM-15 and shush stick went down on the seat between him and the Able Team leader.

Both Schwarz and Blancanales worked their door handles, unhooking the latches but holding the doors closed as the sedan raced on. As if to berate them for such an unsafe act, an automatic buzzer began humming and a red light on the dashboard flashed on and off.

"That's the FBI for you," Lyons muttered under his breath. "More concerned with covering their ass than getting the job done."

"Now, Ironman," Blancanales said. "That old LAPD blue is showing through."

Lyons didn't have time to answer. A split second later, he had pulled the Chevy up into the driveway of the house next to the one with the Kia parked in the driveway. From there, he twisted the wheel and the car shot out over the grass.

The Able Team leader hit the brakes and the sedan tore up the grass, skidding to a halt in front of Zaid Baharlou's front door, which was still open. Schwarz and Blancanales bailed, and as Lyons threw the Chevy into park and dived out of the car himself as he saw both men enter the house.

The Able Team leader was right behind them. And as he leaped up onto the front porch, the heavy sound of the unsuppressed 6.8-caliber rounds from the new Yankee Hill Machine Company's Model 15s thudded in his ears.

Ramesh, Radestan

"I'M HALF SURPRISED they haven't rushed us," Encizo said as he and Manning joined McCarter, James and Hawkins next to the table.

"They don't need to risk the casualties," said James. "They know we're trapped. And they know sooner or later we'll run out of ammo."

"Keep in mind that these are government troops,"

Hawkins drawled. "And they aren't all that enthused about going straight to paradise. Part of this screwed-up, three-way war is being fought because al Qaeda doesn't think the government is religious enough."

"Let's leave the religious and political discussion for later, shall we?" McCarter said. "Right now, I think we've got more immediate problems on our hands." He reached down and grabbed one end of the table. "James," he said, motioning to the other end of the table. The Phoenix Force medic took two steps and lifted the other end of the table. It had been hit by multiple rounds and creaked and crackled as they raised it, threatening to break in two. And it did. But not until the two Phoenix Force warriors had tossed it off the Persian carpet and into the opposite corner of the large room.

Manning and Encizo reached down and grabbed the carpet. They jerked it out and away from where it had rested, revealing the trapdoor beneath.

"You suppose there's one of these under the tables in the other two places we were in?" Hawkins wondered out loud. "It would have saved us a lot of effort. And saved the boss from his dirt bath."

"There's no sense in speculating," McCarter said as he knelt at the trapdoor. "Just be thankful we found this one. If the rounds coming in hadn't curled up the corner of the carpet we'd have never noticed it." The door had no handle and McCarter withdrew his Applegate-Fairbairn dagger. Working the tip into the crevice between the door and the floor, he used the sturdy six-inch blade to pry it up enough to slide a hand beneath the wood.

Manning reached down and opened the trapdoor, accompanied by more creaking and groaning of ancient wood and rusty hinges. McCarter held his breath. The trapdoor might not have been opened for centuries, and if it crumbled into pieces as the walls had done, there would be no way to clear a way through the opening.

That brought another dark thought to the former SAS man's mind. Where did this trapdoor lead? Was there a tunnel through which they might escape? Or was it nothing more than a cellar that would keep them trapped every bit as well as the walls falling all around them?

But the trapdoor stayed in one piece as it opened, creaking loudly again at the end of its ancient hinges and stopping at roughly a forty-five-degree angle. Below, even in the darkness, the Phoenix Force leader could see a set of rickety-looking rotten wood steps. For once, he was thankful for the gunfire going on all around him. He didn't know if the Radestani soldiers knew about the trapdoor or not. But if they heard its creaks and groans as it opened, they'd realize something was going on.

McCarter rubbed his eye gently, trying to get a little more of the orange dirt out of the corner. He still didn't know where the trapdoor led. But he was about to find out.

Looking down into the hole, McCarter said, "Hawk, find out where this leads." Then, as Phoenix Force's youngest warrior began climbing carefully down the aged steps, he looked up again. "The rest of you, keep firing. We don't want to tip them off that we've found a way out."

The men of Phoenix Force, Abdul Ali and the few men from Jabbar's faction of the PSOF who still had ammunition returned to their windows and resumed their end of the firefight.

Hawkins had dropped out of sight into the darkness, but suddenly a light went on twenty feet below. McCarter stared down into the hole and could see Hawkins aiming the beam of his small TechLite Lumen Master flashlight out of sight beneath the surface. He could tell by the way the light traveled rather than bouncing back around Hawkins that they had found a tunnel rather than just a cellar.

Hawkins looked up and switched the position of his flashlight beam to illuminate his face. Then he smiled.

That was all McCarter needed to confirm the tunnel theory.

The firing from Phoenix Force and their allies was noticeably slower now, and David McCarter suspected that the government troops had guessed they were running short on ammo. Another personnel carrier arrived, and more soldiers piled out and took cover. McCarter guessed there had to be at least 150 enemy combatants surrounding them now.

Unless the tunnel led them to safety, this was going to be Phoenix Force's last gunfight. In fact, it looked to become their last action of *any* kind.

As it sometimes did when the odds against McCarter and his team seemed insurmountable, the Phoenix Force leader's mind traveled briefly to Mack Bolan. The Executioner had once told the Brit that, much like the samurai of old Japan, he considered himself already dead. Every day that he still lived, every breath that he still took, was *borrowed*.

McCarter felt the same way. As did the rest of his team, he knew. It was an inescapable fact that someday their luck would run out and they would fall to enemy fire. But rather than frighten them, that knowledge somehow cast a calmness over the men.

They knew they had been created to protect good but weaker men and women. It was that knowledge that gave their lives purpose. And what could not be changed had to be endured. McCarter couldn't remember who had said that. But he knew in his brain, and felt in his heart, that it was true.

Hawkins had disappeared somewhere beneath the floor of the ancient dwelling but now he reappeared and looked up. "This thing leads under all of the houses in this row," he shouted upward over the never-ending gunfire. "Then it connects with another, wider tunnel. There are other small tunnels like this one that I'm assuming come from the other blocks of connecting houses in this neighborhood. They feed into the wider one, too."

"You know where the main route leads eventually?" McCarter asked.

"Uh-uh," said Hawkins. "I didn't think we had time for me to go exploring any farther." He coughed and a fine mist of dirt floated out of his mouth. "But wherever it leads has got to be better than where we are now."

"You'll get no argument from me," said McCarter. He stopped for a moment to think. Then he said, "Okay, I'm going to send Ali and Jabbar and his men down first." If nothing else, he thought, it would get the useless PSOF men out of their way. He started to voice that sentiment, then realized Jabbar had moved up beside him.

From below in the tunnel, however, Hawkins couldn't see Jabbar. "Send them on," he called up. "They won't need a guide. I'll just stay here and make sure they don't freeze and clog up the tunnel for the rest of us."

If the Oxford-educated Jabbar heard his criticism, he pretended not to.

Several of Jabbar's men had now noticed the open trapdoor and made their way over to where McCarter and their leader stood. The PSOF leader barked at them in Arabic and they started down the rickety steps into the tunnel. When the other rebels saw what was happening, they came crawling in a mad rush to follow. Two of the men stood in their hurry to escape.

Both died from fire coming in through the windows.

The others screamed in terror as their comrades fell, pushing and shoving each other across the packed dirt floor in desperation to get to the tunnel. One man reached the edge, then froze in place on his knees and stared down the hole.

McCarter had crawled back to the entrance to the underground. He was quickly losing his patience with the cowardly men. "Afraid of heights, are you, mate?" the Phoenix Force leader said. "Well, let me help you with that." Grabbing the man by the back of the neck, he shoved him over the edge of the hole.

The terrified man screamed on the way down. But once he hit the bottom of the tunnel, he took off out of sight like a frightened jackrabbit.

One by one, the rest of Jabbar's PSOF men dropped down into the tunnel and disappeared from sight. Some were solemn about the ordeal. Others had tears in their eyes like mothers whose newborn babies had been torn from their arms. McCarter found them annoying but tried not to judge them any further. Not every man had the temperament to be a warrior; it simply wasn't in their DNA. Still, he couldn't help wishing that the cowardly men had simply stayed home and out of the way of the rest of the fighters. They were far more of a burden than any kind of help.

While the rebels made their way into the tunnels, McCarter thought about the underground passageway. Someone, many centuries ago, had carefully planned the tunnels out with just this kind of siege escape in mind. He didn't think Genghis Khan or Attila the Hun had ventured into this area. But there had been dozens of lesser known raider-kings, as well as brigands of every race and nationality, who had roamed the Middle East over the years. So the Phoenix Force leader doubted that this was the first time the tunnels had been utilized in the way they had been dug to be used.

The gunfire from both sides of the house was taking its toll and the walls were starting to show giant fissures and a few gaping holes. McCarter stood and ejected his magazine, wishing he'd chosen to bring along the clear plastic mags through which he could actually see how many rounds were left. But if wishes were horses, as the old saying went, beggars would ride. By the heft of the magazine, he guessed there were somewhere between four and eight 5.56 mm hollowpoints left.

Jabbar was the last of the PSOF men still on the surface. He stood next to McCarter. "I am ashamed of my men," he said. "And I am afraid they will scatter like dry palm leaves in the wind down below."

The Phoenix Force leader ignored the remark. It wasn't Jabbar's fault that his men were all but useless. The man had to work with what he had. "I suspect they *will* scatter once we're out of the tunnel," he said. "*If* we get out, that is. Have you got another central meeting place?" McCarter asked. "Someplace they'll know to go to and regroup again?"

"We have another safehouse," said Jabbar. "They will all eventually find their way there. At least those who do not give up and go into hiding."

Hawkins could not be seen in the tunnel. But he must have stayed just out of sight as he hurried the frightened rebels onward because his voice floated up out of the hole. "If *that* safehouse is no safer than this one I may give up and go into hiding with your men myself."

Even in such dire straits, McCarter couldn't suppress a smile. "Go on, Jabbar," he said. "You and some of your men tried. We don't think any less of you." He motioned with his head toward the opening to indicate the PSOF leader should follow his men.

Jabbar shook his head. "It is better that I stay with you. Otherwise, you will not know where we have gone."

McCarter frowned. "You've got a point," he said.

The gunfire from the government troops outside showed no signs of letting up. And now the ammo shortage had caused the men of Phoenix Force—the only ones still inside the building—to measure their shots to a trickle. "The best thing, I think," said the Phoenix Force leader, "is that we all stay together underground. But we've got to all go and go *now*. Any second now they're going to realize we're almost out of ammo and it's time to rush us. And we still don't know whether or not they have prior knowledge about the tunnel."

Jabbar nodded, then began climbing down the rotten steps. McCarter followed, after which came James, Manning and Encizo, each taking final shots out the

windows before descending. On the way down, Mc-
Carter asked Jabbar, "Do you have more supplies at
this safehouse? Stored ammo, extra magazines and the
like?" Before answering, Jabbar took his last step off
the ancient wooden slabs stuck in the dried clay. "My
men and I can always switch to AK-47s if you don't
have the ammo for our rifles."

The PSOF leader looked up as McCarter finished his
descent. "I am afraid we are out of luck," he said. "We
did have extra supplies. Ammunition of all calibers,
extra Kalashnikovs and other things. But they were
stored at the safehouse that was compromised and we
were forced to abandon them when we fled."

T. J. Hawkins was in sight now, just down the passageway. "I wish you'd quit calling these places *safehouses*," he said. "They're anything but safe."

The men of Phoenix Force started down the tunnel
behind Jabbar's men. McCarter switched his sat phone
on but wasn't surprised when he got no reception so far
underground. Switching it off again, he made a mental
note to call the Farm at the first opportunity and have
Grimaldi drop more ammunition, rifle magazines and
other supplies as soon as they were out of the tunnel
and could find a secure location. They were operating
on bare bones now. Both Phoenix Force and the PSOF
were down to a handful of rifle rounds and their pistols, and that wasn't going to last very long.

"Let's move," McCarter instructed. "There's no way
to close the trapdoor and they'll notice it as soon as they
get inside. Then they'll be after us again."

Jabbar switched on a flashlight he had pulled from
under his robe and smiled, showing a row of perfect
white teeth in the semidarkness. "Yes," he said, "but we

have one advantage." Without waiting for anyone to ask what that advantage was, he continued. "Since we are ahead of them we can move ahead at full speed. They cannot. They will have to be wary of every twist and turn—every corner and side tunnel. They will have to stop and carefully check such places out to make sure they are not walking into an ambush. And each time that happens, we will pick up a little more ground and get further ahead of them."

The Phoenix Force leader wasn't so sure. "I hope you're right," he said as they all started down the tunnel. "But you're assuming they aren't familiar with this underground labyrinth. If they *are* they may send men to the other end—or to any other places that open up to the rest of the world—and attack us from the front."

There was no good answer to that problem. So they continued forward by the light of a dozen flashlights now, each man coming to terms in his own way with the very real possibility that death might lurk only a few steps ahead.

Phoenix Force had mixed in with Jabbar's men and in their *abats,* and the bad light it was difficult to tell who was who. Turning down the tunnel, McCarter pulled his own TechLite from his pack and switched it on. He was surprised at the height of the passageway. He had to stoop over to walk but not as much as he'd have guessed. For the man of average height in the era the tunnel had been dug, it would have seemed like the ceiling in a castle.

Hawkins had ushered all of the men who'd descended past him and was waiting on the Phoenix Force leader. "Nice digs, huh?" he said.

"I'm hot, I'm tired, I'm almost out of ammunition

and a few minutes ago I was buried alive in orange dirt," said McCarter. "At least spare me the bad puns."

"You got it," said Hawkins. He even raised his right arm in a crisp salute—a formality rarely performed by the men of Phoenix Force and then almost always more as a joke than out of respect.

McCarter saluted back, almost laughing again. Men who had fought together as many times as those of Phoenix Force had no need for formalities. They learned to respect each other for what each man could do rather than what rank he wore on a uniform. They became closer than brothers and sometimes even appeared to be able to read each other's minds.

Hawkins stepped back to let McCarter pass. The Phoenix Force leader shined his bright Lumen Master upward as he walked, noting that the other dwellings that had been practically shot down around them did indeed have entrances to the tunnel. He shook his head. As Hawkins had said, knowing that would have saved a lot of time and trouble.

Not to mention a lot of ammo.

The Phoenix Force leader moved on down the tunnel. It curved away from the front of the block of dwellings they'd been in. But McCarter reminded himself that there had been government troops behind them, too. Had the passageway passed under where those enemy combatants still were? He doubted it. But he couldn't be sure.

As the curve straightened again, McCarter saw the rest of Phoenix Force and at the front of the line the flustered men of the PSOF.

"We need to get to the front of the pack," McCarter told Hawkins and quickened his pace, reaching out and gently shoving other men out of the way as he went. When the two men reached the front of the underground pack, McCarter turned around and waved for the other members of Phoenix Force to join them. Encizo was the first to arrive. "Gives you a whole new respect for the tunnel rats in Vietnam," he said, referring to the men who had crawled through the labyrinth of tunnels in the Vietnam jungle, armed only with a flashlight, a pistol and a knife.

Jabbar, who had walked a few feet further into the tunnel, now stopped and pointed upward. "Look," he said in his Oxford-accented English. The Phoenix Force leader moved up next to him and shot his light upward.

Above them was another trapdoor.

Where did it lead? Into another ancient house? Into the sandy desert area that surrounded Ramesh? To escape and freedom? Or did this trapdoor open straight up to where a hundred government soldiers would blow the head off the first man who raised his eyes over the hole?

It was impossible to know.

David McCarter stared at the packed dirt to the right of the door. A few remnants of wood remained but for the most part, the steps had rotted away. He turned back toward the men behind him. He called for Manning in a quiet voice.

The barrel-chested Canadian hurried forward and looked up at the trapdoor, then at the broken steps. He didn't have to be told what to do. Lacing his fingers together in front of him, he formed a flesh-and-blood step for McCarter to put his boot in. And as soon as the Phoenix Force leader had regained his balance, Manning lifted him upward with no more trouble than if the former SAS man had been made of feathers.

McCarter looked down. The biceps in both of Manning's arms were bulging as if some surgeon had cut his arms open, implanted a fifteen-pound shotput, then closed the cut and erased the scar. What the Canadian was basically doing was "curling" McCarter with both hands.

Any assault team that didn't have a man who could bench close to five hundred pounds needed to get one, McCarter thought. Then, when the top of his head reached the rotting wood above him, he tilted his head sideways and pressed an ear against it.

He heard nothing, and considered risking an opening. But they had gone only a relatively short distance underground, and couldn't be too far away from the enemy soldiers. Besides, the Phoenix Force leader's gut instinct told him not to open the door. And that gut instinct had saved him, and the others on his team, too many times to ignore. Looking down, he caught Manning's expression in the light of his Lumen Master. Shaking his head, the big Canadian lowered McCarter back to the packed-dirt floor.

"What's wrong?" James asked.

"I don't know," said McCarter. "But something."

James nodded. "That's good enough for me and Bobby McGee," he said. "Want me to take point for a while?"

McCarter shook his head. "I'm still good. Wait until I—" A sudden creaking noise sounded from somewhere in the direction they'd come. The Phoenix Force leader held out his hands, palms down.

The rest of the men in the tunnel understood and went stone-cold silent.

The creak sounded again. It was the familiar sound

of old wood that had started to rot but had not yet given in completely to age. And the only wood they'd seen since they'd entered this underground passageway were the trapdoors and the steps leading to the tunnel where they were now.

"Mates," David McCarter whispered, "I think we've got company."

CHAPTER FOURTEEN

Herman Schwarz was behind a chair in the living room. Rosario Blancanales had taken refuge behind an upholstered sofa. And what looked to be at least five dark-skinned men with Arabic facial features were scattered around the living room. They all wore the coats and ties of businessmen, bureaucrats, plainclothes law-enforcement officers or other honest citizens. But there was a distinct disparity between their law-abiding appearance and their actions.

They might look okay. But they were firing a variety of weapons at Schwarz and Blancanales as Lyons charged through the door.

Schwarz and Blancanales had already started returning fire by the time Lyons dived to the ground. He slid across the carpet and next to Blancanales as the heavy explosions from Able Team's 6.8 SPCII caliber tactical loads flew across the room at the yet-to-be identified men.

Lyons took a half second to catch his breath, then held his own Yankee Hill Machine Model 15 over the back of the sofa and fired a blind eight-round volley. Using the full-auto blast to create the opening for a quick recon, he rose and glanced over the back of the couch.

Two of the unknown men were dying on the floor

in front of the sofa facing the one he and Blancanales were using as a shield. Paralyzed, their blood stained the light beige carpet in pools as they bled out. Other places around the room were now splattered and spotted with crimson that had blown out and away from the men.

Overall, the scene was one of near-total ongoing carnage.

Two more of the men were firing pistols—both looked like Glocks to Lyons. The fifth man had disappeared, presumably taking his own cover somewhere out of sight and laying low.

The Able Team leader and his men opened up again at the same time. Suddenly .30 caliber semijacketed hollowpoint bullets slammed into the two men, jerking them up, down, right and left. As the trio of full-auto onslaughts went on, the men looked as if they were engaged in some macabre dance of death.

Able Team didn't stop firing until both men had finally hit the floor.

Lyons, Schwarz and Blancanales were all on their feet now. The Able Team leader regretted his decision to leave the sound suppression off of the YHMs; his head was chiming as if he might have been the hunchback of Notre Dame in another life. He looked down at the stubby ten-inch barrel of the 6.8 caliber weapon in his hand and saw a thin wisp of smoke trickling out the end and up into the air.

Quickly, his ears still ringing, Lyons swept the room with his eyes. To his right, an open door led into what looked like a kitchen. Straight ahead of him was a sliding-glass door to the backyard. It was obvious that this was the route the men from the rear had taken into the house. Since they couldn't very well kick a sliding-glass door, they'd just broken out the glass.

But where had they gone? Lyons wondered. Kurtzman's drone had spotted eight men. He could account for only four, now dead on the floor. The fifth man—who had been in the living room when he'd entered the house but hidden when he'd dropped down behind the couch—and three more were nowhere to be seen.

To his left—almost directly behind where Schwarz now stood, was a hallway. Most of the unaccounted-for men had to have fled that way. There might be one or more in the kitchen. But while these Arabic-looking strangers might have expected some resistance from inside the house, they had been taken completely by surprise when it followed them through the door from behind. And the hallway had been closer than the kitchen.

Lyons sprinted to the kitchen doorway and stuck an eye around the corner. The room was empty. He turned back to the living room.

It was then that he spotted the dead man on the sofa behind which he and Blancanales had taken cover. The body had been out of their sight when they'd been on the carpet behind the sofa. But now he had a clear look at it.

Was this the fifth man he had wondered about? Somehow he didn't think so. Something didn't quite add up. Lyons frowned down at the dead man. His legs were still hanging off the seat and his feet were flat on the floor. But he had fallen to the side at the waist, and his upper body rested weirdly on the couch.

This man had been sitting when he'd been shot. And

he'd been facing away from the position from which Lyons and Blancanales had been firing.

What caught the attention of the Able Team leader even more, however, was the condition of the blood on, and around, the corpse. Unlike the fresh red blood from the men he and the other members of Able Team had just shot, the blood on the back of the head, and under the chin, of the man on the sofa had dried into a hard crusty black.

Able Team had not shot this man. And neither had the men in suits who they now fought. The man on the sofa had not died in this gunfight at all. He'd been dead before these mysterious men or Lyons and his warriors had entered the house.

For *hours*.

Carl Lyons felt his eyebrows lower as he tried to make sense of what he was seeing. He couldn't remember where he'd heard the expression and it didn't matter. But as he prepared to join Schwarz and Blancanales and go after the rest of the men who were hiding somewhere in this house, the words, "Curiouser and curiouser" began pounding in his head beneath the roar still raging in his ears.

Lyons knew he wouldn't solve this mystery, or the one concerning the men wearing the coats and ties, standing still and gaping at the dead body on the sofa. So he hurried back to where Blancanales and Schwarz stood—covering the opening from the living room to the hallway. Pulling the Kissinger-designed YHM-15's suppressor from his belt, he began screwing it onto the ten-inch barrel.

He didn't need to give the other two men of Able

Team the order to do the same. As soon as he'd finished and was able to cover the hallway himself, both men attached their own suppressors to their weapons.

Lyons didn't want to shout so loud that the men in other parts of the house would hear him. But he knew Schwarz and Blancanales were as deaf—at least temporarily—as he was. So he used hand signals to get them started down the hall toward the remaining men.

Whoever those remaining men were.

Schwarz went first, rounding the corner as Lyons covered him from a standing position and Blancanales dropped to one knee and aimed low. They met no resistance, and all three started down the hallway. The pounding roar of the unsuppressed gunfire still sounded in Lyons's ears, and he knew it must be the same for the other two men on his team. So they would not be able to rely on hearing as they searched the house. They would have to make do with their other four senses if they planned to stay alive.

The first of the final four men made it easy for them. Appearing suddenly from a bedroom door, the man aimed a Caracal automatic pistol at Schwarz. Lyons was half surprised to see the weapon—made in the United Arab Emirates—in the man's hand. But that didn't slow him, or the other two Able Team warriors, down.

The man with the Caracal got off one wild 9 mm shot, which sailed high over the heads of the men of Able Team and buried itself in the ceiling, sending a light sprinkle of white Sheetrock dust down. A split second later the Stony Man Farm warriors teamed up with their YHMs, filling him full of 6.8s.

And this time, with the suppressors threaded onto

the barrels, none of the men from Able Team felt as though their own ears were exploding.

Five down, Lyons thought. Three to go.

Silently, the men from Stony Man Farm moved down the hall as one unit. It was little different than the kill house where they'd first tested out their new weapons. The main difference, however, was that these targets were not paper or three-dimensional mannequin-like enemies.

The three men left in this house were alive. And they would shoot back.

As they neared another door, Lyons stepped past the other two men and dropped to one knee. The Able Team leader kept the longer-but-now-suppressed barrel of the YHM close to his body as he peered around the corner. Another bedroom. It looked empty.

On the other hand, there was enough room between the bed and the far wall to hide a man or men. And one or more could be under the bed for that matter.

A closet door stood open in a side wall. But it was shallow, and while shirts, jackets and pants hung from a clothes rack, Lyons could see through them to the back wall. There was no one hiding there.

If any of the enemy shooters were in this room, they had to be under or behind the bed.

Glancing back over his shoulder, Lyons saw that Schwarz now stood and covered him high. Blancanales was the one on one knee now, his YHM aimed to Lyons's side and ready to rock'n'roll.

The Able Team leader's ears still hummed as he walked slowly toward the bed. Again, if there was any noise, it passed him by. With each step he focused ever more clearly on the bed itself, doing his best to take note of even the slightest movement in the bedskirt that hung from the box spring to the floor or the mattress several inches from the wall.

He was halfway across the bedroom when he saw the material between the carpet and the bed frame rustle ever so slightly. Then a tiny black spot appeared just under the box spring.

A tiny black spot with a hole in the end of it.

Lyons cut loose with a full-auto volley from the YHM, spraying the underside of the bed with 6.8s. His ears were starting to clear now and he heard a scream. It sounded faint and far away. But he knew it had to have come from the bed area.

A hand holding a Turnbill 1911 fell out from under the bed and the .45 fell with it.

A split second later the Able Team leader felt the pressure to his sides as his teammates opened up with their YHMs. He stood perfectly still, trusting his men's skill but knowing that to move to either side would mean his own demise. The rounds passed him by and tore into the mattress, sending frazzled pieces of sheets and white stuffing into the air.

As soon as the assault stopped, Lyons led the way forward.

Behind the bed, he found two more bodies.

"That's all of them," Lyons said to his men. "But just to make sure, let's check the rest of the house."

Schwarz and Blancanales nodded and took off. Lyons followed them out of the room, checking a final bedroom but finding no other signs of the mysterious men. Backtracking through the bodies, he searched all of the men but found no passports, driver's licenses or any other form of identification. Schwarz and Blancanales met him back in the living room.

"How are your ears?" Lyons asked.

"They're clearing up," said Blancanales. "But it's going to be a long time before I shoot this thing without the suppressor again."

"I'll concur with that," said Schwarz.

Lyons felt the familiar vibration of his sat phone and reached inside his jacket pocket for the instrument. Holding the phone to his ear, he turned the volume up as loud as it would go and pressed the on button. "Yes?" he said.

"Where have you been?" Kurtzman's voice sounded muffled. "I've been trying to reach you for fifteen minutes."

"We've temporarily blown out our hearing," Lyons said. "These Yankee Hills work great— as long as you use the suppressors."

"I can tell," said Kurtzman. "You're practically shouting into the phone."

"That's because we can barely hear our own voices," Lyons said.

"Well, listen as best you can, Ironman," said Kurtzman. "I think I've ID'd your guys. I took still photos from the drone and ran them through facial recognition. Most of them came up a big fat blank. But that's to be expected when you combine that knowledge with the two whose faces *did* find a match." He stopped speaking for a moment, then said, "Did your burned-out eardrums take all that in?"

"Facial recognition on two," Lyons said. Slowly, his hearing was coming back.

"One of them is a former Radestani army colonel," said Kurtzman. "But I checked further. He seems to have dropped off the grid the past five years or so. The other guy is Radestani secret service. So I'm guessing that's where the colonel went, and that's who all the rest of the guys in the house must be."

"They aren't actually in the house anymore, Bear," said Lyons, looking around the room. "Their bodies are. But Elvis has left the building and their souls have left their bodies."

"Well, I won't speculate on where those souls have gone," said Kurtzman. "But I will take a guess at what they were doing here."

"The same thing we are," said Lyons. "Looking for the backpack nukes."

"That'd be my guess," said the man in the wheel-chair. "You haven't mentioned him, so I'm assuming Mussawi is not in the house."

"Uh-uh," said Lyons and felt his ears pop as if he'd just changed altitudes. "His Cadenza is here but he's in the wind. You didn't find another rental car for him anywhere, did you?"

"No," said Kurtzman.

"We've got another weird thing going on here," Lyons told the computer genius. "There's a body right here in front of me that's been dead for hours. He looks as Arabic as the others but he was dead long before these guys arrived."

"Can you send me a picture of him?" Kurtzman asked.

"Ten-four," said Lyons. He walked over to the body on the couch and grabbed a handful of the dead man's hair, lifting him back up to a sitting position. The bullet that had killed him had gone in under the chin and out the back of the head so the face was relatively undisturbed. Once he had the man balanced, Lyons switched his phone to camera mode and snapped a closeup. A few more buttons sent the encrypted picture flying through cyberspace to Stony Man Farm.

"Got it," Kurtzman said a few seconds later, and Lyons heard the man's fingers immediately start tapping his keyboard. "Good…from the looks of this he was shot from close range. It had to be somebody he trusted."

"That's what I'm thinking," said Lyons. "And my guess is it was the mysterious Mussawi himself."

The line went silent for several seconds. Lyons waited impatiently. Then he asked, "You got anything yet, Bear?"

Kurtzman chuckled. "Give me a *little* time, Ironman," he said. "This picture has to go into outer space and back and then get compared to hundreds of thousands of—" He stopped in midsentence then said, "Bingo. The man's name is Zaid Baharlou. And he's a suspected al Qaeda agent. Last spotting from Homeland Security was in Denver a couple of months ago." The man in the wheelchair blew air out so loud even Lyons's blasted ears could hear it. "Things are starting to fall into place a little better, you know?"

It was almost as if the knowledge cured Lyons's hearing problems. "You bet I know, Bear," he said. "If Baharlou was al Qaeda, and Mussawi was here, it means that he was al Qaeda, too. And if Mussawi has the nukes, which we're ninety-nine percent certain he has…" His voice trailed off to let Kurtzman come up with his own conclusion.

"The question now is," Kurtzman said, "where is Mussawi and what's he planning to do with the bombs?"

"I doubt we'll know that until we find him," said Lyons. "But if there are two backpack nukes already in al Qaeda's hands, there's no place in the country that's safe." He felt his jaw tighten and his upper teeth began to grind against his lowers. "You said you didn't find another rental car under one of Mussawi's credit cards, right?"

"Right," said Kurtzman. "And I've got an automatic check running on all his cards every ten minutes."

"Tell you what then, Bear," Lyons said. "How about we combine a little old-fashioned low-tech flat-foot work with your magic machines and see what we come up with?"

"What do you mean?" Kurtzman asked.

"I mean that Mussawi's gone but his Cadenza is still here. Can you find out what kind of vehicle Zaid Baharlou owned?"

"That's easy enough," said Kurtzman.

Again, Lyons heard the tapping of the keyboard. But this time, as he listened, he walked out of the living room, through the kitchen, and looked through the glass window in the door to the garage.

"Baharlou, Zaid," Kurtzman said over the airwaves. "The only vehicle listed for him is a year-old black Nissan Maxima. You want the license number?"

Lyons felt the blood rush to his temples now. "No,

but *you're* going to want it," said the Able Team leader. "The garage here is empty, Bear."

"That means—" Kurtzman started to say.

"That Mussawi took the Maxima to cover the trail he knew he'd left renting the Cadenza," interrupted Lyons. "You'd better reprogram your drones, my friend. There's a black Nissan carrying two nuclear weapons somewhere on the road."

Somewhere under Ramesh, Radestan

THE FIRST CREAKING sound had come from their rear. The second from somewhere ahead of them in the tunnel.

David McCarter didn't know exactly who was where or what they had planned. But it was obvious that Phoenix Force, Abdul Ali and Jabbar and his men were sandwiched between enemy forces belowground.

Luckily, the tunnel was an almost constant series of twists and turns, and it seemed that every twenty yards or so a smaller passageway—like the one they'd come out of beneath the four-home block of centuries-old dwellings—appeared. That fact served both as blessing and curse. On the upside it meant the beams from Phoenix Force's flashlights weren't visible, and with a little luck they might be able to take one of the side tunnels and lose whoever it was coming down after them from both sides.

But there was a downside, too. They needed to switch off their flashlights as soon as possible. Otherwise, the same beams that helped them navigate would light them up like bull's-eyes. And how would they know where they were or where they were going then?

McCarter motioned for all of the men to crowd in

around him so he could lower his voice. "Everybody hear that?" he asked.

All of the heads nodded silently.

McCarter looked to Abdul Ali. "You were in the Radestani army," the Briton said. "Did you know about these tunnels?"

"Everyone in Radestan has heard rumors about ancient tunnels in the old part of the city," he said. "But most of us have passed them off as just that—rumors."

"Well, they know they're real now," said McCarter. "You have any idea how they'd plan to handle this situation?"

Ali's eyebrows furrowed in concentration. "I never drilled in securing tunnels," he said. "And I do not know of anyone else who did, either." He reached up, grabbed a strand of his long beard and pulled on it. "But I cannot help but think they will handle the situation like the closest thing to it for which we *did* train."

"And that is?" McCarter prompted him.

"Attacking an enemy on a mountain pass," said Ali. "There are many similarities. When you think about it, a mountain pass is just a tunnel without a roof. Instead of being confined by two walls, you are caught between the side of the mountain and a drop-off. Either way, you are limited in horizontal movement."

"Go on," said McCarter.

"They have already trapped us in between them," said Ali. "And they will come at us from both ends just like they would in the mountains. But they will send a scout—a recon man I believe you call them—first." He paused and dropped his hand from his beard. "Do not make the mistake so many Westerners do because of crazed Islamic suicide bombers. Most Muslims do not want to die. Which is why they will scout things out with one man before endangering the rest."

David McCarter turned away from Ali. Calvin James and Gary Manning were standing next to each other just to his left. The wider tunnel through which they now traveled was higher, too, and neither man had to stoop. Looking from one to the other, McCarter said, "There are a lot of these guys still up there, but they're not particularly motivated. If they were, we'd already be dead from a stampede on the houses." He still had dirt in his hair and on his face and he brushed more of it off his eyebrows. "I think we can spook them if we handle it right."

"What, exactly, do you want us to do?" James asked.

"I want you to take out the recon man behind us," the Briton said. Then, turning his eyes to Manning, he said, "And you get the one ahead of us. "I want it done silently," McCarter continued. "And when the rest of the soldiers finally come upon their scouts, I'm guessing they'll turn tail and run. Those cowards will be terrified the silent killer is targeting them next."

James and Manning knew what they had to do and they both nodded their understanding.

A second later they disappeared into the darkness on both sides of the rest of the men.

CHAPTER FIFTEEN

Gary Manning slid out of his LAR-15 sling and handed the weapon to T. J. Hawkins. In his peripheral vision, he saw Calvin James turn away, draw his Crossada and start down the tunnel. Manning took off into the darkness in the opposite direction.

The Canadian was tired. But he knew all of the men of Phoenix Force, as well as Jabbar's raggedy band of half-fighters—and even the Radestani regulars still hunting them—had to be worn out, too. Overcoming exhaustion was just part of the game. Anyone who was willing to fight *could fight* when they were rested. Experienced warriors knew that it was the ability to keep going after enthusiasm, dedication and esprit de corps was worn out that separated the professionals from the amateurs.

Not to mention determining who lived and who died.

It didn't take long for Manning to outwalk the illumination from the flashlights of the other men. A couple of curves in the tunnel's path and he found himself in total darkness. Reaching to his side, he used both hands on the wall, placing one over the other as his feet continued walking.

Manning had no idea when he'd encounter the enemy recon man. But when he did, he'd have to take him out.

And he would have to do it quickly and as silently as possible.

Ahead, he heard something and it caused him to stop in his tracks. Was it footsteps? He waited but didn't hear the noise again. After a couple of minutes he started forward once more.

The smell of dirt had been in his nose ever since they'd first entered the ancient aboveground dwellings. But now, beneath the earth, it was different. Damper, and for that reason less irritating. For the first time since they'd entered the tunnel, Gary Manning took note of the temperature. It had to be at least twenty degrees cooler down here than on the surface. For the most part his blacksuit wicked sweat away from his body. But no material was perfect at that job, and the light coating of wetness on his skin suddenly made him shiver. The shiver had not come from fear or stress; he had overcome those obstacles to success long ago. It was a purely physical reaction to the colder atmosphere combined with the sweat and it lasted only a moment. But during that moment, he stopped again.

And this time he heard the noise once more. And was sure it was footsteps. Coming toward him.

Manning's hand went automatically to the Beretta at his side. But he stopped with his hand on the grip. McCarter had said he wanted this job done quietly, and Manning knew why. For a moment he wished he had a sound-suppressor for the 9 mm. But then he cast such thoughts aside. The fact was, he *didn't* have one and no amount of wishing would magically produce one. There was a limit to how much equipment any man could carry with him into the field—a limit dramatically brought home to him by Phoenix Force's current ammunition shortage—and it seemed that they were always without something they wished they'd thought to bring along.

That meant that at least once during every mission the men from Stony Man Farm had to improvise. And during this mission, Manning would have to kill the man or men he was about to face *silently* without what the uninitiated erroneously called a *silencer*.

The footsteps in the distance were closer now. Louder. Manning left the Beretta where it was and stretched both hands out in front of him. He no longer needed to walk forward.

Whoever was making those footsteps would come to him.

Manning waited, his arms out, his hands empty, in the blackness. He would go into action like a blind warrior as soon as the man coming toward him walked into his hands. He could index the man's body by touch and take advantage of the first vulnerable area that presented itself.

Seconds clicked away and became minutes. The footsteps continued to grow louder but seemed never to quite reach him. Manning had moved forward on the left side of the tunnel, and now he heard the footsteps almost directly in front of him. A moment later, they were at his side, and then he heard them behind him and just to his right.

The Radestani regular had passed right by his hands to the side.

The big Canadian turned slowly as a waft of body odor—the kind produced from intense stress rather than

the honest sweat that came from physical labor—drifted
up to the Phoenix Force warrior and hit him in the face.

Manning finished his turn, then took a step to the
side. He reached out and felt his right hand fall on the
back of a shoulder.

The man in front of him screamed in the darkness.

Manning moved his right arm on past the shoulder
and wrapped it around the man's throat. His left arm
came across the back of the man's neck and grabbed his
own biceps muscle. Then, with every ounce of strength
in his body, the big Canadian twisted the neck between
his arms and heard it snap.

The body went limp in his arms.

Manning let the man fall to the ground, then stood
silently, listening. He heard nothing. And his guess was
that this had been the only man sent to scout out the
tunnel from this end. Reaching into his pack, he pulled
out his flashlight and waited silently for another minute. Then, convinced that there was no one else in the
darkness, he flicked the flashlight on.

The tunnel was empty as far as he could see either
way. And the man whose neck he had just broken—
who was dressed in a Radestani army uniform—lay
at his feet.

McCarter had wanted the backward-thinking Radestani soldiers *scared,* and Manning was sure that the
discovery of the recon man's corpse would accomplish
just that.

Behind him, far away it seemed, he heard more footsteps. This time it sounded like many men rather than
one. Manning switched off his flashlight and reached
out for the wall again.

He had done his job. Now it was time to get back to the rest of the men and help find a way out of the tunnels. For a moment he wondered if Calvin James had fared as well going the other way in this underground labyrinth. Then he shrugged in the darkness. He would find out soon enough.

Gary Manning's boots made their own soft taps as he hurried away from the corpse.

CALVIN JAMES KNEW that Kydex, Concealex and all the other basically PVC plastic sheaths and holsters were like every other aspect of battle. They had their bad aspects as well as their good.

On the good side, the Concealex in which he carried his big twelve-inch bladed Crossada had been specifically molded to that knife and kept it securely in place without the need for any sort of retaining device. Consequently, the man who had first learned to knife-fight on the streets of Chicago's South Side, then perfected the art as a U.S. Navy SEAL, could draw the weapon directly from the sheath without fumbling with a strap or thumb break or similar device.

Which made for a lightning-fast presentation.

On the bad side of things, however, it made no difference how fast or slow, or at what angle, he drew the Crossada—it made *noise* when it came out. Not a lot of noise if he was careful. But more than enough to give him away within the close walls of the tunnel.

Which is why James drew the big knife from its sheath just as soon as he'd handed his near-empty LAR-15 Hunter to Encizo. He would carry it in his hand until he met up with whoever had made the creaking noise earlier.

James rounded a curve in the tunnel and suddenly the light from the flashlights where the rest of the men had stayed vanished. In total darkness now, he clutched the Crossada in his right hand and reached out with his left, letting his fingertips brush the passageway wall. He moved slowly, reminding himself that precision was far more important than speed at this point. And as his fingers trailed along the wall, he felt tiny wisps of packed dirt give way and fall lightly over his hand. He could hear his footsteps. They weren't loud. But he slowed down anyway.

Calvin James believed Abdul Ali's prediction. He believed that the Radestani army would indeed send one man forward to scout the way before risking the lives of the rest of them. And he knew McCarter had been right about the half commitment of the government regulars.

At any one time on Planet Earth, James knew, there were dozens of wars going on. Most were small; local fights between tribes or clans or other such groups. Regardless of size, at one time or another, James and his Phoenix Force brothers had spent time in most of them. But rarely had he found himself in such a strange and confusing conflict as this one going on in Radestan.

James shook his head in bewilderment. The rebel factions of the PSOF—like Jabbar's—couldn't agree on anything long enough to actually organize and do much more to the government than be a thorn in its side. A *big* thorn, perhaps, but just a thorn nonetheless. And the government troops were pitted with men who sympathized with the rebels. That meant, at the very least, they didn't fight as hard as they would have if they truly believed in their cause.

Then there was the al Qaeda presence in the whole mess. James had no idea who was in charge of the terrorist organization inside Radestan. But whoever it was, was doing his best to keep both sides fighting.

It was a trick as old as warfare itself. Let your enemies kill each other off. Help both or none—whichever kept things stirred up. Then go in after both have weakened past the point of recovery and take over. To the masses of people who were only semi-informed, al Qaeda would end up looking like the heroes who pulled the country back from the brink of total anarchy.

James moved on, the odor of stale, long covered dirt, thick in his nostrils. He felt himself rounding another curve and was tempted to turn on his flashlight. Just for a second. Just long enough to get his bearings.

He fought the temptation down. No good could come from such an action. He reminded himself that he had already covered this same path going the other way, with light. There was nothing he was going to see that he hadn't seen already—unless it was the scout sent out by the army. And flipping on the light would mean the scout would see him first.

Today might be a good day to die as some of his Native American friends sometimes said. But Calvin James knew it was even a better day to live.

He had gone what he guessed was roughly a quarter of a mile when he saw the flicker of light ahead. At the same time, the fingers with which he had been tracing the wall fell free of the dirt, telling him he was passing one of the smaller tunnels that fed into the main passageway.

James stopped. The light grew slightly. Then it grew brighter yet.

Someone, carrying a flashlight, was about to round a curve toward the Phoenix Force knife expert.

Calvin James moved smoothly into the side tunnel as the light suddenly shone straight past where he'd stood less than a second before. The Phoenix Force warrior waited, listening to the soft steps of the Radestani recon man. Each quiet footfall brought the scout one stride closer to the intersection of the tunnels where James hid, just around the corner.

Although it was apparent that the man was trying to keep quiet, the footsteps grew louder as he neared. The flashlight in the man's hand grew brighter as the unseen hand holding it swept it back and forth across the tunnel.

James took a deep breath and let it out again. He reminded himself that this man had been shooting at him only minutes before, and that he and the rest of his Radestani government troops had been behind atrocious torture and persecution of their own citizens, as well as the PSOF rebels and anyone else who opposed them.

James raised the Crossada.

A second later the man with the flashlight, wearing a dirt-covered Radestani army uniform, stepped in front of the side tunnel.

James barely had to move before bringing the Crossada across the man's throat. He felt the edge of the big knife slow slightly as it hit the man's skin. Then it sliced on and just kept going.

RADESTANI SERGEANT SALIH Amid walked confidently down the tunnel. To his left, right and rear, trailed two dozen other Radestani soldiers. Amid didn't let it show, but he was as excited as a small boy on his birthday.

Amid was tired of the civil unrest in Radestan. Sick of fighting rebels with whom he pretty much agreed, and sick of risking his life for a government in which he no longer believed. And he knew that somewhere in the midst of all the turmoil, al Qaeda was pulling strings as if Radestan were some giant puppet stage, just waiting to come in and take over.

And that was what made Amid's blood run hot as he led his men down the tunnel. He had friends he knew were involved with the PSOF. Others, he suspected, belonged to al Qaeda. So if the unorganized rebels ever got it together and took over the government, he knew his rank would rise high above sergeant in the new regime set up by the freedom fighters.

But he was playing it safe in case the war went the other way, too. Russia and China were constantly reinforcing the current regime with supplies and secret advisors. And he could not afford to forget that the whole PSOF movement might eventually be crushed. If that happened, there would be hell to pay for any Radestani military men suspected of supporting, or even just sympathizing with, the rebels.

Amid cleared his throat as he walked on, his flashlight leading the way. The AK-47 hanging from his shoulder in the assault position was aimed ahead of him. He and his troops made no attempt to keep quiet, and Amid knew that the men who had escaped into the tunnel from the houses in Old Town Ramesh would hear them long before they were near. Which was exactly what he wanted. During the fighting he had seen that some of the men were ragged PSOF rebels. But several—he had not been able to get an exact count—had been different. He didn't know exactly who they were but he had seen flashes of their strange black uniforms and knew that they fought like men possessed by demons. So he preferred to let them know he and his men were coming so they could scurry back in the other direction or exit the tunnels by one of the many trapdoors above their heads.

Either way, they would no longer be Salih Amid's problem, and he and his men could safely retrace their steps, return to the world above and wait to see who came out on top in this civil war. What he *didn't* want was a shootout with these men. They were simply too good.

Amid waved his flashlight back and forth as he and his men marched forward. The tunnels had many twists and turns, and they blocked out the light almost as effectively as corners would have done. But the sergeant knew that at least a little of the beam reflected off the dirt and curved deeper than the eye could see. Another good way to alert the strange attackers.

The Radestani sergeant marched onward, rounding curve after curve and making sure he and his men made enough noise to be heard as far away as possible. The flashlights in a dozen hands now bounced back and forth like the strobe lights Amid had often seen in one of the secret underground Western-style nightclubs in Ramesh. His thoughts turned to the music, alcohol and easy women in such clubs. He wished he was in one of them now instead of—Amid rounded a corner and almost tripped over something that was blocking the passage. He pushed against the obstruction with his foot and backed away. A chill ran through his body as his brain took a few seconds to figure out exactly what had happened. But when it did, he looked down and saw the shadowy figure lying lifelessly in front of him.

Amid took yet another step back. He raised his flashlight and trained it on the figure. The dead man's broken neck was cocked at an almost unholy angle. Several of the vertebrae that had pierced the skin shone white in the beam of the flashlight.

Another shiver crawled down Salih Amid's spine. He aimed his flashlight straight into the man's face and knew it was the recon scout he had sent ahead of the main force. He did not remember the man's name.

All of the men to his sides and behind him had stopped when Amid did. Now, there was an uneasy rumbling within the group as the whole scene was illuminated by several flashlights.

Amid stared at the corpse for another second, then turned back around. This man had been killed by the men in the black stretchy uniforms; he had no doubt about that. And if he led his men forward they would encounter these strange warriors somewhere in this underground graveyard.

And there was no way Amid was going to risk such an encounter for a government he suspected might fall at any time.

Salih Amid cleared his throat. Then he called out in a loud voice, "We will return to our original point of entry. The men we seek have obviously left the tunnels."

He got no argument from the other men. And a few seconds later the squad of Radestani soldiers was moving back to where they had started. At twice the speed they'd come.

THABIT HABIBI HAD never liked being a soldier. He had not liked taking orders when he'd been a private, and he did not like giving them since he had reached the rank of corporal. Of course he remained at the low end of the military structure, which meant he received more orders than he gave. And his latest order was to lead two dozen men into the darkness of this long-forgotten tunnel to find out what had happened to Dawud.

Dawud had been sent to recon the tunnel and begin tightening the trap that would ensnare the men who had fired from inside the ancient dwellings within Ramesh's Old Town. As far as Thabit Habibi was concerned, Dawud had received an even more unpleasant order than he.

Habibi wondered briefly who the men in the tunnel actually were. Some, he knew, were rebels and another of the Radestani soldiers thought he had recognized someone named Jabbar. But others Habibi had seen looked completely out of place. Westerners. Americans, probably. Americans seemed totally incapable of keeping their noses out of the business of any country in the world.

The thought of going down into the tunnel had frightened Habibi when he'd first received the order. But now, with twenty-three other soldiers, all armed with rifles and plenty of ammunition from their Russian and Chinese friends, the Radestani regular's confidence was returning. Each man had a flashlight of Chinese manufacture, and they lit up the tunnel like the noonday sun. Habibi walked confidently on, leading the way.

The Radestani forced himself to think about Talibah, concentrating his thoughts on her long black hair, matching eyes and the sensual sharpness of her cheekbones. He would marry her soon, one way or the other. Right now, there was an angry debate going on between his parents, Talibah's mother and father, and the parents of Akilah. Thabit Habibi's old-school parents had arranged his marriage to Akilah shortly after her birth, when he had been a mere toddler. Habibi shook his head. Not only was he in love with Talibah, but Akilah also looked like the wrong end of a camel. The thought of kissing her made him shiver in revulsion.

The tunnel curved and the Radestanis plodded on. He and his men made no attempt to keep their footsteps quiet. The fact was, Habibi hoped the rebels and Americans—or whoever the light-skinned men were—would hear them and run the other way. He had no desire to continue the firefight that had raged above where they found themselves now.

Thabit Habibi felt no sense of patriotism to Radestan. It was led by corrupt politicians. Why should he risk his life for them? He might get *killed*.

The thought made Habibi's shoulders shake again and he forced his mind back to Talibah. He realized that in a sense their situation was a metaphor for all of Radestan. The country was in a state of change. But which way would it go?

On the one hand, the rebel factions including the

PSOF wanted what the Americans called "separation of church and state." Of course, in the case of an Islamic country, that would be "separation of mosque and state." But there were many Radestanis—both young and old—who cried out for a theocracy similar to the one set up in Iran in the late 1970s.

Habibi didn't like that idea. Under such a system, he and Talibah could legally be executed for some of the things they had done. If it came to that, he reasoned, they would have to flee Radestan for some other country. Perhaps even America.

When he thought of America in that light, the Americans didn't seem nearly as bad.

Habibi and his men rounded a curve in the tunnel. Suddenly, far in the distance, a soft light glowed. "Flashlights off!" Habibi ordered. Slowly, without concern, and completely without any sense of military discipline, the men turned off their lights.

They had all stopped walking. Now, the man who would marry Talibah moved forward, waving over his shoulder that his men should follow. As he moved quickly down the tunnel toward the light, he could see it was coming from one of the smaller side tunnels.

Something—Habibi didn't know exactly what—suddenly made the hair on the back of his neck stand up. He lifted the AK-47 from the end of the sling and gripped it so hard his hands hurt. Slowly, he moved closer to the light from the side tunnel. It didn't move.

Habibi took a deep breath, stuck his index finger inside the trigger guard of his AK-47 and reached under the weapon with his left, making sure the rifle was on full-auto. The creepiness increased even more as he stopped just in front of the small side tunnel and took another deep breath.

Thabit Habibi had to force himself to step out, swing the AK-47 around and aim it into the side tunnel. There, he saw Dawud. The man was spread-eagled on the packed earth floor, his throat slit from side to side. A flashlight stood on its end, illuminating his body and the pool of blood that surrounded him.

Habibi had fired over half of his rifle's magazine into the man's body before he regained control of himself and could hear his own screams.

CHAPTER SIXTEEN

Emad Nosiar held one of his suitcases. Harun Bartovi grasped the other as the two men walked across the tarmac toward the plane. The roar of the Radestani-government-owned Boeing 727's three engines warming up forced them to shout slightly as they spoke.

"It is ironic, is it not," said Nosiar, "that I will be flown in a Radestani aircraft to pick up the nuclear bombs that will destroy this country?"

"It is," said Bartovi. "But it is a good reminder that we have infiltrated the current Radestani regime. And it is symbolic, in a sense, of how incredibly confused this civil war has become, and how the government and rebels are both infiltrated by traitors." He paused for a moment and spit on the ground. "May God cast them all into eternal fire."

"Ah, but the incompetence on both sides is fortunate for us," said the al Qaeda leader as he got ready to walk up the portable steps to the passenger entrance. "The same government that provided this aircraft informed me of an attempt by the Secret Service to intercept the bombs from Mussawi. It was at his handler's—Zaid Baharlou's—house, in America."

Bartovi smiled. "The fact that you are smiling and still heading that way tells me they were not successful," he said.

"No," said Nosiar. "In fact they were all killed in the process. Apparently by some American commando team. No one seems to know exactly who they were." He turned and started up the steps.

Harun Bartovi followed. "All Americans still think they are cowboys," he said. "It was probably an FBI team. Or perhaps even the abominable CIA."

Nosiar reached the top of the steps and entered the passenger area of the 727. It had been gutted of seats and redecorated to look more like a living room than the inside of a passenger carrier. He dropped his bag to the side and took a seat against the wall.

Bartovi stepped inside and placed the man's other bag next to the first. He would not be staying, so when Nosiar nodded that he should take a seat, he shook his head. "I would just have to get up again in a moment," he said. "Besides, I spend too much time sitting these days. I am not in the same kind of shape I was when I was younger."

"None of us are," said Nosiar. "But when God takes away muscle he replaces it with brains." He crossed his legs. "We are far more effective—far more dangerous to the Western infidels—now than we were when we were young."

Bartovi leaned against the door, half in and half out of the plane. "Is there anything else you need?" he asked.

Nosiar shook his head. "No. Only for you to look after things until I return." He paused, frowned in thought, then added, "You might begin removing our people from Ramesh," he said. "Of course you will not tell them why. Give them some kind of assignments far enough away that when the explosions occur they will not be affected."

Bartovi smiled. "We are making history," he said. "There has never been such an event—not even when the forever-damned Americans dropped the bombs on Japan at the end of World War II."

"You are correct, my friend," said Nosiar. "May God be praised."

"May God be praised," Bartovi repeated.

"So, we have our cell phones if you need to reach me. But there is a special phone locked away in the safe in my office. I have never used it, and no one but me even knew of its existence until now. For that reason it is one hundred percent secure."

"Why do you tell me this?" asked Bartovi.

"Just as a backup in case our regular phones—which are still secure as far as I know—are somehow compromised." Nosiar paused for air. "It does not hurt to be careful. You know where the safe is, of course."

Bartovi nodded. "Of course."

Nosiar gave the man the combination. "And it is time that I shared with you the rest of my itinerary."

"Only if you feel you should," said Bartovi.

"I *do* feel I should," said Nosiar. "Just in case you need to speak to me and we have trouble with our phones. It is unlikely but possible. And I would hate for anything to stop, or even delay, what is planned after we have come this far."

Harun Bartovi waited.

"The plane will land in Canada," Nosiar said. "In Vancouver."

Bartovi's face showed his surprise. "Canada?" he said. "I do not understand."

"It is a safer place to land, and certainly a safer place from which to take off again after I have taken possession of the nuclear weapons. We do not hate the Canadians the way we do the Americans. And while their officials might search the plane upon landing, it is doubtful they will before we depart."

"Yes," said Bartovi. "But that means Mussawi must cross from the U.S. into Canada. That will mean another search."

Nosiar shook his head. "No," he said. "In Vancouver, a boat will be waiting for me. Our operatives will take me by sea to the coast near Bellingham, Washington. It is there I will take possession. Mussawi will not have to cross into Canada."

"I see," said Bartovi. "But do you not worry about the United States Coast Guard, Emad?"

"It is a short trip over the water," Nosiar said. "I do not think it will be a problem." He sighed and looked at the ceiling of the plane. "And some chances must be taken or nothing is ever accomplished. I will depend on God to protect me during this phase of the mission."

"I will pray for you," said Bartovi.

Nosiar's eyes came down from the ceiling to meet Bartovi's. "Thank you," the al Qaeda man said. "I cannot tell you how comforting it is to know I am leaving things in your hands. I know of no one else I would entrust with either our operations here or the knowledge about my plans, which I have just given you."

"It is my honor," said Bartovi.

The pilot, wearing the official uniform of the government-controlled Radestan Airways, stuck his head through the door. "We are ready," he said.

Bartovi recognized the pilot but could not think of

his name. He did know, however, that he was another al Qaeda operative. He looked over the uniform. It was official right down to the collar brass. Another gift from one of Nosiar's government infiltrators, he suspected.

"Then let us go," said Nosiar.

Bartovi stepped quickly forward and grasped the seated man's hand. "I will see you back here in Ramesh in approximately two days," he said.

Nosiar nodded. "And soon after that *no one* will ever see Ramesh again." He smiled. "Praise God."

"Praise God." Bartovi turned, exited the doorway and walked down the steps. Behind him, he heard the door to the aircraft close and seal.

Harun Bartovi walked quickly across the tarmac to the BMW that had brought him and Emad Nosiar to the airport. Sliding into the backseat, he leaned forward and addressed the driver. "Take me back to our headquarters," he said.

Fifteen minutes later he was in Nosiar's office. Locking the door behind him, he went directly to the painting behind the al Qaeda man's desk and took it down. In the wall, he saw the door to the safe and carefully dialed in the combination Nosiar had given him only a few minutes earlier.

The secure phone was right where Nosiar had said it would be.

Bartovi pulled it out and looked at it, a wide smile stretching across his face. Then he tapped in the number he had memorized several months ago and waited for it to connect. After three rings, a female voice said, "Hello?"

"This is Mr. Smith," Bartovi said, using the code

name the CIA field operative who had recruited him had said to use. "I would like to speak with Mr. Jones."

"One moment," said the woman on the other end of the phone.

Bartovi's smile stretched farther than he thought would have been possible as he waited. But then ten million dollars would make anyone smile, he assumed. And that was the amount of money the United States of America's CIA had promised him for any information they deemed big. And Emad Nosiar completely destroying a city of more than two million people with nuclear bombs stolen from America would have to be considered big. "Praise God, indeed," Bartovi whispered softly. "I am going to be rich."

MANI MUSSAWI CAME out of the liquor store in Twin Falls, Idaho, and returned to the Maxima. The half-gallon bottle of Jack Daniel's in the brown paper bag went onto the seat next to him as he started the engine. With the Nissan still parked, he picked up the bag again and pulled the neck of the bottle out above the brown paper. Twisting off the cap, he looked at the glass it had hidden.

It was clean. No germs could have gotten under the seal. He glanced quickly around to make sure no one—especially any small-town law enforcement officers—was watching, then held the bottle to his lips and tipped it back.

The familiar burn soaked into the membranes around his teeth. He swallowed, and the whiskey warmed his stomach and calmed his nerves almost immediately.

Mussawi closed his eyes as the whiskey raced through his veins. He had been unable to sit still after shooting Zaid Baharlou the night before and decided to drive through the night rather than attempt sleep. He had looked at a map, then decided he would wait until he reached Boise before drinking any more alcohol. And he'd gotten close. But as he'd slowed the Maxima to glide through this tiny Idaho village he'd caught sight of the word Liquor on a sign just off the highway and pulled in without thinking about it.

The al Qaeda mole glanced around once more, took another long pull from the bottle, then twisted the cap back on the neck. He set it down on the seat once more and covered it with the sport coat he had taken off earlier. As he did, he leaned back and felt a sharp pain hit the small of his back. It took a moment for him to identify the cause. But then it hit him that he had entered the liquor store, bought the whiskey, and left with the Makarov 9 mm sticking out of his belt, exposed. The old man working the counter inside had looked half blind and had not noticed the gun. But that had to have been only by the grace of God.

Mussawi pulled the Makarov out and hid it under his jacket next to the bottle. His heart pounded like thunder inside his chest. He was getting careless. And at the worst possible time. If he could just hold it together for a few more hours—maybe a day or two at most—this would all be over. The two nuclear backpack bombs would be turned over to Nosiar and Mussawi would be free to return to Radestan. His old friend Emad would detonate the first bomb in the desert and then take over the government with the threat of an identical bomb going off in Ramesh.

The al Qaeda mole was about to pull out of the parking lot and return to the highway when he felt a sudden presence at his side. When he turned toward the seat, he saw that his gun, the bottle and his sport coat were all on the floor of the vehicle. Next to him sat the man in the white robe.

The man's eyes looked sad again. And while his lips didn't move, Mussawi heard him anyway. *You're drinking far too much,* the man communicated to him.

"I know," Mussawi said out loud. "And you, too, are against the use of alcohol."

The man's eyes remained sad but he smiled. *I am against drunkenness,* he seemed to say. *I turned water into wine when it was appropriate.*

"I will quit drinking as soon as I return to Radestan," said Mussawi. "I will not even toast the nuclear bomb that goes off in the desert."

You know it's not really going to go off in the desert, came the message from the man in the white robe. *Emad Nosiar is going to detonate both bombs in Ramesh and kill over two million people.*

Mussawi lunged for the bottle at the man's sandaled feet. "No, he isn't!" he yelled out loud. "Be quiet! You are not even real!"

I am real, came the next message. Then he smiled the most beautiful smile Mani Mussawi had ever seen. But rather than make him feel better, the expression filled the al Qaeda mole with guilt and dread.

There is still time. I can save all those people, the man seemed to say. *I can save you.* Mussawi took another slug of whiskey, then screwed the top back on the bottle. When he looked to his side again, the Makarov barrel was visible under his sport coat on the seat. He returned both it and the Jack Daniel's to hiding and threw the Maxima into drive.

A few seconds later he was on the highway again. He would drink no more until he reached Boise. Perhaps that would keep the man in the white robe away. Besides, he would need to have a clear head for what he had decided needed to be done when he reached that city. And looking or smelling or acting drunk in any way could ruin the whole operation at this point.

As the Nissan Maxima picked up speed so did the alcohol flowing through his body. Mani Mussawi settled in behind the wheel once more.

AARON "BEAR" KURTZMAN had been paralyzed for years. But he had never let his disability get him down—either mentally or physically. And on the rare occasions when there was a lull in activity at his computers, he kept the parts of his body still operating in tip-top shape.

At the moment, while the drones searched the highways and several other automatic scanning programs operated, Kurtzman had picked up a forty-five pound dumbbell he kept beneath the computer cabinet and was doing one-armed curls. He did ten, then switched arms and did ten more. He was about to start a second set when Hal Brognola came striding up the ramp, the ever-present cigar stub sticking out of his mouth.

Kurtzman leaned to his side and set the dumbbell down on the floor. And as he did, a computer three feet behind him suddenly buzzed, the red light on its side flashing.

Kurtzman nodded at Brognola as he swiveled his chair around and rolled toward the flashing light. A moment later he settled in front of it and saw that he had trapped an incoming call from Radestan to a secret CIA "Hello" number. Hello numbers were used by many agencies and had gotten their name from the way they were answered. Instead of saying the name of the agency, the man or woman monitoring them simply said hello. They were used in undercover operations and the advantages to agents in the field were obvious.

Stony Man Farm had its own Hello numbers, of course. But as the top-secret installation that it was, Kurtzman knew about those of other federal agencies, as well. And he ran a continuous scan of those numbers, often flagged with certain words to alert him of activity in the areas where operatives from the Farm were working.

It all boiled down to the same fact of life that operated in all areas of Stony Man Farm. The Farm knew everything about the other agencies. But the other agencies didn't even know the Farm existed.

"What are you getting, Bear?" Brognola asked. He had followed the man in the wheelchair down the row to the flashing light.

"Hello from Radestan," Kurtzman said. "To the Company." In the corner of his eye, the man in the wheelchair saw Brognola frown.

"Do we know what the spooks have going over there?" the director asked.

"They've got a few plants," said Kurtzman. "And some of them, along with a group of Special Forces troopers, were trying to train the rebels. But you knew all that already. And they've had a standing reward out for several months now that has hooked a few low-level al Qaeda maniacs. Nothing very big so far, though."

"Well, let's see what's going on now."

Kurtzman tapped a few keys, shoved the mouse around the screen and hit it twice, and a speakerphone came to life. There was no sound. "Whoever called in must be on hold," Kurtzman said. "We should—" A voice suddenly came on and the man in the wheelchair stopped speaking.

"Mr. Jones," a heavily accented Arabic voice said. "This is Mr. Smith. It is good to hear from you."

The two men at Stony Man Farm listened to the conversation. When it was over, Brognola looked at Kurtzman. "I'd better have Barb pull Phoenix Force out of Radestan and have them head this way," he said. "And your drones have got to find the Maxima. If it's at all possible, Able Team has got to grab the nukes before they're turned over to this Nosiar character." He chomped down harder on his cigar. "Once they're in his hands it's going to be a real bitch getting them back."

Kurtzman was busy typing. "It's already a real bitch now if you ask me." He nodded.

"And I'd better talk to the President," said Brognola. "He's going to have to tell the CIA to either take a backseat to us or stay out of it altogether."

"They're going to *love* that," said Kurtzman.

"They always do," said Brognola as he hurried back down the ramp.

CHAPTER SEVENTEEN

With Lyons on his secured sat phone, Hal Brognola briefed the Able Team leader on Bartovi's call to the CIA as they returned to Mechner's Field and the waiting SAB helicopter.

"We're at the chopper now," the former LAPD detective said as they rolled to a stop. He, Schwarz and Blancanales left the FBI sedan and boarded the helicopter once more. Lyons took the shotgun seat as before. The other two Able Team warriors squeezed in behind him and Charlie Mott. "Have Bear contact me in a few minutes when we're in the air, will you?" Lyons said as he fastened his seat belt.

"Affirmative," said Brognola and both men ended the call with a click.

The SAB helicopter rose quickly. It took less than a minute for it to be high enough in the air that Kurtzman's voice came clearly over the radio without interference from the mountains. "Stony Man to Able One," it said. "Come in, Able."

"Able One here," said Lyons, picking up the radio mike in front of him on the chopper's control panel. "We're listening."

"What's your 10-20?"

"Due North out of Colorado Springs," said the Able

Team leader. He settled back into his seat. "Surrounded by mountains. Lots and lots of mountains."

"Tell Mott to angle northwest," said Kurtzman.

The SAB angled slightly to the left as the Farm's second ace pilot altered course.

Lyons pressed the microphone button again. "Does this mean you've found the Maxima?"

"I *think* so but not for sure," said Kurtzman. "You have any idea how many Maximas there are on the road? And you remember I said these programs might have a few bugs to iron out?"

"Yeah, I remember that," said the Able Team leader. "And you bringing it up again now sounds like you've run up against one of those bugs."

"I have. The program's having a little trouble distinguishing between the Maximas and a couple of other Nissan models."

"Can you fix it?" asked Lyons.

"Sure," Kurtzman came back. "When I have time. Right now it's more practical to work around the problem than shut down the whole op to try to fix it."

Charlie Mott looked at Lyons and said, "Press the little red button for me, will you, Ironman?"

The Able Team leader did as requested and held the microphone across the chopper, close to Mott's face. "I can hear you direct, Bear," he said. "Any route in particular you want me to take?"

"Whatever gets you the fastest to Boise, Idaho," said the man in the wheelchair.

Lyons pulled the mike back in front of his own mouth now. "That's where the car you *think* is the right one is, Bear?"

"Yeah," said Kurtzman. "It hasn't reached Boise yet

but it's on the highway headed that way. Should get there about the same time you do." The airwaves went silent for a few moments, then Kurtzman's voice returned. "It's got a Colorado license tag but the numbers and letters are partially blocked with mud. My guess is it's on purpose."

"How about facial recognition?" Lyons asked. "Please don't tell me we're at the mercy of tinted windows."

On the other end of the line, Kurtzman cleared his throat. "No, no tinted windows," he finally said. "But the man sits straight up in his seat all the time and I haven't been able to position a drone camera at the right angle to catch his face."

"That leaves your new long-range fingerprint program. Tell me I can have faith in that at least."

Kurtzman cleared his throat again. And Lyons knew the computer genius well enough to know that such a delay meant more bad news. "It hasn't picked up on any prints yet," Kurtzman said. "I'm assuming that's because Mussawi—if it really is the right Nissan and it's Mussawi inside—hasn't been driving it long enough to leave prints on the dashboard. And in addition to sitting perfectly straight, whoever the driver is keeps his hands at the ten-o'clock and two-o'clock position all the time."

The cop in Carl Lyons kicked back in. "How's his speed?" he asked.

"Three to five miles under the speed limit," said Kurtzman. "Consistently."

"Well," Lyons came back. "You put all that together—the straight posture, the hands positioned as if he's in a driver's-ed program and the speed—not too fast, but not too slow, either, and you can be pretty sure whoever's driving that car is worried about getting stopped."

"It's either a man with two nuclear bombs in his car or a man who's been drinking," said Kurtzman.

There were a few moments when the airwaves became silent. Then Lyons said, "How about the original owner of the Maxima? The guy we left molding on the couch. He was al Qaeda."

"Zaid Baharlou?" said Kurtzman. "Yes, he was."

"Then how about programming *his* fingerprints into whatever thing that is, that does what it does?" Lyons asked.

His strange wording made Kurtzman laugh out loud. "I can't believe I understood that but I did," said the man in the wheelchair. "And I'm proud of you, Ironman. You're actually starting to sound like a man living in the twenty-first century."

"Well, listen good," said the Able Team leader. "I doubt it'll last very long." He let up on the transmit button but pressed it again almost immediately. "Do you have a set of this Zaid guy's prints?"

"I'm checking now," said Kurtzman.

Lyons could hear the man's quiet breathing as he kept the line open. "Nothing from the CIA…" The man in the wheelchair sounded more like he was thinking out loud than talking to someone else. "Okay…wait a minute… Bingo. NSA's got a file on a Zaid Baharlou, al Qaeda. No full set of prints but they lifted three from a pistol used in a Saudi Arabian assassination seven years ago." He stopped talking again but Lyons could hear him typing. Finally he came back on the air. "Okay, Ironman. I've entered those three prints into the program. Let's pray we get lucky."

Lyons swiveled halfway around in his seat. "You two have been unusually quiet back there," he said to Schwarz and Blancanales. "You have anything you want to add?"

"Nope," said Blancanales. "Sounds like you covered everything pretty well."

"I agree," said Schwarz.

The Able Team leader pressed the transmit button once more. "Keep us informed, Bear," he said.

"Will do," said the man in the wheelchair before ending the call.

Ramesh, Radestan

DAVID MCCARTER REACHED up and ran his hand over the back of his head. While he couldn't see it, he could feel dirt fall out of his hair and trickle down his neck. The Phoenix Force leader suppressed a smile. The experience in the ancient mud dwellings and then in the tunnels below had been the epitome of a "dirty fight." He kept the bad pun to himself.

His team had suffered enough.

McCarter, the other men of Phoenix Force, Ali Abdul and Jabbar and his rebels had emerged from the tunnels a half hour earlier. For once, luck had been with them and they'd found themselves on the same side of Ramesh that they had originally entered. No Radestani soldiers appeared to be in the area, so they had double-timed it back to the tall grass and vehicle graveyard where their first battle had occurred. The Phoenix Force leader had waited until they were roughly three klicks from Ali's small cottage and the corral where

Hawkins had "christened" his boots, before pulling his sat phone from his pack to call the Farm.

The Phoenix Force leader had requested a parachute drop of more 5.56 mm ammunition.

What he heard, however, had surprised him.

"That's a big negative, David," Hal Brognola had said. "Grimaldi's on his way to pick you up right now. You're coming back to this part of the world."

Now, as McCarter led his men up a small rise in the countryside outside of Ramesh, the Phoenix Force leader saw a helicopter in the distance. With the chopper in sight, McCarter broke into another double time. His men and those who followed Jabbar's PSOF faction ran behind him. McCarter stayed focused on the chopper as it settled. McCarter smiled, imagining a little shut-eye would be in order as they flew back to the U.S. The Phoenix Force leader stopped at the chopper and turned around. "Say goodbye and go on up, mates," McCarter told Manning, Hawkins, Encizo and James. He stepped to the side to let them pass, then extended his hand to Ali and Jabbar. "Keep fighting the good fight," he told the PSOF man. "We may meet up again one of these days."

Jabbar's men looked lost and confused as McCarter turned and climbed inside the chopper. He had no idea what would become of Radestan. The men he was leaving might finally organize with the other rebel groups and take over. Or the current regime, still backed by Russia and China, might prevail. Either way, McCarter knew that al Qaeda was planning to make its move once both sides were weakened.

And from what he'd learned from Brognola, Mc-

Carter knew that they were about to be weakened as no other country in history had ever been. And soon.

The Phoenix Force leader stopped and stared behind him. He hated leaving the country in the shape it was in. But he could best help Radestan now by going directly after the madman who was on his way to pick up the two nuclear bombs. If Phoenix Force and Able Team failed to stop Emad Nosiar, there would be no Ramesh, or much of Radestan, left for *anyone* to govern.

Boise, Idaho

THE SAB WAS a fast little chopper and Charlie Mott got the men of Able Team to Boise just as the Maxima was about to enter the city from the south.

"Stony Man to Able One," came over the radio as Mott hovered the craft in the air. "Come in, Ironman."

"Able One, Stony Man," said Lyons. "What's up?"

"The driver of the Maxima just leaned in slightly and I got facial confirmation," said Kurtzman. "Looked like he was taking a drink of something in a brown paper bag."

Schwarz leaned forward behind Lyons. "That's wino behavior," he said. "Isn't this guy a Muslim? And aren't they supposed to abstain from alcohol?"

"A fanatic will do whatever he wants in the name of jihad," said Blancanales. "None of that's important right now," Lyons growled. Then, thumbing the red button on the mike again, he said, "You have any luck with the prints, Bear? Not that we really need it now."

"It never hurts to double-check things like this," said Kurtzman. "And the answer to your question is yes. When he took his hand off the steering wheel to grab the bottle, the drone camera zoomed in on the steering wheel." He stopped speaking for a moment, then summed it all up with, "It's Mani Mussawi's face, and it's Mani Mussawi's fingerprints, so it's Mani Mussawi behind the wheel of the Maxima."

"Not for long," said Lyons. He nodded at Mott and the pilot took the chopper slowly forward, pacing the black Nissan below. "I don't want to take him out in town," the Able Team leader went on. "Too many civilians around. We'll wait until he leaves the city limits again and then come down ahead of him and block the road."

"Ten-four, Ironman," said Kurtzman.

Schwarz leaned forward again. "I hate to have to ask, but…" he said. "What are the chances he sets the nukes off in the car when he sees us blocking his path?"

"Extremely unlikely," said Kurtzman. "The backpack nukes aren't stored 'cocked and locked.' There has to be several more steps taken before the bombs are actually activated for ignition. Even the pros don't take chances with those things. He'd be a fool to be driving around with them ready to go. Especially when they still have to travel all the way to Radestan."

Mott continued to fly just slightly above and behind the Maxima. Lyons could look down and see it in the light traffic. He heard a noise above them and looked up to see a large Predator drone cruise by. It would not be armed with anything more than the camera Kurtzman was using. Not in U.S. airspace, anyway.

"Wait a minute… What?" came Kurtzman's voice over the radio.

Lyons looked down and saw the black Nissan Maxima turn off the highway running through town and take a secondary road, passing houses and then businesses before coming to a medium-size parking mall.

"Oh, *man*," said Blancanales. "Tell me he isn't going to do what I think he's going to do."

"I'm afraid he is," said Schwarz. Both men were now almost in the front of the SAB with Lyons and Mott.

"You seeing this, Bear?" Lyons said.

"Unfortunately," said Kurtzman.

The men of Able Team and Mott watched helplessly as the Maxima followed an older Buick into a covered parking lot. Three more cars followed it in fast succession.

In the meantime, a half dozen other vehicles of different makes, models and shapes exited the unseen parking area on the opposite side of the mall.

Lyons shook his head. "He'll change vehicles," he said with his teeth gritted together. "And they're going and coming too fast for the drone camera to check all of them before they get away."

"Okay," Kurtzman said. "So scratch that plan. I'll do what I can with the camera. But it'll be nothing but luck if I ID him again."

MANI MUSSAWI WAS feeling proud. He had promised himself that he would not take another drink until he reached Boise, Idaho. And he had not. Oh, he had been tempted to—especially when the alcohol he had already consumed began to wear off and his hands became shaky and his stomach wanted to turn upside down. Twice he had moved to pick up the bottle. But both times he had refrained.

And the man in the white robe had not appeared since he'd stopped at the liquor store. For that he was grateful.

The second he passed the sign announcing the Boise city limits, however, Mussawi had grabbed the brown paper sack with the bourbon bottle in it and pulled it to his chest like a mother might do a child. His hands shook as he tried to twist the cap off with one hand and steer the Maxima with the other. Finally, it came off. But the half-gallon bottle was so big that he was forced to lean forward over the steering wheel to have room to tip it up. When he did, however, he was able to guzzle down several mouthfuls of whiskey.

Then he sat back. And stopped shaking. It was almost like magic.

Mussawi followed a small Datsun as he screwed the cap back on the half-gallon bottle. He knew he had to be careful. He could not afford to be stopped by the police or to get into any sort of traffic accident. He had work to do here in Boise. Important work. A task he had devised himself for which God would undoubtedly reward him later.

For it would further the jihad.

Mussawi had driven through Boise several years ago on a vacation trip to Oregon. He had made a wrong turn at a stoplight in town and found himself at the entrance to a shopping mall. It had been a large mall; too large, he would have thought, for a town this size. He had decided to go in and look around. And he remembered the underground parking lot where he had parked.

The al Qaeda mole also remembered where to turn, and when he got to that corner he stopped at a red light. Then, seeing no cross traffic coming toward him, he carefully turned the Maxima and drove on through a residential section of town and finally to the mall. It looked just as he remembered it and he found himself laughing in glee. But even as he laughed he realized he was breaking down emotionally and suddenly tears of sorrow were flowing down his cheeks. He stopped to let a worn-looking Buick turn right into the underground parking, then made a left and followed the car in. For a moment he studied the Buick through his tears. No, it was not the vehicle he wanted. Too old.

Mussawi took another quick drink and stopped crying. He parked beneath the concrete ceiling on the second level of the lot, shrugged into his sport coat and stuck the Makarov into his belt. He left the Jack Daniel's bottle on the front seat and the two nuclear bombs on the back, hidden in their nondescript black cases. Then he got out of the car.

The man in the white robe was waiting on him, leaning against the car next to which he'd parked. He smiled at Mussawi. *You don't have to do this,* he let Mussawi know.

"Yes, I do," Mussawi said. "It is God's will."

It is not my father's will. "I know who you are," Mussawi said to the man. "You were a prophet. But that's *all*."

The beatific smile stayed on the man's face. *Follow me,* he whispered. *I can save you.*

Mussawi turned away from the man in the white robe as a dark red Toyota Tundra pickup pulled up onto the second level of the underground lot and parked three spaces down.

He reached inside his sport coat and gripped the Makarov as he walked that way. An elderly man with white hair and a matching beard, wearing a striped "lumberjack" work shirt, faded brown work jeans and a straw cowboy hat was just stepping out of the truck as he arrived. His keys were in a liver-spotted hand.

Mussawi drew the pistol and dropped the front sight on the man's nose.

Before he could pull the trigger, the man in the white robe appeared to the older man's side. His face was serious now. *Do not do this evil thing.* "I have to do it," Mussawi said.

The old Idaho cowboy thought Mussawi must be talking to him. He stared the al Qaeda man in the eye. "No, you don't, son," he said in a low, gravelly voice. "You ain't gotta do it at all." His eyes traveled from Mani's to the gun. Mussawi's own eyes jerked back and forth from the cowboy to the man in the robe.

The man in white just shook his head.

Mussawi lowered the Makarov slightly but kept it trained on the old cowboy's chest. "Come with me," he ordered the man.

The old cowpoke raised his hands without being told to. His keys still dangled from the fingers of his right hand and Mussawi stepped forward quickly, pulled them away, and dropped them into the pocket of his jacket. But as he did, he kept his eyes on the weathered cowboy, and was surprised to see no fear as he walked the man back to the Maxima. "Pick up the two black cases in the backseat," he ordered his hostage.

The man opened the Maxima's rear door and hauled out both innocent-looking black nylon bags.

Mani opened the front door and took possession of the brown paper bag himself.

"Now carry those things back to your pickup," the al Qaeda mole told the old cowboy. He wanted another drink from the half-gallon badly. But at the moment his hands were too busy covering the old man with the pistol.

The white-haired cowboy limped slightly as he lugged the backpack nukes to his truck, never knowing what he carried was meant to murder two million people on the other side of the world. "What you got in here, boy?" he asked over his shoulder. "Drugs? Some of that crack cocaine or one of them designer drugs I keep hearing about?"

"It is none of your business," Mussawi said sharply.

"No," said the old man as he stopped next to the Toyota and set the nylon bags down on the concrete. "But I do gotta know one thing before I go on."

Mussawi stared at the man, his eyes squinting slightly. "And what is that?" he demanded.

The old man with the white hair and beard smiled, and that smile made the al Qaeda mole think of the man in the white robe. "You want these bags in the bed of the truck or the backseat?" he asked.

Mussawi looked briefly at the pickup. It had one of the tiny, almost "half" backseats in which people could ride but not very far. At least not in anything any reasonable man would call comfort. There would be plenty of room for the two black cases, however. "Backseat," he said.

The cowboy had left the driver's door open upon first seeing the man with the pistol and now all he had to do was swing open the half-door in back. Once the nylon bags were on the seat, he closed that door, then the one leading to the driver's seat, and turned to Mussawi.

"I will be taking your pickup, now," Mussawi told the man.

His words brought a sharp laugh from the old man.

"You know, son," he said. "I'm just an old Idaho country boy. But I'd pretty much figured that one out all by myself." The old cowboy grabbed the brim of his well-worn straw hat, swept it off his head and ran the fingers of his opposite hand through the thin white hair atop his head. "I suppose this is the part where you shoot me," he said.

Mussawi lifted the Makarov and sighted it in between the old man's eyes. The aged cowboy had showed no fear since first getting out of his truck. Mussawi couldn't help wondering why.

"You seem to be at peace with what is happening to you," Mussawi said. "Tell me why."

"Well," said the old cowboy, placing his hat back on his head and then looking Mussawi straight in the eyes again. "I've had a pretty durn good life. Got a little spread about ten miles from here. Run a few cattle. Raise some potatoes." He reached up into the pocket of his work shirt and pulled out what looked like a hand-rolled cigarette. "You mind?" he asked, but before Mussawi could reply he had produced a wooden match, struck it with his thumbnail and lit the end.

As soon as he saw that the cigarette was burning, he went on. "But my children are all grown. Son's a doctor in Seattle. Daughter just got her Ph.D. in physics last year and went to work for the government doing something in Hawaii." He took a deep drag off the hand-rolled cigarette and let the smoke drift out through his mouth and nose. "My wife passed on goin' on two year ago. Breast cancer. The doctor didn't take it seriously enough and didn't do a biopsy when she first went in and a year later—when he finally *did* take it serious it had done spread and was too late." He took another hit from the hand-rolled, then said, "But you don't want to hear my life story, do you, son." It was a statement rather than a question. The old cowboy dropped what was left of the smoke on the concrete and ground it out with the heel of a well-worn boot.

"So you are not afraid of death because you are alone?" asked Mussawi.

The tanned and weathered face looked up from under the cowboy hat. "No, son," the man said. "I'm not afraid of death because I'm *not* alone. Jesus Christ has been with me every step of the way since I was twenty-five years old."

The statement suddenly filled Mussawi with rage. Satan was attacking him again, trying to confuse him. Get him to give up the plan that al Qaeda had worked on so long and hard in order to further strike against the enemies of Islam. He felt his finger tighten on the Makarov's trigger and take up the slack.

The old cowboy just smiled back at him.

And the man in the white robe suddenly stood next to the cowboy.

Do not do this evil thing. In overwhelming rage and frustration, Mani Mussawi raised the Makarov into the air and brought it down on the old cowboy's head. The man was still smiling as his eyes closed and he fell to the ground in the covered parking lot.

Mussawi stuck the pistol back in his belt and reached down, grabbing the unconscious man under the arms and dragging him back to the Maxima. He felt the man's pulse in his throat. It was strong.

The old Idaho rancher would wake up with a headache and probably need some stitches. But that was all.

Mussawi left the man sleeping in the backseat of

Zaid Baharlou's Maxima. As he walked back to the
Toyota Tundra he passed the man in the white robe,
leaning against another car again.

Not perfect. But it's a start, Mussawi heard.

Mani Mussawi got behind the wheel of the pickup
and inserted one of the keys he had taken from the old
man into the ignition. He took time for one more long
pull from the half-gallon bottle, then backed out of the
parking space and headed for the exit of the underground garage.

CHAPTER EIGHTEEN

Another impromptu meeting was being held in front of Aaron "Bear" Kurtzman's bank of computers. But this time, along with Hal Brognola, Barbara Price had come up the ramp, as well. She stood next to Kurtzman's computer as Brognola went back down the ramp and returned pushing a wheeled desk chair in front of him and dragging a second behind. A moment later, all three Stony Man Farm experts were seated.

Kurtzman glanced at the shapely, honey-blond mission controller who had been quietly coordinating the operations of both Able Team and Phoenix Force. And, while he evidently hadn't needed to contact the Farm in several days, Mack Bolan was undoubtedly off somewhere in the world, fighting evil and risking his own life so others could live theirs. Price would be monitoring the Executioner's progress, as well.

"Barb's been busy," Brognola said. "You need to bring her up to date in regard to the state of our union, Bear. Especially Nosiar's schedule. We'll start from the very beginning to make sure we've got everything straight. Nosiar is running the al Qaeda operation in Radestan and on his way personally to pick up the two backpack nukes."

"Take a look here," said Kurtzman. He tapped a few keys on the keyboard in front of him and a map of the world appeared on the screen. "We've got a basic idea of what's going to happen and when," he said. "Intercepting that phone call to the CIA was like a big giant Christmas present. But we don't know all of the details. And there could be last-minute changes in al Qaeda's plan that we haven't, and won't, hear about, either. At least not until they've already taken place."

Price smiled, and Kurtzman couldn't help but smile back. The woman was as competent as they came. Coolheaded, creative under pressure and possessing a mind that could keep every aspect of a mission compartmentalized and then know when to bring them all together at the right time.

Kurtzman dropped his hand onto the mouse next to the keyboard and moved it until the curser flashed on and off to indicate Ramesh, Radestan. "Phoenix Force is headed back to us but Grimaldi's taking the long way home," the computer man said. "He's swapped the helicopter for a Concorde and is going to head across India, then cut down between Indonesia and Australia." He dragged the mouse across the map, showing Price the general route Grimaldi would be taking.

"Any particular reason for that?" Price asked.

"Couple of reasons," said the man in the wheelchair. "That route won't take them across the airspace of as many Islamic countries. We know al Qaeda has infiltrated the Radestani government. And we know that they've done the same thing in Saudi Arabia, Egypt, Libya and Algiers. Maybe not to the same extent, but our boys will have to get clearance from each country they fly over, and an unusual craft like a Concorde will draw attention. Attention that might well be passed right on to al Qaeda."

"And the second problem you mentioned?" asked Price, crossing her legs with a *whoosh* of her stockings.

"Any suspicious terrorist—particularly al Qaeda—will see them going *away* from America. If they take notice of the plane, we can assume they'll think whoever's on it is headed somewhere else. At least for a while."

Brognola's mouth had been empty but now he pulled a new cigar from the breast pocket of his suit coat, and began unwrapping the cellophane in which it was encased. "You know that old saying about the word 'assume' making an ass out of 'u' and 'me'?" he half muttered.

"Of course I do, Hal," Kurtzman said. "But we've got to get Phoenix Force back home *somehow*. Looking several moves down the line in this giant apocalyptic chess game, they could be our last resort in getting the nukes back."

"Please explain," said Price.

"According to the phone call, Barb," Kurtzman said, "Nosiar is to land in Vancouver, then take a fishing boat to Bellingham, Washington."

"Won't he have to check in with the Coast Guard or customs or the border patrol or *someone?*" asked Price.

"He *should* take the fishing boat through customs," said Kurtzman. "But he won't. We—and by 'we' I mean the United States—don't monitor our Canadian border nearly as close as we do Mexico. Fishing boats and other craft up north come and go and most don't even know for sure when they cross into foreign waters. It would only be by chance that he'd get stopped and checked. Anyone who's studied the goings and comings of the Coast Guard and other agencies could avoid being noticed with ease."

"And you can believe that al Qaeda has done their homework in that area," said Brognola. He bit down on the new cigar and an audible click-like noise sounded as his teeth pierced several layers of tobacco leaves.

Kurtzman nodded his agreement. "Then Nosiar plans to take the bombs on the boat back to Vancouver and fly off with them again." The computer wizard rested both of his hands on the wheels of his wheelchair. "The way I see it, Able Team will have a first chance at getting the bombs from Mussawi when he arrives in Bellingham to wait for Nosiar. Assuming—and there's that word again—we can locate him in Bellingham. If that falls through there'll be another chance on the boat while he's returning to Vancouver."

Kurtzman's fingers tightened around the wheelchair wheels. "Able Team's last chance will be there, in Vancouver, before Nosiar takes off again." The man raised his wrist and looked at his watch. "If none of that works out, by my calculations Phoenix Force should be about halfway across the Pacific by that time. If we haven't taken them out by then, it'll be up to McCarter and his troops to do so in the air. Their Concorde's outfitted with twin M-61, 20 mm machine guns and AGM-65D IIR Maverick precision attack missiles."

Price frowned. "They—and by 'they' I mean Nosiar—are flying the other way, aren't they? Crossing the Atlantic rather than the Pacific, and then flying across all of Canada before landing?"

"They are," said Kurtzman. "They don't have to play hide-and-seek with the Islamic governments like we do. Grimaldi will bring Phoenix Force in from the west. When the Radestani 727 takes off again they'll have to follow Nosiar back east, all the way past Halifax before they shoot them down somewhere between there and Europe."

"I can't be the first person to wonder about this," Price said. "But none of us are nuclear physicists. If it turns out that Phoenix Force has to shoot them down, what are the chances of the plane exploding triggering the nukes in turn?"

"I've already checked, and double-checked, on that," said Kurtzman. "The bottom line is there's that chance. But my source on such subjects says an explosion such as the airplane's would be about as likely to *disassemble* the nukes as it would be to set them off." He took in a deep breath, then let it out through clamped teeth. "It seems to be determined by exactly what stage the bombs are in when the initial explosion takes place. We've been pretty certain they wouldn't go off while Mussawi had them because it wasn't likely he even knew how to arm them."

"But what about if they do get to Nosiar?" asked Price.

Kurtzman looked the woman in the eye. "That," he said, "is hard to tell. I did a little more digging and learned at least one thing I didn't like at all. Like Mussawi, Emad Nosiar went to college in the U.S. Got a Ph.D. from M.I.T. Want to guess what in?"

"Nuclear physics," said Brognola.

The man in the wheelchair nodded. "Exactly," he said. "So, we can be sure Nosiar knows how to activate the nukes. Whether he has, or hasn't, we don't know.

Logic would tell us that he'd wait until right before he set them in place to do so in order to avoid a premature accident. But we've learned from Islamic suicide bombers and other terrorists that logic doesn't always enter into the equation. That's another reason we'd prefer to shoot the 727 down over the ocean rather than land."

Brognola chomped down on his cigar once more and spoke through gritted teeth. "So what you're telling me, Bear, is that what we're doing by shooting down the Radestani plane is similar to walking into a casino, going to the roulette table and placing our chips on either black or red. If you forget about the green 0 and 00, it's pretty much a fifty-fifty chance."

"That's pretty much it," said Kurtzman.

Price sat forward slightly in her chair. "If the explosion does trigger the nukes, Bear," she said to Kurtzman, "what'll happen to the Concorde?"

Kurtzman felt his eyes fall to the floor as if of their own accord. "If they're close enough to shoot the plane down, and the nukes go off," he said, "they'll be incinerated."

A moment of silence fell over the room. There was nothing more to be said about the situation.

"That means I'd better pick them up on radar and keep track of them," said Price. "And I'll need to do the same with Grimaldi and Phoenix Force." She stopped speaking and recrossed her legs. "There are a *lot* of aspects that could get in the way of our timing, Bear," she said as she smoothed out her skirt with both hands. "Such as, how long will the fishing boat trip take? How long will it take for the Radestani plane to clear Canadian customs? I'm glad David and his men are in one of the Concordes. They fly roughly twice as fast as the plane Nosiar's in so they can catch up or lag back—whichever turns out to be necessary." The mission controller stood and turned to Brognola. "What did you find out about the CIA?" she asked.

"The President cleared the way," said the SOG director. "They've opted to just stay out of the whole mess and leave it to the 'ghost patrol' as they've started calling us."

Price smiled. "They don't know who we are," she said, "but they can't help knowing there's *something* out there that sometimes takes over and leaves them high and dry."

"And as my mother used to say," said Brognola, "they're madder than wet hens."

"One more question, Hal," said Price as she straightened the collar on her white blouse. "Do you want to bring the Canadians in on this?"

The big Fed closed his eyes for a moment. Finally he opened them and shook his head. "It's not that I don't trust them, Barb," he said. "But unless Able Team ends up in Vancouver, it's kind of like the CIA—we just don't *need* them. And we may not need them with Able Team north of the border if they can get in and out fast enough." He chomped down again on the new cigar.

"All right," Price said. "Bear, the timing's going to be close on all this. We'll need to stay in touch."

"You got it, Barb," said the man in the wheelchair.

Price and Brognola walked out of the Computer Room.

All three Stony Man Farm veterans knew that within the next few hours they were likely to lose both the men of Phoenix Force and Jack Grimaldi. Men who were not only top operatives but six of their best friends.

MANI MUSSAWI WAS almost sober by the time Bellingham, Washington, came into view. On the edge of town, he saw another run-down motel like the one he'd stayed in the night after stealing the two backpack nukes. The sign said Bellingham Courts.

He pulled the Toyota Tundra off the highway and onto the gravel in front of the sign that read Office.

Mussawi reached under his sport coat on the shotgun seat and pulled out the near-empty half-gallon bottle of Jack Daniel's. He finished it off in two large swallows, threw the empty container on the backseat and stared briefly at the two black nylon cases resting side by side. He had stopped just north of Seattle in a little town called Everett and purchased a new half-gallon bottle of bourbon. He looked at it now, hidden inside another brown paper bag on the floor of the backseat. Part of him wanted to grab it and take another drink. But he would make himself wait until he checked into one of the cottages lining the shore behind the office building.

The smell of the sea salt refreshed Mussawi as he opened the door and concentrated on walking steadily. He had spoken to Nosiar less than fifteen minutes earlier and his old friend had scolded him, maintaining that Mussawi sounded drunk again. He had assured Nosiar that he was fine, and the al Qaeda leader had promised to meet him in Bellingham in three hours.

As he neared the office door, Mussawi glanced at his wrist. That had been thirty minutes ago. He had two-and-one-half hours more and it would all be over.

If the motel manager noticed that Mussawi was drunk he didn't say anything about it, and four minutes after he had entered the tiny building Mussawi was back in the pickup and heading for cottage D. He parked on the gravel, barely noticing the dilapidated condition of the cottage. And for once, germs did not even enter his mind.

It took several tries but Mussawi finally got the old-fashioned skeleton key into the lock and opened the door. A moment later he had hauled in his luggage and the nylon cases. Locking the door behind him, he lay on the bed with the cell phone in his hand and closed his eyes.

The room swirled behind his eyelids.

Mussawi forced his eyes open and his arms to pull him up into a sitting position. Just across the small room from the bed was a cheap scarred and chipped pine desk. An equally marred chair was pushed into the chair well facing away from him.

It took two tries but a minute later Mussawi had Nosiar on the phone again. "I'm here," he said into the instrument.

"Where, exactly?" asked Nosiar.

Mussawi couldn't remember the name of the motel. "Wait a minute," he slurred into the mouthpiece as he forced himself off the bed and walked haphazardly to the door. Through the glass in the top he could see the sign on the highway. "Bellingham Courts," he managed to get out before burping. "Cottage D."

"You are even more drunk than before," accused Nosiar. "Stay where you are and *do not move*. I will find you."

Mussawi had pulled the half-gallon bottle out of the brown paper sack and was working on the cap. "How long?" he asked.

It seemed to Mussawi that there was an overly long pause on the other end. But then he knew Nosiar was right—he *was* drunk. So his perception of time might be faulty. Luckily, he could depend on his life-long friend to take care of such things until he could sober up again.

"Approximately two more hours," said Nosiar. "Perhaps a little longer. Again, stay where you are."

Mussawi looked at the new half-gallon of bourbon in his hands and wondered why he would ever want to go anywhere else. He had everything he needed right here. "I will be waiting," he said. He heard a click as his old friend ended the call.

Mussawi got the cap off and held the bottle to his lips, letting swallow after swallow gulp down his throat. There was a just-right amount of alcohol, he had learned, during his years in America. But it was *so* hard to find. Somehow, he always never quite reached it. Or else he shot past it into a sort of "no man's land" where instead of feeling good, he just went numb.

On the other hand, numb wasn't all that bad. It beat sober and the pain that came from the knowledge of what he was about to do.

This time when the man in the white robe appeared, he literally glowed with light. He had pulled the desk chair out, turned it around, and was sitting facing Mani. He looked gentle and loving and kind, as he always did when he appeared. But now, he also looked concerned.

The word *Mani* seemed to come directly from the man's brain to Mussawi's. *I offer forgiveness to all who ask. But eventually when I come to save, if the heart has been hardened and I am rejected over and over, I quit coming.*

Mussawi let the bottle fall from his hands and spill

some of its contents over the bedspread. "What should I do, Lord?" he asked through his drunken haze.

Follow me, came the answer. *Accept me and repent of your sins.*

"I do, Lord," said Mussawi. "I am sorry for so many things."

And you must not carry through with what you are about to do.

"But Emad is only going to use the first bomb," Mani slurred through his drunken lips. "No one will be hurt."

The face of the man in the white robe became stern. *That is a lie and you know it. He intends to detonate the bombs in Ramesh and slaughter over two million sheep in my flock.*

"But what can I do now?" Mussawi asked out loud again. "Emad is on his way."

Take the nylon cases to the Bellingham Police Department. They will keep them safe.

"I don't know where the police department is," Mussawi tried to argue. "And I am afraid of Emad."

I will show you the way. And you need not fear. I will be with you no matter what happens.

Suddenly, Mussawi felt himself grow sober. And in his chest he felt a new strength; a new presence. He didn't understand it. But there was something inside him that hadn't been there before.

He didn't bother with his clothes or the Makarov. Lifting one of the nuclear weapons in his right hand, the other in his left, he moved them next to the door. He had to set one of them down to twist the doorknob. But once the door was open he lifted the nylon case once more and stepped outside.

Standing just outside the single concrete step leading up to his cottage, Mani Mussawi saw Emad Nosiar. And now, in his sober state, Mussawi realized that the man had lied to him about his time of arrival to gain the upper hand. And what he had come to know in the last minute or so—that Nosiar really did intend to murder two million people—became abundantly confirmed.

Nosiar raised his arm and in his hand Mussawi saw the pistol.

Without thinking, Mussawi's had went to the cross around his neck; the cross Jason Hilderbrand had given him several years before when he had pretended to be interested in Christianity as part of his cover. A strange comfort came over him.

A second later Mussawi heard the explosion and it felt as if something had slapped him in the chest. He dropped both of the nylon cases and fell to the ground on his side. Looking up, he saw Nosiar aiming the handgun down at his head. In his own hand, he could feel the silver cross that was now slippery with blood.

Mussawi closed his eyes again. But he could see the man in the white robe on the back of his eyelids. *It is not the first cross to be covered with blood,* the man said.

Another explosion sounded. And as he took his last breath, Mani Mussawi's heart was content and he could feel the smile on his own face.

THEY HAD BEEN a half step behind the backpack nukes since reaching Bellingham, Washington. That fact had made Carl Lyons—never particularly known for a happy-go-lucky nature or a carefree attitude—even angrier than usual.

They were *so close* to the stolen nukes.

Yet they were still *so far away.*

While they had not known what Mani Mussawi was driving when he'd left the underground parking lot in Boise, they had at least known from Kurtzman's intercepted phone call where the al Qaeda mole planned to end up. The question: would Mussawi take the most direct route toward the little Washington State village that was almost in Canada? Or would the long-term mole choose a more roundabout pathway to further throw off any pursuers?

So Mott had headed them that way in the SAB, scouting the highways below for any clue as to which vehicle carried the nuclear bombs. Several cars and trucks that they remembered watching exit the mall had looked like likely candidates for a while. But each had eventually turned off the main route and headed in some other direction.

The problem was twofold, as the Able Team leader saw it. First, they could not be certain that Mussawi hadn't stayed underground for minutes or even hours after Mott had flown them away toward Washington. If that was the case the man with the nukes might be way behind them for all they knew. The second flaw in their surveillance strategy was that when Mussawi left the parking area he could have purposely turned in another direction just to throw them off. He might well have driven twenty, thirty, fifty—maybe even a hundred miles—in another direction just to get rid of a tail.

There was no way to be sure.

But since the Kurtzman-intercepted call *had* told them that Bellingham was the final destination, it was to Bellingham Mott had taken them. And they had arrived just in time to look down and see Mani Mussawi come out of one of the cottages of a rat trap known as the Bellingham Courts.

Lyons, Schwarz and Blancanales had even watched as the man had taken a bullet to the chest and then another to his head from a man they had to believe was Emad Nosiar.

Mussawi had dropped two identical black nylon bags when he'd gone down after the first shot. And the men of Able Team had no doubts as to what they contained.

Brognola had phoned ahead and this time it was the U.S. Border Patrol instead of the FBI who had met them at the small airport with a ground vehicle. They had arrived at the docks in time to see a fishing boat round a curve in the shoreline and disappear.

Several fishermen still on the docks had described the boat as being Canadian and told the men of Able Team that while it was not an everyday occurrence, it was hardly unheard of that a fisherman should wander off course and find himself in the U.S. illegally.

There had only been two men on the boat, as far as the other fishermen could tell. And both had spoken English but with an accent unfamiliar to the locals. They had been happy to provide that information to Able Team.

They had been less enthusiastic when Lyons and his men showed them their Justice Department credentials and commandeered one of their boats to go after the strange-talking men.

The fishing vessel had been docked in Vancouver when they arrived. And it had been swarming with Canadian officials. But the two men who had docked the commercial craft had left before they'd arrived. The cooperative Canadians did, however, take the men with the U.S. Department of Justice credentials to the closest landing strip. And they had arrived just in time to see the Radestani Airlines aircraft take off.

"Can you tell me," Lyons asked, "what a foreign-government-owned 727 jet is doing on this out-of-the-way airstrip in the first place?" Lyons had asked.

None of the officials had an answer.

Carl Lyons had pulled his sat phone out and pressed it to his ear. As long as he didn't give away any secrets about Stony Man Farm it mattered little now what the Canadians, or anyone else, heard him say. A moment later he had David McCarter on the line.

"What's your 10-20?" the Able Team leader asked.

"About two hundred miles out," said McCarter.

"How about dropping down here and picking us up?" said Lyons.

The line went silent for a few seconds but Lyons could hear McCarter's British accent conversing with someone in the background. Grimaldi was his guess.

It turned out that his guess was right.

"Can do," said McCarter when he came back on. "Jack says we can still easily catch up to the 727."

"We'll be waiting," said Lyons.

"Be there as quickly as we can, Ironman," McCarter finished. "Phoenix Force is always happy to help you blokes out when you get yourselves into a jam." His chiding was light. But it was definitely there.

Lyons ended the call and switched off the phone. The Canadians had moved away a distance and Schwarz and Blancanales were standing next to him, alone. "You know, guys," he said in a quiet voice, "I don't mind going after this airplane. And I don't mind taking the chance that we'll all three be vaporized into trillions of

completely different molecules in a few more hours."
He stopped talking for a moment, then finished with,
"What I *really hate* is having to listen to McCarter and
his boys act as if they saved the day after we fell short."

Blancanales smiled. "Don't worry, Ironman," he
said. "It was all just pure dumb luck that things worked
out like this. The important thing is the job will get
done."

"We've pulled their butts out of the fire more than
once," said Schwarz.

"And," said Blancanales, "we'll do it again."

EPILOGUE

Getting air clearance from each of the Canadian provinces they flew over was no problem. Canada was one of the few countries that didn't seem to have a chip on its shoulder for the United States. One by one, the Concorde followed the Radestani Airlines Boeing 727 over British Columbia, Alberta Saskatchewan, Manitoba, Ontario, Quebec and out into the Gulf of Saint Lawrence.

Jack Grimaldi, assisted now by Charlie Mott as copilot, kept their plane far enough behind to be out of sight from the foreign-owned jet with the backpack nukes on board. Also in the cockpit were David McCarter and Carl Lyons, representing both Phoenix Force and Able Team.

The rest of both teams were back in the middle of the bird-looking aircraft, strapped into the reclining chairs bolted to the deck in the main cabin.

The Concorde and the Boeing were both flying at roughly 30,000 feet when they passed between Newfoundland and Nova Scotia and continued out over the Atlantic Ocean. McCarter, Lyons, the pilots and the other members of the Stony Man Farm strike teams all knew the score.

In less than an hour they would shoot down the Radestani aircraft. There was no other choice. If they allowed it to reach Europe they would be taking the chance that the exploding aircraft might trigger the nukes over inhabited areas. And if they waited much longer than that the plane carrying Emad Nosiar might land in some Islamic nation and the nukes would disappear from their grasp altogether.

At least until the al Qaeda operative set them off in Ramesh as part of his mad plan to take over that warring nation.

McCarter and Lyons watched the radar screen in front of them as Grimaldi guided the Concorde on. Above, they saw nothing but blue. Below, the peaceful white clouds over the Atlantic seemed contradictory to the violence that was about to take place.

Few words were exchanged by the men. They all knew what had to be done. And they all knew the chance they had to take.

The Concorde had been slowly catching up to the Radestani aircraft since they'd left Canadian airspace, and now Jack Grimaldi unwrapped the headset and looked over his shoulder at Lyons and McCarter. "Well, guys," the ace pilot said, "it's now or never. We're as far from inhabited land in all directions as we're going to get. And if we wait much longer we'll be—"

Never one to waste words, Carl "Ironman" Lyons said, "Do it."

McCarter nodded his agreement.

Grimaldi wrapped the headphones back around his ears and lifted the secured radio microphone. "Birdman to One," he said into the mouthpiece in front of his face.

"Go ahead, Birdman." It was Barbara Price who responded.

"Getting ready to fire," said Jack Grimaldi. "Thought I'd say goodbye for all of us—just in case."

He got no response from the mission controller and ended the call.

"You guys ready?" Grimaldi asked over his shoulder.

"Let's do it," McCarter said.

"And get it over with," said Lyons.

"No point in wasting 20 mm ammo when we don't have to," Grimaldi said. "Charlie, you want to do the honors?"

"Why not?" said Mott. He reached forward and touched a fingertip to one of the buttons on the Concorde's weapons control panel. "One," he said softly. "Two...and three."

The Stony Man pilot pressed the button and an AGM-65D IIR Maverick precision attack missile took off from the Concorde. The men in the cockpit watched it rocket away from the underside of the plane, leaving a white trail of smoke in its wake.

A few seconds later a loud explosion rocked the Stony Man aircraft. And in a few more seconds they were flying through a rainfall of debris that had once been a Boeing 727.

Somewhere within the scraps were the now harmless remnants of what had once been two nuclear bombs.

Charlie Mott turned and smiled at McCarter and Lyons. "Anybody need to pinch themselves to make sure they're alive?" he asked.

Carl Lyons shook his head. "Not me," he said. "Just seeing you guys still here convinces me I'm not in Heaven."

McCarter laughed. "Tell Barb we're heading home, Jack," he said. Then he and Lyons turned and walked back toward the main cabin to tell the other warriors from Stony Man Farm that they were home free. Just like the men in the cockpit, they had been aware that this might turn out to be their last flight.

"You want to tell them or you want me to, Carl?" the Phoenix Force leader asked.

"Let's wait," said Lyons. "I hate to wake them up."

* * * * *

Don Pendleton
TRIPLECROSS

An American body found in a devastated Indian village raises suspicions of conspiracy

Tensions erupt between Pakistan and India after an Indian village is massacred and bodies from both parties' troops are found in the rubble. But when neither country claims responsibility for the attack, and an American businessman is found among the dead, a warning flag is raised in the White House. While StonyMan's Phoenix Force hunts down the rogue armies overseas, Able Team must uncover why a U.S. mining company representative was at the massacre, and eliminate the deadly role the company plays in this game of war.

STONY MAN®

Available June wherever books and ebooks are sold.

GOLD EAGLE®

GSM131

Don Pendleton's Mack Bolan

JUSTICE RUN

Europe is targeted for attack...

A conspiracy to topple the European Union is being spearheaded by a powerful German industrialist and his underground cabal of fascist business, military and government officials. The plan is backed by money, weapons and power, and launch time is in less than forty-eight hours.

The head of the United Front prepares the opening salvo, a plot to shatter the first line of defense when Europe is attacked: the U.S. government. Bolan runs this mission hard, furiously chasing a burning fuse across Europe and America to stop an explosion that will alter history in the wake of fascist horror.

Available June wherever books and ebooks are sold.

The Executioner

Don Pendleton's®

PATRIOT STRIKE

Superpatriots decide Texas should secede with a bang

After the murder of a Texas Ranger, Mack Bolan is called in to investigate. Working under the radar with the dead Ranger's sister, he quickly learns that rumors of missing fissile material falling into the wrong hands are true. The terrorists, die-hard Americans, are plotting to use the dirty bomb to remove Texas from the Union. As the countdown to D-day begins, the only option is to take the bait of the superpatriots and shut them down from the inside. You don't mess with Texas. Unless you're the Executioner.

GOLD EAGLE®

GEX425

JAMES AXLER

DEATH LANDS

End Program

Newfound hope quickly deteriorates into a fight to save mankind

Built upon a predark military installation, Progress, California, could be the utopia Ryan Cawdor and companions have been seeking. Compared to the Deathlands, the tortured remains of a nuke-altered civilization, Progress represents a fresh start. The successful replacement of Ryan's missing eye nearly convinces the group that their days of hell are over—until they discover the high tech in Progress is actually designed to destroy, not enhance, civilization. The companions must find a way to stop Ryan from becoming a willing pawn in the eradication of mankind….

Available May wherever books and ebooks are sold.

AleX Archer
GRENDEL'S CURSE

A politically ordered excavation unearths more than expected

Skalunda Barrow, rumored to be the final resting place of the legendary Nordic hero Beowulf, is being excavated, thanks to charismatic—and right-wing extremist—politician Karl Thorssen, and archaeologist Annja Creed can't wait. But with the potential to uncover Hrunting and Nægling, two mythical swords the politician would kill to possess, the dig rapidly becomes heated. As Thorssen realizes the power of possessing Nægling, he is quick to show how far he will go to achieve his rabid ambitions. And when Thorssen marks Annja for death, the only way she can survive is to find a sword of her own.

The legend of Beowulf could tear a country apart...

Available May wherever books and ebooks are sold.